SUNKER'S DEEP

DEEP

LIAN TANNER

SCHOLASTIC INC.

ISBN 978-1-338-23173-1

12 11 10 9 8 7 6 5 4 3 2 1   17 18 19 20 21 22

Printed in the U.S.A.   40

First Scholastic printing, September 2017

Book design by Anna Booth

For Deb, Pam, and Margie, with love.

MAIN CHARACTERS

The Sunkers

SHARKEY — a seemingly heroic boy, born on a lucky tide and destined to be admiral one day

GILLY, PODDY, AND CUTTLE — Sharkey's young cousins and greatest admirers

ADMIRAL DEEPS — a woman who will do anything to protect her people

The Oysters

PETREL — who used to be Nothing Girl, but is now a valued member of the crew

FIN — an ex-Initiate of the Devouts, and Petrel's best friend

THE CAPTAIN — a mechanical boy with a mind full of wonders

MISTER SMOKE — a rat, and a law unto himself

MISSUS SLINK — another rat, with a talent for stitching wounds

DOLPH, *Third Officer* — a girl trying to live up to her late mam's reputation

KRILL, *Head Cook*   a huge man whose gruffness is all on
the surface

SQUID, *Krill's daughter*   a young woman with quick wits and a
kind heart

ALBIE, *Chief Engineer*   a cunning, vicious-tempered man, and
Petrel's uncle

SKUA, *Albie's son*   a bully, but not as dangerous as his da

OTHERS

BROTHER THRAWN   the wounded leader of the
fanatical Anti-Machinists known
as the Devouts

BROTHER POOSK   a nondescript man disliked by
his fellows

RAIN   a timid girl, and Brother Poosk's niece

BRAN   an Initiate of the Devouts, and Rain's
little brother

PROLOGUE

THEY CAME TO THE MEETING SHORTLY AFTER MIDNIGHT, separately and secretly. Professor Serran Coe was the first to arrive, and he greeted the other three with his finger to his lips. Not a word was spoken until they were in the basement, and even then, with the university abandoned above them and a dozen locked doors between themselves and the outside world, they were reluctant to name the things they were talking about.

"Has he gone?" whispered Professor Surgeon Lin Lin, a small, sharp-eyed woman with night-black hair.

Serran Coe nodded, and a flicker of regret crossed his face. "Two weeks ago. The ship sailed under cover of darkness."

Ariel Fetch leaned forward, her long earrings tinkling. "Did you give him the instruction? The one we agreed upon?"

"I built a compulsion into his circuits," said Serran Coe. "It will come into play when he crosses the equator on the return voyage."

"If there *is* a return voyage," growled Admiral Cray, who was Lin Lin's husband.

The others began to protest, but the admiral spoke over them. "Nothing is certain, and you cannot tell me otherwise. I have just learned that five of our best ships were sunk last night, and their officers murdered! By their own crews, mind you, who then deserted en masse to join the Anti-Machinists." The admiral's waxed mustache twitched in disgust. "This whole thing is spreading quicker than anyone thought possible. There are even rumors that the government is teetering! And what do we four do about it? We run, we hide, we send a mechanical child to the far southern ice, hoping that one day he will return and be compelled to seek out—"

"Hush!" said Lin Lin, and her husband broke off his rant. The building above them creaked ominously.

"It is only the wind," said Serran Coe in a tired voice. "It has been rising all week."

The admiral grumbled, "Look at us, jumping at shadows! Why are we not out there fighting the mobs?"

His question momentarily silenced the other three. Then Ariel Fetch sighed and said, "You may be a fighter, Admiral, but we are not. And even if we were, we could not turn back the Anti-Machinists. Their time has come. All we can do is try to preserve as much knowledge as we can, so it is there when people want it again."

"Pah!" said the admiral. "They will never want it again! They are fools and criminals—"

His wife interrupted him. "Then you should be glad that we are leaving them behind."

Her words fell like a blow on the tiny gathering. Serran Coe loosened his stiff white collar and said, "You are going to do it? I thought you might change your minds. It is so—extreme."

"Extreme it may be," said Lin Lin, sitting up very straight, "but I refuse to live under the rule of the Anti-Machinists, and I am not the only one who thinks that way. Besides, the medical papers we are taking with us must be preserved for the future. Even your mechanical child does not know everything."

"When will you go?"

Lin Lin's calm voice gave no hint of what lay ahead. "Another week, at least. It will take that long to gather family and friends." She smiled wryly at her husband. "Which means there is still time for a little fighting if you wish it, dearest."

The admiral took a deep breath through his nose—and let it out again. "Nay," he said. "Nay, you are right. We must follow our plans to the very end. I just hope—" He scrubbed his fists against his knees until the blue cloth crumpled. "I just hope it is worth it."

NINE DAYS AFTER THAT MEETING, PROFESSOR SURGEON Lin Lin and her people left. They told no one where they were going, and no one had time or inclination to ask; the government was on the brink of collapse, and the city was in uproar.

Screaming mobs rampaged through the streets, determined to destroy the machines that they blamed for all the wrongs in the world. They smashed automobiles and typewriters, omnibuses and telephones. The police were helpless against them. The army, brought in by the collapsing government, destroyed its own gun carriages and joined the mobs. Everyone else, frightened and confused, barricaded their doors, telling each other that the madness *must* stop soon.

BUT THEY WERE WRONG. The long, harsh reign of the Anti-Machinists was only just beginning.

CHAPTER I

THREE HUNDRED YEARS LATER

SHARKEY SQUINTED ONE-EYED THROUGH THE THICK GLASS porthole. He was searching for scraps of metal—metal that'd be covered in weed by now and colonized by barnacles, so that it looked no different from the rocks around it. But it was here somewhere, seventy-five feet below the surface of the sea, and he was determined to find it.

"Two degrees down bubble," he murmured.

"Two degrees down. Aye, sir!" cried eleven-year-old Gilly as she turned the brass wheels that tilted the little submersible's diving planes.

In the bow, eight-year-old Poddy's hands flew across the control panel, trimming the boat and keeping the direction steady as it sank. Farther aft, Gilly's younger brother, Cuttle, braced his bare feet on the metal deck, waiting for orders to change speed. Pipes gurgled. Dials twitched. Above the children's heads, the ancestor shrine maintained a silent watch.

"Ease your bubble," said Sharkey.

"Ease bubble. Aye, sir!" Gilly turned the wheels the other way.

Outside the porthole, the green light that filtered down from above touched thick strands of kelp and a school of codlings. The throb of the *Claw*'s propeller was like the beating of Sharkey's heart.

He straightened his eye patch and sang the last part of an old Sunker charm under his breath:

"Below to find,
Below to bind—"

It must have worked, because almost straightaway he saw something out of the corner of his undamaged eye. "Starboard twenty," he said.

"Starboard twenty. Aye, sir!" cried Poddy, and the *Claw* began to turn.

When they were on the desired heading, Sharkey said, "Midships."

"Midships. Aye, sir!"

"All stop."

"All stop. Aye, sir!" And Cuttle threw himself at the motor switches.

Gilly came for'ard, ducking past the periscope housing and wriggling around the chart table. "Have you found something, sir?"

Sharkey wasn't sure, not really. But he always sounded confident, even when he had no idea what he was doing. "Aye. There, where the kelp's thickest," he said.

Young Poddy hooked her toe under the control panel and

leaned back on her stool. "Adm'ral Deeps *thought* you'd be able to find it, sir. And she was right!"

"'Course she was," said Sharkey, hoping that the strange-looking bit of rock really was scrap metal from the giant submersible *Resolute*, which had broken up somewhere near here ninety-three years ago.

"Has he found the boxes?" called Cuttle.

"Not yet," said Gilly. "But he will." She bobbed her head in the direction of the ancestor shrine. "Thank you, Great-Granmer Lin Lin. Thank you, Great-Granfer Cray."

For the rest of the morning, the *Claw* cruised back and forth through the ropy kelp while Sharkey stared out the porthole, half-dizzy with concentration.

At the end of the forenoon watch, Gilly struck the bell eight times. *Ting-ting ting-ting ting-ting ting-ting.* "It's midday, sir. We're due back on the *Rampart* soon."

"Mmm," said Sharkey. "I want to find at least one of the boxes before we go."

From the helm, Poddy said, "You could ask Lin Lin and Adm'ral Cray where they are, sir."

Sharkey said nothing. His fellow Sunkers venerated their dead ancestors, but at the same time they seemed to think that the spirits were like some sort of boat crew, and all he had to do was whistle and they'd come running.

Poddy glanced out the helm porthole. "Look, sir, there's a dolphin! Maybe it's the spirit of Lin Lin! Maybe she's going to show you the boxes!"

Sharkey sighed in a long-suffering sort of way. "Lin Lin

talks to me when it suits her, Poddy. So does First Adm'ral Cray—"

The younger children bobbed their heads respectfully.

"—and *that* is just an ordinary dolphin."

"Oh," said Poddy, disappointed.

The dolphin swam idly away from them, and Sharkey watched it go. His eye flickered downwards. There was something—

"There!" he said. "Port full rudder."

"Port full rudder. Aye, sir!" Poddy's small hands brought the *Claw* around, as smooth as sea silk.

"All stop."

"All stop. Aye, sir!" shouted Cuttle.

"Hold us right there," said Sharkey, and he gripped the lever that worked the retrieval device.

Like the underwater vessel that housed it, the device was called "the claw." Sharkey pulled the lever back, and it ratcheted out from the side of the little submersible and spread its talons. It wasn't easy to use with only one eye; Sharkey had to compensate for the fact that he couldn't judge distances as well as he'd been able to before the accident. And he didn't want to wreck the box. Now that he'd found it, he was sure it'd be a good one, crammed full of surgeons' secrets, with not a drop of water seeped in to spoil it.

Gilly eyed the chronometer. "We're due back on the *Rampart* now, sir," she said.

Without looking up, Sharkey said, "Send a message turtle. Tell 'em we'll be late."

"... Aye, sir."

There was no argument, of course. Discipline on the submersibles didn't allow for arguments. But as Gilly scratched out a note and took one of the mechanical turtles from its rack, Sharkey knew what the middies were thinking.

He won't get into trouble. But we will, even though we're just following his orders!

It was true. Because of who he was, Sharkey could get away with being late, whereas the middies couldn't.

Still, that was their problem, not his.

It took him another ten minutes to juggle the box into the side air lock. As soon as it was secure, he murmured, "Mark the position."

Gilly squeezed past the ladder to the chart table. "Position marked, sir!"

"Half-ahead. Take her up to periscope depth."

As the *Claw* moved forward again—the planes tilting, the bow rising—Sharkey sat back on his stool, pleased with himself. He knew what the other Sunkers would say when they heard about the box.

Sharkey can do anything. Sharkey can find *anything. Sharkey's a hero, a future adm'ral, born on a lucky tide and blessed by the ancestors. Thank you, Lin Lin!*

The submersible leveled out, and he grinned. "Up periscope."

There was probably no danger from their enemies, not so far from terra. But caution was drilled into the Sunker children from the day they could crawl. Gilly crouched, her face pressed against the eyepieces, her feet swiveling in a circle.

Halfway around, she stopped and rubbed her eyes. "Sir, there's something strange in the Up Above. Like huge bubbles—"

Sharkey was already moving, snatching the periscope handles away from her.

"Sou'west," said Gilly.

The breath caught in Sharkey's throat. Gilly was right. There were three enormous white bubbles floating through the sky with woven baskets hanging beneath them! And figures leaning over the edges of the baskets, pointing to something below the surface. And lines tethering the bubbles to—

To skimmers! To a dozen or more skimmers with billowing sails and their hulls low in the water, following those pointing fingers with a look of grim purpose.

"It's the Ghosts!" cried Sharkey, and his blood ran cold. For the last three hundred years, the Sunkers had dreaded this moment. "It's the Hungry Ghosts! And they've found the *Rampart*!"

CHAPTER 2

EARLIER THAT SAME DAY

As dawn broke, twelve-year-old Petrel leaned against the rail of the ancient icebreaker *Oyster*, staring into the distance. Somewhere over there, beyond the horizon, was the country of West Norn.

"Will there be penguins, Missus Slink?" she murmured.

"Probably not," said the large gray rat perched on her shoulder. A tattered green neck ribbon tickled Petrel's ear. "But if my memory serves me correctly, there will be dogs and cats. And perhaps bears."

"Bears is farther north," said Mister Smoke, from Petrel's other shoulder. "Don't you worry about bears, shipmate. There's worse things here than bears."

"You mean the Devouts?" asked Petrel.

"Don't frighten the girl, Smoke," said Missus Slink.

"I'm not frightened," said Petrel quickly. But she was.

For the last three hundred years, the *Oyster* had kept its course at the farthest end of the earth. Its decks were rusty, its hull was battered, and its crew had broken down into warring tribes and forgotten why they were there. All that had remained of their original mission was the myth of the Sleeping Captain and the belief that the rest of the world was mad and therefore best avoided.

But the Devouts, fanatical descendants of the original Anti-Machinists, had traced the *Oyster* to the southern ice and sent an expedition to destroy the ship and everyone on board. Thanks to Petrel, they had failed, and the Sleeping Captain had woken up at last.

The Devouts thought the *Oyster's* captain was a demon. But really he was a mechanical boy with a silver face and a mind full of wonders. He knew sea charts, star maps and thousands of years of human history. He could calculate times and distances while Petrel was still trying to figure out the question, and he could mend or make machines and lectrics of every kind. On his orders, the *Oyster* had left its icy hideaway and headed north.

"We are going to bring knowledge back to the world," he had said.

The voyage had taken more than twelve weeks, with several engine breakdowns that had tested even the captain. But now Petrel was about to set foot on land for only the second time in her life.

She heard a rattling in the pipes behind her and turned to listen. It was a message in general ship code. SHORE PARTY PREPARE TO BOARD THE *MAW*. SIGNED, FIRST OFFICER HUMP.

With the rats clinging to her shoulders, Petrel slipped through the nearest hatch and onto the Commons ladderway, which took her from Braid all the way down to Grease Alley. She ran past the batteries, which were fed by the *Oyster*'s wind turbines, and past the digester that took all the ship's waste and turned it into fuel.

And there was the rest of the shore party, making their way towards the *Maw*.

"Here she is!" boomed Head Cook Krill, in a voice that was used to shouting over the constant rattle of pots and pans. "We thought you must've changed your mind, bratling."

"Not likely!" said Petrel, putting on a bold front. "Don't you try leaving *me* behind, Krill."

"We would not go without you," said the captain in his sweet, serious voice. "I knew you would come."

Fin just smiled, his fair hair falling over his eyes, and handed her a woven seaweed bag.

"Ta," said Petrel, and she smiled back at him, though her heart was beating too fast, and her mouth was dry at the thought of what lay ahead.

The *Maw* was an enormous fish-shaped vessel set to watch over the *Oyster* by its long-ago inventor. It traveled underwater, and the only way onto it was through the bottommost part of the ship. As the small party climbed through the double hatch, Chief Engineer Albie was giving last-minute instructions to his son, Skua.

"No mucking around, boy. This is a big responsibility, taking the cap'n and his friends ashore." In the dim light, Albie's eyes were unreadable, but Petrel thought she saw a flash of white teeth through his beard. "You set 'em down nice and gently."

It wasn't at all like Albie to be so thoughtful. By nature, he was a cunning, evil-tempered man, who until recently had made Petrel's life a torment. But Petrel was so excited and nervous that she didn't think much of it. Not until later, and by then the harm was already done.

"Aye, Da," said Skua.

"And come straight back when you've dropped 'em. You hear me?"

"Aye, Da. Watch your fingers, Da!"

There was a clang as the double hatch was clamped shut, and a moment later the *Maw*'s engines roared to life and the interlocking plates of its hull began to move.

Thanks to Albie's instructions, their passage towards land was smooth and uneventful. Skua brought them right up close to the headland, where the drop-off was steep, and they jumped onto the rocks without getting wet past their knees.

"I'll be back at noon," said Skua as he stood in the mouth of the *Maw*, tugging at his sparse red whiskers. "Watch out for trouble, Cap'n. And the rest of you!"

His expression was suitably serious, but it seemed to Petrel that as he stepped back into the shadows, it turned into something else. A smirk, maybe. Mind you, that was normal for Skua, who smirked at everything, and once again she thought nothing of it. A moment later, the *Maw*'s huge mouth closed, and the monstrous fish dived below the surface.

Petrel felt a tremor run right through her. *We're on land!*

She took a cautious step forward, and the ground seemed to sway under her feet.

"Mister Smoke," she hissed. "The ground's moving!"

"Nah," said the old rat. "It's because you've been on the *Oyster* for so long, shipmate. It'll stop soon."

Fin had been staring at the surrounding countryside with uncertain pride. Now he turned to Petrel and said, "This is West Norn. What do you think?"

The landscape stretched out in front of them, muddy and inhospitable. There were patches of snow on the ground, and the air was cold, though not nearly as cold as Petrel was used to. A few straggly trees were scattered here and there, with a bird or two huddled on their branches, but there was no other sign of life.

Petrel would've liked it better if there'd been a good, solid deck under her feet, and the familiar rumble of an engine. But she didn't want to hurt Fin's feelings, so all she said was, "It's big, ain't it. Reckon you could fit the *Oyster* in its pocket, and it wouldn't even notice."

Behind her, Krill said, "What now, Cap'n? We head for the first village?"

The captain pushed back his sealskin hood and nodded. "Once we have introduced ourselves, we will explain the workings of water pumps and other simple machines that will make their lives easier. We will find out what they want most, and go back to the ship for supplies and equipment." He paused, his beautiful face gleaming in the early-morning light. "Of course, I will ask them about the Song too."

Krill scratched his chin until the bones knotted into his beard rattled. "Now, this is where you've lost me, Cap'n. I still don't understand this stuff about a song."

"There is nothing mysterious about it," said the captain. "Serran Coe, the man who made me, must have programmed it into my circuits. As soon as we crossed the equator, I became aware of its importance."

"But you don't know *why* it's important?"

"I know that it will help us bring knowledge back to the people. I know that I will recognize it when I hear it—the Song *and* the Singer. If I do not know more than that, it must be because my programming has been deliberately limited, in case I am captured."

He pointed due west. "Three hundred years ago, there was a prosperous village in that direction. We will start there."

EVERYTHING PETREL SAW THAT MORNING WAS STRANGE AND unsettling. She was glad of Mister Smoke and Missus Slink, riding on her shoulders, and of Fin, who walked beside her, naming the objects she pointed to.

"That is a fir tree," he said. "It does not lose its leaves in winter, like the other trees. That is an abandoned cottage."

Petrel clutched the seaweed bag, which contained dried fish in case they got hungry, and a telegraph device that the captain had built so they could talk to the ship. "Folk used to live in it?"

"Yes."

"What happened to 'em?"

"I do not know. They probably got sick and died."

The mud slowed them down, and the village they were heading for seemed to get no closer. But at last Fin nudged Petrel and said, "*That* is a tabby cat."

Mister Smoke's whiskers brushed Petrel's cheek. "You sure it's a cat, shipmate? Looks more like a parcel o' bones to me. I can see its ribs from 'ere."

My ribs were like that not so long ago, thought Petrel, and she took a scrap of dried fish from her bag and tossed it to the cat.

"Captain! Krill!" called Fin. "If there is a cat, the village is probably close by. Beyond that row of bare trees, perhaps. But we should be careful. There might be Devouts."

The captain nodded and waited for them to catch up. "That position accords with my knowledge. Mister Smoke, will you go ahead and see if there is danger?"

"Aye, Cap'n," said the rat, and he leaped down from Petrel's shoulder and scampered away.

"D'you really think there might be Devouts here, lad?" Krill asked Fin. "We're a good hundred miles or more from their Citadel."

"They have informers everywhere," said Fin. "And there are always rumors that someone has found an old book or un-earthed a machine from the time before the Great Cleansing. The Devouts travel the countryside, trying to catch them."

Petrel listened to this exchange carefully. Fin knew all about the Devouts. He used to be one of their Initiates and had traveled to the southern ice with his fellows to destroy the

Oyster and her crew. But Petrel, not knowing who he was, had befriended him, and bit by bit Fin had changed.

Now he's one of us, thought Petrel. *And we're going to find his mam.*

Her heart swelled at the thought. She knew that the main purpose of the *Oyster*'s voyage north was to bring knowledge back to a world that had sunk deep into ignorance and superstition. But as far as *she* was concerned, the search for Fin's mam, who had given him to the Devouts when he was three years old to save him from starvation, was just as important.

Mister Smoke returned with mud on his fur, and his silver eyes shining. "No sign of Devouts, shipmates. Village is quiet as a biscuit."

Petrel looked towards the trees, feeling nervous all over again. "But what about the informers?"

"The Devouts who attacked us down south know we weren't beaten," said Krill. "I reckon they could guess we might come after 'em. And what with all that engine trouble we had on the way, I wouldn't be surprised if they passed us and got here first. So we're not giving up too many secrets by showing ourselves to a few villagers, informers or not." He cracked his knuckles thoughtfully. "All the same, it won't hurt to take it slowly. How about I go in by myself, chat to a few folk, see what's—"

But the captain was already striding towards the village.

"Wait!" cried Krill. "Cap'n! Wait for us!"

In the end, they entered the village in a tight group, with the captain's silver face hidden under his hood. For her part,

Petrel was glad they were sticking together—and not just because of her fear of the Devouts.

For most of her life, she had survived by pretending to be witless. Shipfolk had called her Nothing Girl and believed that she couldn't talk. Then the Devouts had attacked, and Petrel had spoken up at last, to save the *Oyster*.

Since then, she had grown used to speaking her mind, to proving over and over again (to herself as much as anyone else) that she was *not* Nothing. But that was on the ship, where everything was as familiar and comforting as her own two hands.

This was different. This was *land*, and these villagers were strangers. She already felt out of place. *What if they take one look at me and decide I'm not worth talking to?*

To take her mind off such an ugly possibility, she whispered to Fin, "Wouldn't it be good if your mam was right here, in the first place we stopped?"

"She will not be," said Fin. "Look! There are the cottages!"

"They're small," said Petrel.

"And *dirty!*" Fin sounded shocked. "I knew people's lives were hard, but I had forgotten—"

He broke off, and they all stared in dismay at the little settlement. The cottages were made of earth and reeds, with more reeds for the roofs. Most of them leaned one way or the other, and the ones that didn't lean, slumped in the middle as if they could no longer be bothered standing upright. The snow between them had turned to sludge, and in some places it was hard to tell where the houses ended and the muddy ground began.

"Is this the place you were thinking of, Cap'n?" murmured Krill. "It don't look prosperous to me!"

Petrel thought she saw movement, but when she jerked around, there was just a scrap of filthy curtain trembling over a glassless window. "Where's all the people?" she whispered.

"Watchin' us," said Mister Smoke, from her right shoulder.

"Scared," said Missus Slink, from her left.

They're not the only ones, thought Petrel. *Blizzards, I wish I was back on the ship!*

"Come," said the captain, and they waded through the mud to what seemed like the middle of the village. Krill looked relaxed except for the muscles in his neck, which were as taut as stay wires. Fin eyed the mean little cottages with a mixture of fascination and disgust.

They saw no one.

"Don't reckon they want to talk to us," whispered Petrel. "We might as well go—" Her whisper turned to a yelp as a rock flew out of nowhere and hit her on the leg.

Her instinct, honed by years of survival, told her to run for her life. But Fin grabbed her hand, and the captain stepped forward and cried, "We do not mean you any harm!"

A whisper came from one of the cottages. "Go away!" A man, from the sound of it, not wanting to be heard by his fellow villagers.

"We wish to help you," cried the captain. "We will teach you how to build a water pump so you do not have to carry—"

Another rock splashed into the mud by his foot. "Scat, the lot of yez!"

Somewhere a baby started to wail and then was instantly silenced. The air was sour with fear.

Petrel swallowed. More than anything else, she wanted to be back on the ship. "Let's go," she whispered.

But the captain did not move. He raised his voice again. "We are also searching for the Song—"

"Scat!" hissed the man again.

At which Fin suddenly lost his temper. "Is that all you can say?" he shouted. "You ignorant peasant!"

"Shhh!" said Krill.

But Fin wouldn't be silenced. "We came here to help you, and you will not even—"

A woman's voice interrupted him. "Our beloved leaders, the Devouts, are on their way." Unlike the man, she spoke loudly and carefully, as if she had tested each word beforehand to see how it would sound. "They will be here shortly after midday. They are always interested in travelers; you must wait and speak to them."

That stopped Fin in his tracks. "Let's go!" urged Petrel again. And this time the captain listened to her.

"D'you reckon they'll tell the Devouts about us?" she asked when they at last reached the headland. She felt horribly exposed standing there in the open, with the hostile land at her back.

"'Course they will," said Krill. "Didn't you hear what the woman said? She was warning us, which was right kind of her. Especially after the way a *certain person* spoke to 'em."

Fin reddened. "I—I did not mean to shout. But they *are* ignorant. That is the truth."

23

"They're scared," said Krill severely, "and with good reason, from the sound of it. And if they're ignorant as well, who made 'em that way, hmm? The Devouts, that's who. Seems to me you're in no position to go around shouting insults at folk, lad."

Fin was a proud boy, and Petrel knew that apologies did not come easily to him. But he swallowed and said, "You are right. I am—sorry."

Krill glared at him for a moment longer, then softened. "Ah, you're not doing too badly, considering where you came from."

"It is not long till noon," said the captain. "By the time the Devouts arrive, we will be gone." He looked over his shoulder in the direction of the village. "But I wish the people had liked us more. How are we to help them if they will not talk to us? How are we to find the Song?"

"Look at it this way, Cap'n," said Krill. "We mightn't have got any further with the Song or the water pumps, but those poor folk told us more by their silence than they could've done with a thousand words. We've got a huge task ahead of us."

That stopped the conversation dead, and they waited for the *Maw* in silence, staring out over the water. Petrel kicked at a rock, wishing Skua would hurry up and take her back to the ship, where she belonged.

Noon came and went.

"D'you think he's forgotten us?" asked Petrel after a while. She shaded her eyes with her hand. "Can you see any sign of him, Mister Smoke? Look, over there, is the water moving?"

"That's the tide, shipmate," said the rat. "It's on the turn."

Petrel made herself wait another few minutes, then said, "He should be here by now. We'd best remind him." She took the telegraph device from her bag. "How does this thing work, Cap'n?"

"It is quite simple," said the captain, sounding pleased that she had asked. "I took a spark gap transmitter and changed the—"

"Sorry, Cap'n, I'm sure that's really interesting, but it's not what I meant. How do I *use* it?"

"Oh," said the captain. "It is like banging on the pipes. You tap the key, and it sends that same tapping to the device on the bridge."

"Dolph'll be on duty by now," said Krill. "Ask her what's happening."

But before Petrel could begin, the telegraph key began to move by itself, clicking out a message in general ship code.

At first Petrel thought it must be a joke. She looked at Krill, and he was obviously thinking the same thing. But then his smile died. Because Third Officer Dolph would never joke about something as serious as—

"Mutiny!" whispered Petrel. The word tasted so foul in her mouth that she could hardly continue. But Fin didn't understand general ship code, not when it was rattled out fast, so she had to translate the whole message, stumbling over the dreadful meaning of it.

"Albie's locked the First and Second Officers in their cabins and taken over the ship!"

"What?" said Fin.

"He told everyone that—that Skua came to fetch us—but we were dead—murdered on the rocks and—and the cap'n smashed to smithereens!"

"But that is not true!" said the captain. "I am not smashed. Why would he say it if it is not true?"

The tapping continued. Petrel felt sick. "Albie's saying we should never have left the ice in the first place, and—and he's demanding that the *Oyster* go south again!"

Krill roared like a wounded sea lion. But the captain said, "Why would he *do* that? It is not logical."

Petrel thought of Albie's uncharacteristic helpfulness and Skua's smirk. She thought of all she knew about the Chief Engineer, from a lifetime of hiding from him. "Reckon he prefers the way things *used* to be on the *Oyster*, Cap'n," she whispered. "With the payback and the treachery and everyone being scared of him. Since you woke up, he's had to take orders, and he's not an order-taking sort of man." She stared blindly at the telegraph. "I *knew* he wasn't to be trusted. I did! I should've seen this coming!"

Small paws patted her shoulder. "So should we all," said Missus Slink. "But we didn't—"

"Hush, there is more!" said Fin, as the telegraph began to click again. "What is it saying?"

Petrel listened. The thought of the *Oyster* sailing south without them filled her with such horror that it was hard to concentrate. But the next bit of news was not quite so bad. "Dolph and Squid and a few others have—have barricaded themselves—on the bridge. They've got a bit of food and water—which means—which means Albie *can't* go south! Not yet, anyway—'cos they control the steering—"

The tapping stopped abruptly. Petrel shook the device, but there was no further sound from it. Quickly, she sent a return message, begging Dolph not to go south without them—*please* not to leave without them! But there was no reply.

"Cap'n," she said, thrusting the device into his hands, "it ain't working! I think your spark thing's broken!"

The captain inspected the device, then shook his head. "There is nothing wrong with it. The fault must lie at the other end, on the *Oyster*. A loose wire, that is all it would take."

"So, did Dolph get my message?" asked Petrel.

"Probably not," replied the captain.

Petrel stared at her companions, and they stared back. Krill looked as if he were going to explode. Fin's face was deathly white. Even the captain seemed dumbfounded.

"Then we're stranded," whispered Petrel. And suddenly the countryside around her looked more hostile than ever. "We're stranded, and the Devouts are coming."

CHAPTER 3

A DUTY TO STAY ALIVE

At that very moment, two hundred miles northeast of Petrel and her friends, Sharkey was shouting orders. "Up aerial!" There was no time for a message turtle. "Send a comm to the *Rampart*!"

Cuttle leaped for the aerial crank, and Gilly tapped away at the comm key. ATTENTION *RAMPART*! HUNGRY GHOSTS OVERHEAD! ATTENTION *RAMPART*! HUNGRY GHOSTS OVERHEAD!

"Tell 'em they've been spotted," cried Sharkey. "Tell 'em to get under way before the Ghosts eat 'em!"

YR POSITION DISCOVERED, tapped Gilly. GET UNDER WAY!

Sharkey cursed the clearness of the sea hereabouts, which had allowed the Ghosts to spot the big submersible from their strange bubbles. And then he cursed the big submersible because there was no answer to Gilly's message, which meant the

Rampart was below aerial depth. And comms didn't pass through water.

"Try again," he snapped, and as Gilly tapped out the futile message, he pressed his eye to the periscope.

All Sunker children knew the tale of the Hungry Ghosts by heart. They'd heard it from Granfer Trout, who was the oldest of all the old salts on the *Rampart* and had no duties at all except to eat, sleep and tell stories.

Three hundred years before, a horde of Ghosts had escaped from the darkness of Hell and invaded the Up Above. These ghosts had bellies as big as mountains! They were always hungry, and their favorite food was machines. They ate automobiles, trains and buses; steamships, rockets and flying machines. And when that didn't satisfy them, they gobbled down the people who *invented* the machines, and the people who used them.

Anyone who tried to stop the Hungry Ghosts was killed and eaten. Nowhere in the Up Above was safe. And so Professor Surgeon Lin Lin and her husband, First Admiral Cray, built a fleet of giant submersibles and took to the Undersea, along with family, friends and a hundred waterproof boxes of surgeon papers.

Things were fearfully hard for that first generation. They weren't used to being crammed into such small spaces, sharing bunks and bumping into their neighbors whenever they turned around. But they gritted their teeth and stayed. And it was only at night, with the fleet running on the surface, renewing air and batteries, that they gave in to their homesickness and stood on the outer decks, straining their eyes to see the land from which they were exiled.

Sharkey couldn't imagine feeling homesick for terra. The Undersea was the only world he'd ever known. Like all the Sunkers, he ate mussels, oysters, seaweed and fish, cooked and raw. His clothes were made from sea silk, and any metal he needed was mined from the ocean floor and smelted in one of the onboard workshops.

Life was still dangerous, of course, and smelly, and either too hot or too cold, depending on the season. The water from the distillers always tasted of oil, the air was usually a little stale, and over the centuries, most of the submersibles had been destroyed by storms or rust or accidents, until only the huge *Rampart* and the tiny *Claw* were left.

But no one complained. It was what they were used to, and, besides, it was a hundred times safer than the Up Above. In all those years, the Sunkers had seen the Hungry Ghosts' skimmers from afar any number of times. But the Ghosts had never seen the Sunkers.

Until now.

The skimmers were furling their sails, revealing immense structures on their decks. Sharkey had a bad feeling about those structures—which worsened when he saw rocks being loaded onto them, and figures hauling at a winch, turning it tighter and tighter.

"Looks like some sort of catapult," he muttered.

"Still no answer," said Gilly. "What now, sir?"

Sharkey's mind was awhirl. Would the rocks damage the *Rampart*? Maybe not! They'd lose some of their force when they hit the water, so maybe they'd bounce off the hull, leaving nothing but a few dents.

But then the first catapult fired its load—and a moment later the children heard a muffled *whoomp*, like an undersea avalanche. The *Claw* shuddered. A gout of water spurted upward.

Sharkey groaned. "They've got explosives!"

The second catapult fired. And the third. Then the first again! *Whoomp. Whoomp. Whoomp.* Explosives tumbled into the water all around the *Rampart*.

"Sir?" said Poddy. "We're going to help 'em, aren't we?"

Sharkey hesitated. He was horrified by what was happening, but he was also pretty sure that the *Rampart* was doomed— and he wasn't about to risk his own precious skin for a lost cause. "Nay," he said.

The three middies stared at him. He knew what they were thinking. *But it's Ma and Fa they're attacking, and Granfer Trout and Ripple and Adm'ral Deeps and Surgeon Blue—*

"It's not going to help anyone if we get eaten as well," he said. "If the *Rampart* goes down, we'll be the last of the Sunkers. We'll be the only ones who know where the boxes are, and what's in 'em. We've got a duty to stay alive."

It sounded good, which didn't surprise him. His mind was always calculating, even in an emergency. Always thinking about what things *sounded* like, and how to survive, and how to fool people so that he came out the other end looking like a hero.

The three middies nodded. Poddy's eyes were brimming, but Sharkey knew she wouldn't cry. Sunkers hardly ever cried. They just followed orders and made the best of things.

He put his good eye to the periscope again. "The *Rampart* must be trying to get away," he said, keeping his voice flat and sensible. "But the Ghosts are pointing to her—the skimmers have caught up—"

He stopped as a roil of water, like the breath of a dying whale, broke the surface. The skimmers rocked from side to side. The Ghosts rushed to re-aim their catapults.

"The *Rampart*'s surfacing!"

And now at last the comm began to work. First came Admiral Deeps's call sign. Then the quick, desperate message.

RAMPART HOLED AND TAKING ON WATER. ABANDONING SHIP. POSITION FIFTY-ONE DEGREES TWENTY-FIVE MINUTES NORTH, FOUR DEGREES TWENTY-TWO MINUTES WEST. SAVE YOURSELVES. GO! THAT'S AN ORDER!

None of the middies moved.

Sharkey snapped at them. "You heard the adm'ral! All ahead two-thirds! Ten degrees down angle!"

At that, Cuttle, Poddy and Gilly rushed to their posts. "All ahead two-thirds. Aye, sir!"

"Ten degrees down angle. Aye, sir!"

As the *Claw*'s bow sank, Sharkey took one last look through the periscope. He thought he saw one of the giant bubbles break from its moorings and blow towards the *Claw* . . . and then the sea washed over the glass, and the Up Above, with all its hatred and destruction, was gone.

"Make your depth sixty feet." Sharkey stood over the helm, snapping out orders and watching the depth gauge. No one spoke except to acknowledge his instructions, but the air in the little submersible was thick with grief.

There'll be no survivors, thought Sharkey. *The Ghosts'll get 'em, every one. Which makes us the last of the Sunkers.*

"Steady on sixty feet, sir!" said Gilly.

Sharkey nodded. "Adjust trim. Heading east-sou'-east."

He sounded completely calm. But if he was good at hiding his feelings from his crew, he couldn't hide them from himself. His parents had died two years ago, killed in the accident that sank the *Retribution*, but his aunties and uncles and cousins were still on the *Rampart*, and he couldn't imagine a world without them.

He thought of what it must have cost Admiral Deeps to abandon the giant submersible and let it sink to the bottom. He thought of the Hungry Ghosts, who had eaten so much and were still not satisfied—

To port, something tumbled down through the water.

Sharkey's first thought was that they were under attack, but then he saw the billowing cloth and the thrashing legs. Someone had escaped from the Ghosts!

"Hard port rudder!" he shouted.

The *Claw* turned quickly, though not quickly enough for Sharkey. Those frantic legs touched the seabed and tried to push off, but the cloth had snagged on something and wouldn't come free.

Sharkey threw himself into the retrieval seat and grabbed the lever. "All stop!"

He pulled the lever back quickly, and the mechanical claw shot out towards the frantic figure, knocking the box out of the side air lock and probably losing it forever. But there was no time for regret. No time for caution either, or for worrying about bruised flesh or broken bones.

"Stay still!" he hissed, but the figure struggled harder.

Bubbles swirled around the little claw, and so did sand. It was almost impossible for Sharkey to see what he was doing. The talons closed around something. He hoped it was the figure; he wouldn't get a second chance at this.

Behind him, Poddy opened and shut valves, compensating for the weight of the little claw and whatever it held. Sharkey pushed the lever forward, and the figure was hauled back into the *Claw*'s side air lock.

"Seal outer hatch!" he snapped. "Blow water! Unseal inner hatch!"

He scrambled for the side air lock, which was aft of the chart table. He flung the inner hatch open and dragged the limp, sodden figure into the control room.

It was a girl, her eyes closed, her hair in pale strings around her face. She coughed, and a stream of salt water gurgled out of her mouth.

Sharkey backed away from her in horror, his ruined eye aching behind its patch. In that moment of confusion, he'd thought he was saving one of his cousins. But the girl who coughed and puked on the deck was a complete stranger.

He had rescued a Hungry Ghost and brought her onto the *Claw*.

WHEN THE TELEGRAPH DEVICE STARTED CHATTERING OUT A new message, Petrel almost jumped out of her skin with relief. "It's Dolph!"

But it wasn't.

"That's not ship code," rumbled Krill. He'd been pacing up and down, his face thunderous, ever since the message from the *Oyster* came through. Now he stopped and glared at the device. "Nor is it Cook code."

"It's not any sort of code," said Petrel, her shoulders slumping.

The telegraph fell silent. But a few minutes later, it tapped again.

"I believe it *is* a code," said the captain. "And I have nearly enough information to calculate—" He listened. "Yes, there are numbers. Fifty-one degrees twenty-five minutes north, four degrees twenty-two minutes west."

"That's a chart readin', shipmates," said Mister Smoke. "Someone out there's sendin' their position to someone else."

The members of the stranded company stared at one another. "But that is impossible," said Fin. "They would need another telegraph device, would they not? And such things are unknown outside the *Oyster*."

"*Someone* must know about 'em." Krill ran his fingers

through his beard. "Cap'n, where's fifty-one thingummy? It's not close enough to do us any good, I know that."

"It is two hundred and seven miles, sixty-five yards and two feet northeast of here," replied the captain. "Which puts it forty-three miles off the coast in the Nornuckle Sea. Near the Banks of Kell, which are famous for their fishing."

"A fishing boat would not have a telegraph device," said Fin firmly. "*No one* would have a telegraph device. The Devouts would have found it and destroyed it years ago. You do not understand how clever they are, how persistent. They even found the *Oyster* in the end!"

Krill started pacing again. "But they didn't destroy us, so maybe they're not as clever as you think, lad. Or maybe there's a ship out there that's even better at hiding than we were. But like I said, it won't do us any good, not two hundred miles and more away."

"Two hundred and seven miles is not far, not for Mister Smoke and Missus Slink," said the captain. "They could run that distance in—"

"No!" said Petrel. And then they were all looking at *her*, and she couldn't say what she was thinking—that Mister Smoke and Missus Slink had been a part of her life for as long as she could remember. That without the *Oyster*'s deck under her feet, she already felt as if she'd lost a big chunk of herself. And now here was the cap'n trying to slice off *another* chunk and send it north!

So all she said was, "I don't think we should split up like that. Sorry, Cap'n, but it doesn't sound like a good idea to me."

"All the same, he is right," said Fin. "We must get back to the *Oyster* before Albie goes south and leaves us behind. Which means we need a boat."

"'Course we do," said Petrel. "But there must be one closer than two hundred miles!"

"I thought there'd be boats all along this coast," said Krill, "but I ain't seen a single one."

"The Devouts have probably confiscated them for their own use," said Fin.

Krill peered at the captain from under his heavy brows. "How long would it take the rats to get to this other ship?"

"I cannot give you an exact time," said the captain. "If they keep to the coast, they will have to pass very close to the Citadel, which will slow them down. And then they will somehow have to get from the shore to the ship. My best estimate is twenty-six hours, or perhaps a little more. That is, if the ship does not move from its current position. How long will Squid and Dolph hold out against Albie if they do not hear from us?"

"As long as they can," said Krill gruffly. "That daughter of mine won't believe me dead until she sees my bones laid out in a row, and even then she'd probably tell me to get up and stop lazing around."

"Then Smoke and Slink should go now," the captain said.

"No!" Petrel couldn't believe that they were going to do it. She tried to think of sensible reasons to keep the two rats with them. "What if they can't get from the shore to the ship? What if the weather's bad? What if the crew's hostile or mad or—or just plain nasty, like Albie?"

Mister Smoke winked up at her. "Don't you worry about us, shipmate. We'll find a way."

"But what do *we* do in the meantime?" That was Fin. "We cannot stay here, not with the Devouts on their way."

"We will go up the coast too," said the captain, "but at a slower rate. We will look for villagers who *want* to learn about water pumps and mechanical plows. We will search for the Song. And when Mister Smoke and Missus Slink find the boat—"

"*If* they find it," said Petrel quickly, "which I don't see how they can."

"—they can send us a telegraph to get our new position."

Fin winced. "We will be traveling towards the Citadel. There will be spies and informers everywhere."

"Then we will have to be wary," said the captain. "Mister Smoke, Missus Slink, are you ready?"

It was going to happen, and there was nothing Petrel could do to stop it. She wanted to pick the two rats up and hold them so tightly that they couldn't go anywhere, but she knew she mustn't.

Her hand touched each gray head, as lightly as a snow-flake. "You'll come back, won't you?" she whispered.

"Aye, shipmate," said Mister Smoke. "We'll come back."

"Don't worry about us, girl," said Missus Slink.

And with that, the two of them turned tail and dashed off. Petrel watched them go, wondering if she would ever see them again.

CHAPTER 4

THE HUNGRY GHOST

The four Sunker children stood well away from the Hungry Ghost, studying her warily. They half expected her to leap to her feet and attack them, but once she'd finished puking, she just lay curled up on the deck, with her eyes closed and her fists clamped under her chin.

Which was a nuisance.

The *Claw* was basically a metal tube, no more than twenty-five paces from one end to the other, and every inch of her was packed with instruments, valves, pipes and pumps. Her control room, in the bow, was really just a stool set in front of an array of dials and switches. Her engine room, in the stern, was hot and cramped, and so was her little workshop. Her batteries, with a single bunk perched on top of them, butted up against the dive wheels, which in turn nudged the tiny galley and the chart table. And in the middle of it all, so that everyone had to breathe in as they edged past, were the periscope station and the ladder that led up to the conning tower.

Even without a Ghost on board, there was hardly room to move.

"Maybe the salt water hurt her," whispered Gilly. "Maybe she's dying."

"Ghosts can't die," said Sharkey.

He wasn't sure if that was true, but Gilly nodded seriously and said, "She might sort of melt, though, sir. If we leave her alone. She might disappear."

Sharkey hoped his cousin was right. He had no idea what to do with the Ghost. Granfer Trout had been wrong about "bellies as big as mountains." Apart from her white hair and pinky-brown skin, the girl looked almost human, and Sharkey had to keep reminding himself that she wasn't.

I should shove her back out the air lock, he thought. But he didn't want to touch her again. Didn't *dare* touch her, if he was being truthful with himself. No matter what she looked like, she was a Ghost, and Ghosts were dangerous.

So in the end, he left her where she was, with Gilly standing guard.

Early next morning, they returned to the scene of the *Rampart*'s sinking. Sharkey didn't want to go, but he gave the order all the same. If it'd been the *Claw* down there on the seabed instead of the *Rampart*, Admiral Deeps would've gone back to check. It'd look bad if Sharkey did anything else.

They surfaced forty-five minutes before sunclimb, with the periscope showing a dark, overcast sky and no sign of skimmers or giant bubbles. Sharkey ordered the diesels started, to recharge the batteries and air. Then he edged past the Ghost.

Right up to that moment, he hadn't been sure about leaving the middies alone while he went to check on the *Rampart*. But apart from flinching when the diesels roared to life, the Ghost still hadn't moved. *Maybe she* is *dying,* thought Sharkey. *Or maybe she's just too sick to hurt us. Wish Surgeon Blue was here; I bet he'd know.*

He beckoned Cuttle and Poddy. "Watch her carefully," he said over the clatter of the diesels.

"Aye, sir!"

"If she moves, call Gilly—she'll be up on deck, keeping watch."

The two middies saluted and took up guard positions.

With a weight belt and a waterproof lantern slung over his arm, Sharkey climbed the ladder inside the conning tower. Then he unsealed the two hatches and stepped out onto the small, flat deck, just two feet above the waterline. Gilly followed him.

The sea was calm, and the horizon was a dark line. Sharkey screwed up his good eye and said, "You've got the conn while I'm gone."

Gilly saluted. "I've got the conn. Aye, sir!"

"Keep an eye on Poddy and Cuttle. Make sure the Ghost doesn't try anything. And watch out for skimmers and bubbles."

"Aye, sir."

Sharkey took off his sea-silk pants and jerkin and hung them over one of the stay wires. He undid his eye patch and tucked it into the pocket of his pants. Then, with his back to his cousin, he strapped on the weight belt with the waterproof lantern attached, slipped out of his smallclothes and jumped over the side.

The water was so cold it made his teeth hurt, but he'd been swimming in temperatures like this since before he could walk, and thought nothing of it. He hung on to a porthole, taking in lungfuls of air and letting them out again. Then he took a deep breath—and dived into the darkness.

His strong legs drove him down and down and down. Fish darted across his path. Strings of kelp brushed against his hands. When his ears felt as if they were going to burst, he held his nose and blew, to even the pressure.

On that first dive, he found nothing except the rough seabed. On the second, he thought he saw something to the east—something gray and silent—but when he brought the lantern closer, it turned out to be an outcrop of rock.

He went up again, for another breath. He felt sick and angry, and the rumble of the diesels seemed to drag on him like an anchor chain.

It took him another ten minutes to find the *Rampart*. By then the horizon was growing light, and Sharkey was so cold he could barely think. *One more try,* he told himself. And he drew the air into his aching lungs and dived.

The *Rampart* was lying on her side, some way west of where Sharkey had been looking for her. Even in the semidarkness, he could see the battering she'd taken. There was an enormous, jagged hole just behind the conning tower, and another two farther for'ard. The water must have rushed in like a king tide. It was a wonder Admiral Deeps had managed to get a message sent. It was a wonder anyone had got out.

If they *had* got out.

Sharkey picked up a rock and banged on the bow hatch, in case someone was still alive in one of the watertight compartments. There was no answer. He banged again on the stern hatch, trying to remain hopeful. But he couldn't ignore what he knew in his heart. The holes in the hull were too big. The watertight compartments weren't watertight, not anymore. Anyone who was left on the *Rampart* was dead.

He dropped the rock and swam for the surface. His fingers and toes were numb, but he didn't *feel* cold. He'd lost his fear of the dying Ghost girl too. There was a ball of rage inside him, and he wanted to grab hold of the girl and shake her until she rattled.

It wasn't until he had dragged himself back onto the deck of the *Claw*, with the diesel engines thumping away under his bare feet, that he realized Gilly was no longer there.

Sharkey hated it when crew weren't where they were supposed to be. Life on the submersibles was dangerous enough as it was. There were so many things that could go wrong—a stuck valve, a hot bearing, a loose connection. There was no room for half measures, no room for inattention. For the Sunkers, it was all or nothing. Watertight or holed. Alive or dead.

Which meant that Gilly wouldn't have left her post unless there was some sort of emergency.

The Ghost! thought Sharkey.

And with murder in his heart, he threw on his smallclothes and leaped for the conning tower.

CHAPTER 5

RAIN

SHE WAS NOT A FIGHTER, BUT SHE DID HER BEST. As the three savage children pummeled her from all sides, she put her arms over her head and pressed forward. She thought she had nearly made it, but then, without warning, one of the children kicked her behind the knees. Her legs crumpled, and she tumbled to the floor.

"That'll teach you!" cried the child, sitting on top of her so she couldn't move. "Stinking Ghost!"

Rain said nothing. She had retreated into her own world and was doing what she always did when things turned bad: singing under her breath.

Her name was Rain,
And like rain
She fell from the sky . . .

She heard a thud of footsteps, and the fourth savage, the boy with black hair, came hurtling, bare-chested, down the ladder from outside.

"What happened?" he snapped. "Gilly, report!"

The older of the two girls—the one who had kicked Rain—leaped to her feet. She had very short brown hair that looked as if it had been hacked off with a knife, and she wore trousers instead of an overskirt. "The Ghost tried to eat the depth gauge, sir! We barely stopped her in time."

The savages had an odd way of talking. They slurred some of their letters, chopped off others and used strange words, so that at first Rain had thought they were speaking a completely different language. But now, after a day or so of listening, she was used to it.

Depth gauge, she thought, and she automatically started to weave it into a song. She did it silently, in case the savages disapproved of singing, the way Brother Thrawn did.

I tried to break the depth gauge
To save my brother's life—

Rain liked singing, though she was not very good at it. She was not very good at anything, according to her uncle Poosk.

"Nevertheless, Brother Thrawn wants to try you in one of the new hot-air balloons," he had said. "I did my best to persuade him otherwise, but he would not budge. Since returning from the failed demon-hunting expedition, he will not tolerate weakness of any kind, and if you make a mess of it, he might well punish your brother. So please try to get it right."

Of course, Rain *had* made a mess of it, which was why she was here now, trapped in this terrifying underwater ship with bruises rising on her legs and arms. All around her, iron wheels stuck out of the walls, along with a hundred other things she did not have names for. Somewhere not far away, *machines* rumbled out their frightful tune.

She was afraid, of course. She was afraid of most things, including hot-air balloons and throwers and the infernal devices called bombs. Such things had not been seen in West Norn for hundreds of years—hardly anyone even suspected they still existed. But after he came back from the southern ice, Brother Thrawn had ordered them dug out of buried storehouses and had set teams of men to test and repair them.

For the last few weeks, everyone in the Citadel had been repeating his words with a mixture of awe and excitement. "The demon is coming, and we must protect ourselves. We will use the devil's tools to fight the devil."

The balloons and the bombs were frightening enough. But the machines at the far end of the underwater ship were far worse. They hadn't stolen Rain's soul, not yet, but it was only a matter of time. She imagined them stalking stiff-legged towards her, like savage dogs—

She shuddered. *What will happen to Bran when I am no longer there to protect him?*

"It was our fault, sir," said the boy sitting on Rain's ankles. He looked a bit like the girl, though his face was narrower and he seemed younger. "We weren't watching her close enough. Sorry."

The boy they called "sir" nodded. Then, without a word, he found a rope and bound Rain's feet together.

The other two children stood up cautiously, but Rain made no move to escape. After all, where could she go? She was trapped and helpless, and her captors were both stronger and fiercer than she was.

The bare-chested boy trussed her arms behind her back, then pulled her into a sitting position and tied her to the leg of a table. Like the other savage children, he was streaked with oil, but beneath the dirt his skin was as white as a winter grub.

"What are we going to do with her, sir?" asked Gilly.

"Sir" did not answer. Instead, he leaned closer to Rain and tapped his face. "See this?" he hissed.

Rain looked directly at him for the first time—and gulped. His eye socket was puckered and hollow, and the skin around it was a web of scar tissue.

"I fought a Massy shark," whispered the boy, baring his teeth in a vicious grin. "A big one. Bigger than you could imagine."

Rain had no idea what a Massy shark was. She tried to slide away from the boy, but the rope held her tight.

"And you know who won?" he asked, still grinning. "Me. Shark got my eye, but I got its guts. That's why they call me Sharkey. So when we're safely away from here, you're going to tell me everything I want to know. And don't try holding anything back, 'cos if you do, I'll slice you open like I sliced that shark. And then I'll chuck your dead body overboard. You understand me?"

Rain nodded jerkily. The machines growled as if they could smell her fear.

"Good," said Sharkey.

Then he stood up and said to the other children, "The

Rampart's busted wide-open. There's no one left on board. Not alive, anyway."

Rain peeped at their faces, expecting tears and other signs of grief, but saw nothing.

"It's close to sunclimb," continued Sharkey. "Poddy, get my clothes. Cuttle, you've got the conn. Take her down."

"Take her down. Aye, sir!" shouted Cuttle as Poddy, a small, round-faced girl, scrambled up the ladder. "Prepare to dive!"

For a moment, Rain thought they were going to leave Poddy to drown. But the little girl was back down the ladder with Sharkey's clothes more quickly than Rain would have thought possible.

And then they were all shouting incomprehensible phrases like "Pressure in the green!" and "Five degrees down bubble!" and "Switch to batteries!" They closed some things and opened others, they turned the huge wheels, they ran back and forth, ducking their heads and edging around the table, and shouted some more.

Or at least the three younger children did. Sharkey tied a black patch over his empty eye socket and then stood with his legs braced and a superior look on his face, watching the activity around him.

As the iron ship sank beneath the water, Rain stole a glance at the patch and gulped again. She was not a brave person. She was shy and timid, and the only way she had ever been able to make sense of the world was by singing at it. She even thought in songs much of the time, as if they were a code that only she could understand.

Now she sang under her breath:

I will tell him everything
I know.
I will tell him names and days
And places—

She stopped, knowing that there was one thing she must *not* tell him, must not tell anyone. Ever. Something she did her best not to even *think* about.

Because she *might* get away from these savages, though she could not imagine how. And her little brother *might* survive without her.

But if anyone learned the truth and traced it back to Rain, Bran's life would be worth less than a scrap of kindling. And so would hers.

SHARKEY DIDN'T REALLY LOSE HIS EYE IN A FIGHT WITH A Massy shark. He didn't lose it in a fight with anything. It was just a dreadful accident.

There were always accidents on the submersibles, but no one expected Sharkey to get caught by one. He was born on a fortunate tide. Not only that, but he came into the world with a head of straight black hair, just like the old engravings of Lin Lin. His ma and fa were so pleased that they named him straight off, rather than waiting a few months in case he didn't survive. They gave him a good, strong name too, instead of calling him Winkle or Sprat or one of the other baby names that got changed to something better as children grew older.

No way was Sharkey changing *his* name. There wasn't a better name to be had, except perhaps for Admiral Deeps.

His straight black hair fell out, the way it usually does with babies. But to his parents' delight, it grew back even straighter and blacker.

"He's Lin Lin's boy, that's for sure," said everyone who saw him. "He's got great things ahead of him. Expect he'll make adm'ral one day."

And as Sharkey grew older, he thought the same. Why wouldn't he? He was clever, keen-eyed and lucky. He had everything on his side—until the dreadful day, when he was eight years old, that ruined everything.

It was an accident; nearly everyone agreed on that. The *Retribution*, where they lived, was old and tired, and there were always gaskets bursting and pipes breaking. Crew usually managed to skittle out of the way in time, but every now and again someone got hurt.

The steam from that particular burst gasket cost Sharkey his right eye and most of the skin around it. He could still remember the agony of it, and how Ma held his hand while Surgeon Blue applied cold water to the burns.

That was the end of "Expect he'll make adm'ral one day." Crew stopped mentioning the fortunate tide and how much he looked like Lin Lin. Instead, Sharkey was reminded over and over again how lucky he was that he'd lost one eye instead of two.

He didn't feel lucky. He didn't want to spend the rest of

his life huddled in a greasy corner of the *Retribution*, doing someone else's bidding. He didn't want crew looking away so they wouldn't have to see his ruined eye, even after his ma had sewn a patch to cover it. He didn't want to be at the bottom of things.

But that's where he had been, and that's where he'd seemed likely to stay—until the night of his tenth birthday, a year and three months after the accident. When the miracle happened.

This is how he'd told it, breathless, on his return to the *Retribution*. He was out swimming, when a turtle spoke to him. Yes, a turtle, a flatback, as pretty as moonlight! It swam right up close, and he was thinking of turtle soup. But before he could kill it, it put its horny head close to his and said, "Do not go west, Great-Grandson, not this week."

Then it swam away into the deep blue, leaving Sharkey half-drowned with shock.

He was still spluttering when Fa dragged him over to the *Rampart* to talk to Admiral Deeps. "Adm'ral, you've got to hear this!" said Sharkey's fa. "It's—" He shook his head, speechless.

Sharkey told the story again. And again, as the Sunkers gathered around him, firing questions.

"It *spoke*? The turtle *spoke* to you?"

"You *sure* it was a turtle?"

"How far down were you? Might've been raptures, if you were deep enough."

"Not far down at all," said Sharkey, standing up for

himself. "Maybe half periscope, that's all. It wasn't raptures, I'm sure of it. And it *was* a turtle."

"Turtles don't speak," said Admiral Deeps, and everyone nodded. That was a fact, on a day when facts seemed few and far between.

"*What* did it call the boy?" asked one of the old salties from the back of the crowd.

"Great-grandson," replied someone else. "It called him great-grandson!"

All of them grew very quiet then, staring at Sharkey as if they'd never seen him before. He stood as straight and tall as he could, trying not to shiver, trying not to flinch when Admiral Deeps turned her cool eyes on him.

"And why would a flatback turtle call *you* great-grandson, Sharkey?" she asked.

It was his ma who answered. "Because it wasn't a turtle at all, Adm'ral. It was the spirit of Lin Lin!"

"That's right," said Sharkey, drawing his ten-year-old bones even taller. "It was the spirit of Great-Granmer Lin Lin!"

And with that, his life changed forever.

Of course, Lin Lin wasn't really Sharkey's great-granmer; she had died too long ago for that, and people had lost count of the generations in between. But everyone called her Great-Granmer, because it was respectful, and respect was important to the Sunkers.

They respected Sharkey once they heard his tale. And their respect grew when, a month later, both Great-Granmer

Lin Lin *and* Great-Granfer Cray spoke to him. This time they appeared in the form of dolphins and warned Sharkey not to go north, which was where the fleet had been heading.

Everyone took the warnings seriously. In three hundred years, the Hungry Ghosts had never found them, but that could change at any moment. So instead of going north, they went east and south and saw no sign of their enemies. None of the submersibles broke down either, and everyone knew it was because of Sharkey and Lin Lin.

It wasn't long before they started mentioning that fortunate tide again. Even Admiral Deeps smiled at Sharkey, and she wasn't a woman who gave her smiles easily.

Sharkey loved the attention, loved being so important. He was allowed to take the *Claw* out whenever he wanted to, and he got the best food and the fewest hard duties. And whenever he came back from a swim, someone was sure to ask, "Any word from Lin Lin or Adm'ral Cray?"

Sometimes there was and sometimes there wasn't. And right now, with the *Rampart* lying broken on the ocean floor and the rest of the Sunker community dead, Sharkey's honored ancestors weren't talking.

Which was no great surprise to Sharkey, who had made the whole thing up.

CHAPTER 6

THE LAST OF THE SUNKERS

MEANWHILE, ON THE BESIEGED BRIDGE OF THE *OYSTER*, Third Officer Dolph was testing the barricades, making sure Albie and his mutineers couldn't break through.

Behind her, a dozen voices went over the same old arguments.

"Maybe Skua's telling the truth. Why would he lie about such a thing?"

"Because his da told him to, why else?"

"But what if they *are* dead? Where does that leave us? We can't hold out against Albie forever, not with the whole ship behind him—"

Squid's sensible voice broke in. "The whole ship's *not* behind him!" she said. "Glory be, haven't you been listening to the pipe messages? The Engineers are behind him right enough, but—"

"Engineers always do what Albie tells 'em."

"Exactly," said Squid. "But it sounds as if a goodly number of Cooks don't want any part of it—didn't you catch that pipe message about barricades in Dufftown? As for the senior Officers, there's no way *they're* behind him. But they can't do much while they're locked up."

"Still, there's an awful lot of folk listening to Albie."

"And who can blame 'em?" said Squid sharply. "Here we are in hostile waters, and the first thing that happens is the shore party gets murdered—at least that's what Albie's telling everyone. And you know how shipfolk feel about the cap'n; he's like a talisman, and losing him just about strips the heart out of 'em. Then there's Krill and Petrel and Fin, and each one of 'em leaves a gap. If First Officer Hump could've taken charge, it mightn't've been so bad, or Second Officer Weddell. But Albie's no fool. He's got 'em both under lock and key, along with anyone else the crew might listen to. Most folk don't *want* to follow him. It's just that he hasn't left 'em much alternative."

"What about Dolph—"

"Dolph might be Third Officer, but she's young and untried, and when things turn bad, shipfolk want someone with a bit of experience in charge. And right now, that means Albie. He's got it all worked out. Mind you, he's not infallible. If the shore party turned up alive, this mutiny'd be over in a heartbeat."

"If Orca was still with us," said Minke, "Albie wouldn't dare pull a trick like this."

It's true, Dolph thought miserably as she went back to

jamming lengths of driftwood into place. *If Mam was alive, she'd've stopped this before it began. Which means I should've stopped it. I might be young, but I'm Third Officer, and it was my job to keep the ship safe till the cap'n got back.*

She rested her head against the driftwood, wondering what to do next. The folk behind her were expecting a decision—she knew that. Some of them wanted to negotiate with Albie. Others wanted to hold out as long as possible.

She turned around and caught Squid's eye. When the older girl strode over to join her, Dolph whispered, "D'you think Skua's lying? Really?"

"I do," said Squid.

"We haven't had a reply to that message I sent."

"Could be something's gone wrong with the telegraph device."

"Albie?"

"Not necessarily," said Squid. "Might just be bad luck. It got bumped around a fair bit when we were rushing to build the barricades. Maybe something's come loose. I've had a look, but it's got all sorts of strange innards and I don't know what I'm supposed to be looking for." She folded her arms. "But message or no message, this is how I see it: I can imagine the cap'n being caught unawares—he's too trusting for his own good. And Fin isn't that canny either, not when it comes to survival. But Da?" She laughed. "It'd take more than a few Devouts to beat him. Same for Petrel. And the two of them combined are a powerful force."

Dolph nodded slowly. "So—what d'you think we should do?"

"That's up to you," said Squid. "You're Third. You're in charge."

The younger girl flushed. Up till now, she'd liked being Third Officer. She'd been learning navigation mostly, and taking her turn at the wheel. And every now and then, when she thought she could get away with it, she'd practiced bossing people around.

But this was different. This was the future of the ship.

"Right," she said. Then "Right!" louder this time, so that the arguments stopped and everyone turned to stare at her.

"Um—Squid thinks her da and Petrel are still alive, at least," said Dolph. "So do I. And we don't abandon our shipmates, do we?"

Dead silence. A few sideways glances.

Dolph summoned up memories of her mam and tried to get that Orca ice into her voice. "*Do we?*"

To her surprise, it worked. Minke said, "No, you're right, girl. We don't."

"So," said Dolph, clasping her hands behind her back, where no one could see them shaking, "we're going to keep sending telegraph messages, um, at the beginning of each watch, just in case they can hear us. And we're *not* giving in to Albie, no matter what he says. We're going to hold out as long as we can."

She paused, expecting argument, and got none. "Squid, you're in charge of food and water."

"There's not much of either," said Squid.

"Then we're on short rations," said Dolph. "It won't be the first time. Minke, you're in charge of pipe messages. Tell the ship that Skua's lying. Tell 'em over and over again and hope they start to believe us. And—and if anyone has any useful ideas, like how we can take the ship back from Albie, I'm willing to listen. But *no more arguing*. We're all in this together."

She glared at them, Orca-style, then dismissed them with a nod, hoping she could reach the nearest seat before her legs gave way and ruined everything.

I'm doing my best, Mam, she thought as she lowered herself carefully into the pilot's chair. *I'm doing my best. I just hope it's good enough.*

As soon as the *Claw* was running smoothly, with Gilly at the helm, Sharkey squatted in front of the Ghost girl again. His anger had not cooled, and it overrode any remaining fears.

"Have you got a name, Ghost?" he demanded.

The girl licked her lips. "My name is Rain."

"What?" said Sharkey.

"My name is Rain."

Sharkey turned to Poddy. "What's she saying? Can you understand her?"

"I think she said her name's Rain, sir," said Poddy. "She's got a funny way of talking. Maybe Ghosts've got another lingo, and she's only just starting to learn human."

Sharkey turned back to the girl. Speaking loudly, to make sure she understood, he said, "Three hundred years and your lot never found us. Why now?"

"Because of B-Brother Thrawn." Her voice was so quiet he could hardly hear it.

"Louder," he said. "Slower."

"Because of B-Brother Thrawn. The leader of the Devouts. He has—he has recently come back from the far south. Where the demons live."

This time Sharkey managed to catch most of it, but it still didn't make much sense. Devouts? Demons? He scowled, and the Ghost girl flinched away from him and said, "He was—he was hurt; the demon hurt his body. But his mind—his mind is as clear and sharp as ever—"

"The truth!" snarled Sharkey.

"The truth," gasped the girl. "The truth is that we—we were not looking for you at all. We were watching for the demon ship! That is why B-Brother Thrawn sent out the balloons and the infernal d-devices. When we saw the big underwater ship, no one knew what it was." Her voice faded. "But we were told to kill it."

Sharkey sat back on his heels and stared at her. She was too foreign, too strange, and he couldn't be sure he was reading her right. She looked terrified, but that was probably just a Ghost trick. She looked as if she was lying about something, but that might be wrong too. For all he knew, she could be laughing at him!

His anger flared up, hotter than ever, and he almost gave the order, right there and then, to chuck her out the air lock.

But even as he opened his mouth, his clever mind was

working away, telling him that it might be *useful* to have a captive Ghost and that he shouldn't be in too much of a hurry to get rid of her.

Cuttle cleared his throat. "Sir, me and Poddy've been thinking. Maybe some of those on the *Rampart did* survive."

Poddy nodded. "And we could rescue 'em!"

"Nay," said Sharkey, standing up. "They didn't have a chance. I told you, they're all gone. We're the last of the Sunkers."

He thought that was the end of it, but Cuttle, who wasn't usually so contrary, said, "But what about the ones who abandoned ship, sir?"

"They drowned," Sharkey said bluntly. "Or else the Ghosts ate 'em."

The Ghost girl made a squeak of protest and said, "You mean the D-Devouts? They do not eat people! They have probably taken them to the camp."

"What camp?" demanded Poddy.

"The reeducation camp. Near the Citadel."

Camp. Citadel. None of it meant anything to Sharkey. "Be quiet," he said. "Don't talk to my crew. Don't try to trick 'em."

"I am not—" began Rain. But Sharkey shot her one of his blackest looks, and she fell silent.

The *Claw* was heading east, towards the Greater Seddley Current. Sharkey set the course with as much outward confidence as he could muster, then kept the middies busy cooking, cleaning pumps and lines and scrubbing away at bits of rust. At night they surfaced to fish, swim, recharge the batteries and renew their air. They slept in shifts, partly owing to lack of room, and partly to keep an eye on the Ghost.

Sharkey spent most of his time in the tiny workshop aft of the diesel engines, hammering out spare parts. It was heavy work, which he usually avoided, but now he hoped it'd stop him thinking too much.

We're the last of the Sunkers.

It was a world that had existed for three hundred years, a world of knowledge, secrets and responsibility. And now the whole thing rested on Sharkey's shoulders. He felt as if he'd fallen into one of the deep ocean trenches, and the pressure of the water above was crushing him. He could hardly breathe from the weight of it.

The last of the Sunkers!

He would never have admitted it to the middies, but he was scared witless. Apart from everything else, he was used to having Admiral Deeps checking his decisions and saving him from mistakes. He was used to taking all the credit and none of the blame and coming out the other side all shiny and heroic.

He wished desperately that the admiral was with them now. She'd know what to do. She'd take this weight off his shoulders.

He wished too that the ancestors would speak to him. *Really* speak to him this time. Give him a sign, a hint. Anything.

And on the third night, they did. Or so it seemed . . .

It was past sunfall, and they'd seen no skimmers or giant bubbles since the attack. But Sharkey wasn't taking any risks.

"Up periscope," he said, and Gilly heaved the periscope into place and snapped its handles open.

The Ghost girl watched silently, as she watched everything. Sharkey had been surprised to discover that she ate real food, instead of just chewing on machines and people. He hated wasting fish on her, and he still wondered if it'd be best to simply push her out the air lock.

"All clear, sir," said Gilly, after turning in a circle twice, once quickly and once slowly. "It's raining."

"Take her up," said Sharkey.

But before anyone could respond, something banged against the periscope.

Gilly squawked. Sharkey's heart leaped into his mouth. He was about to shout *Flood the quick-dive tank!* when Gilly cried, "Can't be Ghosts, sir! There's no one out there. Must be something floating."

Poddy, who hadn't been sleeping well since the attack on the *Rampart*, whispered, "Might be a corpse."

Cuttle's mouth tightened. Gilly lowered the periscope a little and said, "Nay. It's too small."

They surfaced cautiously, ready to dive at the slightest sign of danger. But when Sharkey climbed the ladder and opened the double hatch, there was nothing there except gray clouds and rain, and the seawater still pouring off the hull.

A cloud of spray hit him in the face, blinding him for a second or two. He wiped his eye and stepped out onto the deck, bracing himself against the swell. "All clear!" he called.

The object bobbing off the *Claw*'s bow looked like an odd-shaped bottle, though Sharkey couldn't be sure. He shouted down the hatch. "Bring a net, Poddy!"

"Aye, sir!"

They hauled the strange bottle on board, handling it gingerly as if it might blow up in their faces. It had something inside it. A scrap of paper, maybe.

As Sharkey examined it, Poddy gasped. "Dolphins, sir! Look!"

There were two of them, poking their smooth noses above the water as if they had come for a visit. In the rain, Poddy's face shone. "Is it *them*, sir?" she whispered. "Is it Lin Lin and Adm'ral Cray? Are they going to say something?"

Sharkey scowled. "It's not them. Come on, I want to see if there's anything on this paper."

They went below, where the yellow lamps ran on batteries, day and night. "It's a message," cried Poddy as she swung down the ladder. "From Lin Lin!"

"It's *not* from Lin Lin," snapped Sharkey. He dried his face and hands with a rag, propped himself against the berth that straddled the batteries, and unfolded the scrap of paper.

Like all the Sunkers, he had learned to read as a middy. But the spiky scrawl in front of him was nothing like the square, sensible writing of real people.

He turned the paper this way and that, frowning. He didn't want to admit that he couldn't read it, so he said, "Must be in Ghost lingo," and thrust it under the nose of the Ghost girl. "What's it say? And don't lie."

Rain scanned the paper and blinked. "It is from—" She looked up. "It is from Brother Thrawn."

"Him?" said Gilly. "The one who ordered the attack on the *Rampart*? What's he want, a bang on the head? I'll give it to him!"

"He wants"—Rain squinted at the paper—"to make an exchange. For me!"

"What sort of exchange?" demanded Sharkey.

"If you give me back, he will give you one of the *Rampart*'s crew."

Cuttle said, "But they're all dead, sir. He *can't* give 'em back, can he?"

"Maybe he's going to give us a corpse," said Gilly, glowering. "Maybe he thinks it's funny."

But Poddy's face was bright with hope. "They're alive, sir! They *are*!"

"Nay," said Sharkey fiercely. "It's a trap. Ghosts are trying to lure us Up Above so they can eat us too. Don't be fooled, Poddy."

Rain cleared her throat. "The Devouts are not ghosts. And they do not eat people."

Sharkey wasn't listening to her. "How'd they find us? That's the question. One little bottle in such a big ocean?"

"Maybe there are dozens of bottles, sir," said Gilly. "All with the same message. All chucked into the water at different spots. And the current brought one of 'em this way."

"Mmm." Sharkey nodded cautiously.

"And maybe," said Poddy, her face still glowing, "some of the crew *did* survive. Maybe the Ghosts didn't eat 'em all. They might be waiting for us to rescue 'em, sir!"

Sharkey didn't want his crew thinking about rescues. Such things were for real heroes, not fake ones. He ignored Poddy and said to Rain, "What makes you so special? Why does Brother Thrawn want you back?"

The girl reddened. "I—I do not know. M-maybe he is doing a favor for my uncle."

"Who's your uncle? Someone important?"

Rain shook her head vigorously. "He is Brother Thrawn's nurse, that is all. He does the things Brother Thrawn cannot do for himself anymore. He is not the least bit important, but— but he took us in four months ago, when Mama died. My little brother and me. We would have starved but for Uncle Poosk."

"Uncle *Poosk*?" Gilly snorted at the name, but Sharkey watched the Ghost girl, trying to separate lies from truth.

"What's your brother's name?" asked Poddy.

For the first time, Rain's face lit up with a genuine smile. "Bran. He is six. He is the sweetest boy—"

Sharkey pushed himself away from the bunk, saying, "This isn't getting us anywhere. I don't care about *Uncle Poosk* and sweet little *Bran*—"

The girl's smile disappeared.

"—I just want to know if this is a trap or not."

"I don't think it's a trap, sir," said Poddy. "I think it's a sign. I've been asking for one for days. We all have." She beamed up at the ancestor shrine. "Thank you, Lin Lin! Thank you, Great-Granfer Cray!"

"What about the Hungry Ghosts?" asked Cuttle. "How could we make a swap without getting eaten?"

Poddy ignored him. "I bet those two dolphins pushed the bottle towards us!"

"What about the Hungry Ghosts?" asked Cuttle again.

"It *might* be a sign—" began Gilly.

"What about the Hungry *Ghosts*?" This time Cuttle was so loud that they had to take notice.

Everyone fell silent, even Poddy. All their lives they'd known that going Up Above after sunclimb was almost certain death. The Hungry Ghosts would find them and eat them. It was madness to even think about it.

But Poddy wasn't about to give up. "If the ancestors want us to do it, sir, there must be a way."

Sharkey felt like laughing, though there was nothing funny about the situation. Of course it was a trap! He couldn't believe he was even considering it.

But then he started wondering who they might get in exchange for Rain. A middy? An auntie or uncle?

Or Admiral Deeps?

Once the idea was there in his mind, it wouldn't go away. Admiral Deeps, who'd know what to do next. Who'd take this great weight of responsibility off his shoulders.

He glanced at Rain. Was that a flicker of hope in her eyes? Or was it scorn? Did she think he was afraid? Did she think he wouldn't dare go Up Above, not even to get Admiral Deeps back?

I asked for a sign, he thought, *and I got one. Maybe Poddy's right. Maybe there* is *a way.*

Gilly said, "When's the handover? And where?"

"The day before the next full moon," said Rain, reading the scrap of paper. "Early morning, due west of where the Devouts attacked your big ship. Behind the beach, at the grand monument."

Whatever a mon-u-ment is, thought Sharkey. He felt as if he were about to step off the edge of an abyss, into water deeper than he'd ever known. "Four days away," he muttered.

"We could just go and look, sir," said Poddy. "Watch from periscope depth, see if they come."

Sharkey took a breath—and nodded. "Gilly, find the right chart."

"Aye, sir!"

And with that, the decision was made.

CHAPTER 7

WE SHOULD NEVER HAVE LEFT THE ICE

Mister Smoke and Missus Slink had been gone for far too long.

Something's happened to 'em, thought Petrel as she and her friends stumbled along a rough coastal track. *According to the cap'n's calculations, they should've reached that ship by now. They should've sent a message, but they haven't. They ain't coming back—I'm sure of it! I'm never going to see 'em again.*

Her only consolation was the messages from the *Oyster*, which came every four hours and were disjointed and scrappy.

. . . STIL . . . HERE, said each message. ST . . . HOLD . . . OUT. WHER . . . AR . . . YOU?

"There must be a loose connection at their end," said the captain. "That is why they are not getting our replies. I wish they would fix it."

"So do I, Cap'n," said Krill grimly. "But at least they're alive, and they've still got the bridge. Albie hasn't won yet."

All the same, he was dreadfully worried, and so was Petrel.

Between one message and the next, she imagined Albie storming the barricades, Squid and Dolph dead and the *Oyster* turning south.

As bad as the situation was, hunger made it worse. The dried fish was long gone, and this particular bit of coast seemed to offer nothing but stunted trees, low thorny bushes and rocks.

Last night, Petrel had dreamed she was eating a toothyfish, so sweet and juicy that she could still taste it when she woke up. The withered roots called taters, which Fin had found halfway through the morning, were a poor substitute.

What's more, the captain insisted on going into every village they passed. The others did their best to dissuade him, but on this one matter he would not be budged. "We are here to change the world," he said.

The trouble was, they *weren't* changing the world. They weren't even changing a tiny part of the coast of West Norn. No one in the villages would talk to them, no matter how politely they offered information about water pumps, mechanical plows and windmills. Fin had been sure that folk would be grateful for simple machines that made their lives easier, but it seemed he was wrong. The villagers of West Norn were too frightened of the Devouts to be grateful for anything.

It bothered Petrel to see them so cowed and voiceless. It reminded her of the way *she* used to be, which she didn't want to think about, and she found herself getting angry with the villagers and blaming them for their own misery—which made her feel even worse.

The only one not dispirited by their failure was the captain. He simply grew more determined to find the Singer and the Song, which, he said, would make all the difference.

And now they were walking again. The snow had melted, the day was damp and miserable, and everyone except the captain was snappish. To take her mind off her worries, Petrel trotted up close behind Fin and said, "What does your mam look like? What color's her hair?"

Without turning, Fin said, "You have asked me that a dozen times since we left the ice."

"And I'm asking again."

"I cannot remember her hair."

"What about her eyes?"

There was an edge to Fin's voice now. "I cannot remember her eyes either."

Petrel knew she should give up. Instead, she walked closer, so she was almost treading on his heels. "How about her name?"

Fin stopped dead and said, through gritted teeth, "I was three years old, Petrel. Her name, as far as I was concerned, was Mama. Now, can you tell me how, in the whole of West Norn, I am going to find a woman called *Mama*?"

He didn't wait for her reply. As he walked away, Petrel thought she heard him mutter, "Besides, she is probably dead."

There was no answer to that. But Petrel might have kept digging anyway, if the captain hadn't suddenly stopped and picked up something from the path.

"It is a bird!" he said. "A pigeon. Look." And he opened his hands to show them.

The pigeon was smaller than the gulls and albatrosses of the icy south, and its feathers were blue-gray, with dark stripes across the wings and tail. Its eyes were closed, and it lay panting in the captain's grasp.

He ran his clever fingers over its wings. "Nothing is broken," he said. "Perhaps it was chased by a hawk and is exhausted. If I take care of it, it should recover."

He made a cooing sound, and the bird opened its orange eyes and blinked at him.

"It belongs to the Devouts," said Fin. "See?" He gently extended the pigeon's leg, which had a scroll of waxed paper tied to it. "They use them as messenger birds."

"What's it say?" asked Krill.

Fin unraveled the bit of paper. "'Demon and companions sighted in coastal village, District 2. Believed to be heading north.'"

"Just as well *that* didn't get through!" said Petrel. She stroked the bird's feathers. "I'm sorry for you, pigeon, being attacked and all. But it's a good thing you didn't make it."

Fin shook his head. "*This* bird did not make it, but the Devouts always send more than one. Which means they know we are here. They will be hunting—"

He broke off, his eyes darting back the way he and his companions had come. Petrel froze. So did Krill. The captain was as still as a bollard, his hands cradling the bird.

A slow, rhythmic thud reached their ears.

"Horses!" mouthed Fin. "Coming up behind us!"

For a moment, Petrel felt as if she were back on the *Oyster*, and the Officer bratlings coming after her with the tar bucket.

Except she knew every single hidey-hole on the old ice-breaker and could conceal herself easily. Not like here.

She caught her breath. *There must be somewhere to hide!* She stared frantically at the unfamiliar landscape and saw a clump of vines and fallen trees. She pointed. *There!* The others hurried off the track after her, moving as quietly as they could through the low scrub.

The sound of horses grew louder. One of them snorted. A man called out, "Are you sure they were heading this way? If you are wasting our time, you will be sorry."

When she heard that, Petrel just about fell over with fright. *That last village! I* told *the cap'n we should go around it!*

She urged her friends on, scrambling around bushes and over rocks, until she and Fin and the captain were tucked up inside the clump of vines, with the pigeon lying on the ground beside them. Krill was nearly there too; he just had to climb over those last few wet rocks.

Except he was going too fast, and his foot slipped. One of the rocks tipped under him. His weight skewed in the wrong direction—and he fell sideways, his starboard leg suddenly useless, his hands grabbing at the ground so he wouldn't make too much noise as he fell.

There was no time to lose. Fin, Petrel and the captain grabbed hold of Krill and dragged him into the shelter of the vines. He didn't make a sound, not even a whimper, but his face was contorted with pain, and the sweat poured off him in torrents.

And then the horses were passing by no more than fifteen paces away, and all Petrel and her friends could do was crouch behind the thin curtain of vines, hoping they would not be discovered.

The horses were long-nosed creatures with hoofs as big as portholes. The two men who were riding them wore brown robes and wide-brimmed hats to keep the rain off, and had shiny, satisfied faces, as if they'd recently eaten a large meal. Across their backs they carried axes, and tied to each of their saddles was a wicker cage containing several pigeons.

A third man walked in front of the horses. *He* didn't look satisfied. His cheeks were so hollow that it hurt Petrel to look at him.

"I am sure they went in this direction, gracious sirs," said the thin man in an anxious voice. "There is a reward for sighting them, is there not? *I* sighted them, I did. Four of them! What is the reward, gracious sirs?"

"The reward is for *us* sighting them, you fool," said the plumper of the two riders.

The second rider said, "How long ago did you see them?"

"No use asking him that," said the first man. "The peasants are not capable of measuring time."

The villager, his face unreadable, said, "Not long at all, gracious sir. The clouds have barely moved in the sky since they left our village."

"Really?" The second rider shaded his eyes. "They cannot

be far ahead of us, then. Come, let us hurry!" And they disappeared up the track.

Petrel waited for several minutes, to be sure they'd gone, and then she crept out from under the vines. Behind her, she could hear the captain murmuring questions. "Do you have pain *here*, Krill, around the medial malleolus? What about *here*, around the lateral? No? My medical knowledge is not as good as my maps or my telegraphy, but I do not think your ankle is broken."

"We're stuck now, ain't we?" Petrel said to Fin when he followed her out. "Krill's ankle might not be broken, but it's sprained at the very least. He won't be able to walk on it, not for a week or so."

Fin nodded. "And we cannot carry him. Not even the captain is that strong."

Neither of them suggested going on without the big man. He was crew, and they couldn't leave crew behind.

"We will have to stay here," continued Fin, "and wait for Mister Smoke and Missus Slink."

"Which might not be so bad," said Petrel, doing her best to sound cheerful.

But it *was* bad, and she knew it.

She thought back to the time, all those weeks ago, when they had decided to leave the ice and head north. She had had everything she wanted then. Good friends. Good food. The reassuring decks of the *Oyster* under her feet.

And now nearly all of it was gone.

She felt a tear spring to her eye and wiped it away. But she couldn't wipe away the thought that came with it. It sat there inside her like a tater, wrinkled and sour.

Albie was right. We should never have left the ice in the first place.

By THE TIME THE *CLAW* REACHED THE COAST, RAIN HAD been singing under her breath for days, and the world still did not make any sense.

Un-cle Poosk wants me back
Because blood is thicker than water
Un-cle Poosk wants me back
Because blood is thicker than tea—

She had tried to believe it and could not. Uncle Poosk might have saved her from starvation, but beyond that he did not care what happened to Rain. Girls could not become Devouts.

No, it was her brother he wanted—Bran, who was young enough to be an Initiate, young enough to be molded into the right way of thinking.

She tried again.

Bro-ther Thrawn wants me back
Because—

Cuttle was at the periscope, watching the coast road. To her own surprise, Rain was getting used to life on the underwater ship. By listening carefully, she had learned the names of things and had even grown accustomed to the sound of the machines.

What was more, she was beginning to like Cuttle, who was quieter than the others and more cautious. She liked Poddy too. The two younger children did not pinch and bully her the way Initiates would have done, or whip her to show who was in charge. Since the fight, when she had tried to break the depth gauge, they had mostly treated her like a strange sort of animal that had to have its ankles tied to the chart table for its own good.

Rain was still making up her mind about Gilly. But she did *not* like Sharkey, not one bit. She did not like the way he ordered everyone around and the way the other children looked at him as if he could do no wrong.

Right now he was pacing up and down, though he could take only three steps before he had to turn around and go the other way, and with two of those steps, he had to duck his head. Occasionally he paused, jerked his chin at Cuttle and said, "Well?"

"Two Ghosts on foot, sir," said Cuttle, without taking his eyes from the periscope. "Heading sou'west."

"That's all?"

"Aye, sir. That's all."

Rain went back to her singing.

Bro-ther Thrawn wants me back
Because—

"Sir," cried Cuttle, "come and look at this! There's a thing with wheels, and Ghosts marching beside it, heading nor'east—"

Sharkey bent over the eyepiece. He watched whatever it

was for a few minutes, then straightened up and glowered at Rain. "A beast," he said. "Pulling a box on wheels."

"A horse?" said Rain, who had come to realize that the Sunkers knew almost nothing about life on land. "A horse and cart?"

Without a word of thanks, Sharkey went back to the periscope, turning the little knob that made things look bigger and closer. "Three Ghosts walking. And there's a couple more in the—the cart. Least, I think they're Ghosts."

"Must be, sir," said Cuttle. "Can't be Sunkers. They'd've been gobbled up already."

"Aye . . . ," said Sharkey. For once, he did not sound sure of himself.

"The Devouts do not eat people," said Rain. As usual, they ignored her.

"Wake Gilly," said Sharkey. "She's got the best eyesight in the fleet."

Cuttle's sister was curled up on the bunk above the batteries, where the Sunkers took turns sleeping. Cuttle shook her gently. "Gilly."

The girl was awake in an instant, running her fingers through her short hair and rubbing her eyes. "What?"

Sharkey made way for her. "Have a look, Gill. Who's that in the cart? Can you see?"

Gilly yawned, rubbed her eyes again and took the periscope handles. "Where, sir?" Then she stiffened. "It's the adm'ral!"

"That's what I thought," said Sharkey, as grim as Rain had ever seen him. "But it can't be."

"I know it can't," said Gilly, her voice muffled by the eyepiece. "They should've eaten her. But it is, sir! It's the adm'ral and she's alive!"

At the helm, Poddy swung around, her face shining. "Does that mean Ma and Fa might be alive too?"

"They might be—" began Gilly.

"Nay," said Sharkey. "It doesn't mean anything." He snapped out a series of orders, his shoulders stiff. "Cuttle, take us down to eighty-five feet. Heading one three four. Make your speed nine knots. Gilly, get the collapsible skiff ready."

"Aye, sir!" they cried—and Rain put her hands over her ears so as not to hear the orders repeated three or four times.

But when Cuttle came to check something on the chart above her head, she whispered to him, "Where are we going?"

"North," said Cuttle, "to tomorrow's handover. Doesn't look like a trap, but we're going early just in case."

Rain nodded as if she was pleased. And she was! She needed to see Bran again, needed to make sure he was all right. That was more important than anything.

And so, even though she liked Poddy and Cuttle, she did not say a word about the exchange. Not out loud, anyway.

But under her breath she sang one of the oldest songs she knew. One that Mama had taught her, after making Rain promise that she would never sing it where she might be overheard.

Would you walk into the jaws of a tiger?
Would you pat a hungry bear on the snout?
Would you trust a rabid dog
Or walk a rotten log
Or believe the words of a Devout?

CHAPTER 8

TERRA

SHARKEY'S ELBOWS FELT TOO BIG FOR HIS BODY, AND HIS BODY felt too big for the collapsible skiff. He didn't want to go ashore, not at all. The mere thought of it set his teeth on edge, and he wished he could send Gilly in his place, on the grounds that a captain shouldn't leave his ship. But Admiral Deeps would never make an excuse like that. No hero would, and the middies knew it. Sharkey was trapped.

He didn't show his fear, not to the middies left behind on the *Claw*, and certainly not to Rain, sitting wordless in the bow of the skiff with her arms wrapped around herself and the whites of her eyes showing in the moonlight.

Gilly's voice drifted across the water. "Fair tides and clear water, sir! The ancestors go with you!"

Sharkey raised a deliberately casual hand in acknowledgement, made sure that the telling-scope still hung at his waist, and dug the paddle deeper. The skiff shot towards the shore.

I'm going to set foot on terra!

The beach he had chosen for landing was a rocky one, two miles north of the rendezvous point. He maneuvred the skiff between the rocks, with no sound except the *dip dip dip* of the paddle and the hiss of water. Rain hugged herself tighter.

To Sharkey, the rocks still seemed like part of the sea, so it took no great effort to jump out of the skiff onto a flattish one. He dragged the Ghost girl out too, then hauled the skiff from the water and draped it with kelp to hide it. The night was clear and cold, and the moon looked too close.

The scramble over the rocks wasn't so bad either, mainly because he was trying not to slip and fall, and had no time for thinking about anything else.

But then they reached the place where rocks gave way to soil. And Sharkey found himself stopped dead, with his breath hitched in his throat and three words rattling around his brain.

I'm. On. Terra!

It was almost too much for him. He felt dizzy. He felt as if the world had suddenly started speaking a different lingo and he didn't understand a word of it. Where were the fish? Where were the seaweed and the salt water? Where were the diving planes and the depth gauges, and the double hulls that had protected him all his life?

Even the air smelled wrong. And the ground beneath his feet was too solid and the night was too big—and—and the only thing that stopped Sharkey dropping to his knees and crawling back to the skiff as fast as he could was Rain. *She* seemed pleased to be on terra, and Sharkey hated her for it, hated the way she stood so steady while his own legs shook!

"Are you all right?" she asked.

"Of course I am," snapped Sharkey, and he grabbed her wrist and whipped a rope around it, as if he thought she might try to run away. But really he felt as if he were drowning and she was the only thing that could save him.

Two miles was no distance at all in a submersible, but on foot—on *terra*—it seemed a long, long way. Every step took Sharkey farther from the *Claw*, and his Sunker soul howled in protest.

What's more, he saw danger everywhere. When a small gray creature with long ears peered at him from under a bush, he tightened his grip on the rope and muttered, "That thing over there."

"What thing?"

Sharkey pointed. Rain screwed up her face. "You mean the rabbit?"

"It's—watching us."

The corner of Rain's mouth twitched. Sharkey said fiercely, "Don't you laugh at me! In the Undersea, the smallest creatures are often the deadliest."

"I was not laughing. I was smiling because I did not think you were afraid of anything."

"I'm not," said Sharkey.

"I am afraid of everything," Rain said matter-of-factly. "I always have been. Sometimes even getting up in the morning scares me. Mama used to say I would grow out of it, but I have not."

Sharkey couldn't believe that anyone would confess to such

a thing. For a moment his own fears receded, and he almost saw Rain as a real person instead of a Hungry Ghost.

"What about the giant bubble?" he asked. "You went up in that."

"The balloon? I thought I was going to die of fright."

"But—"

"Sometimes you have to do things even when you are scared," said Rain.

Which made sense, though Sharkey would never have said so, not out loud.

The grand mon-u-ment, when they reached it, turned out to be nothing but a gigantic pile of rocks.

"This is where the Great Cleansing started," said Rain. "There used to be a building here, full of soul-stealing machines, but the Devouts pulled it down."

Sharkey wasn't listening. He was peering down the road to where it disappeared in the darkness. *Hungry Ghosts are on their way*, he thought. And he wondered if he would ever see the *Claw* again.

By the time the winter sun came sidling up from the east, Sharkey's belly was clenched so tight he could hardly breathe.

He and Rain were tucked up in a thicket some distance away from the mon-u-ment. In the dark, all those close-growing trees had felt reassuring, but now they seemed like feeble protection. Sharkey wanted to burrow. He wanted to dig a deep hole and crawl into it so the Hungry Ghosts couldn't find him. Or maybe—as the sun touched the horizon—maybe he should just run out into the open and get it over as quickly as possible.

"Are you all right?" asked Rain again.

Sharkey didn't bother answering. The sun was just above the horizon, and his good eye was streaming from the unaccustomed brightness. He heard a clinking sound, followed by a rumble. And around a bend in the road, in ragged formation, came the Hungry Ghosts.

"Don't you shout," Sharkey hissed to Rain. "Don't you give us away, or else!" Then he wiped the tears from his eye and raised the telling-scope.

The first thing he saw was the horse and cart. The second was the tall, familiar figure who sat in the middle of the cart with her arms tied at her sides.

Something unwound in Sharkey's chest. *Adm'ral Deeps. It's really her. We're really going to get her back!*

Beside him Rain twisted her fingers. Sharkey shifted the telling-scope.

A Ghost rode in the cart next to the admiral, and another three walked beside it, wearing long brown robes that flicked out in front with the tramping of their feet. Sharkey looked for a trap and couldn't see one. The Ghosts had knives strapped around their waists, but apart from that, they didn't look particularly dangerous. Their bellies weren't as big as mountains, and they weren't gobbling up everything they passed. In fact, they looked as ordinary as Rain.

Sharkey wondered how they were going to do the swap.

He didn't want to step out from the safety of the thicket, not for anything. But he might have to.

The formation stopped next to the mon-u-ment, and the rumbling sounds died away. One of the Ghosts helped Admiral Deeps down from the cart. In the circle of the telling-scope, her face was hard and closed, and there was a red mark across her cheek, as if she'd been struck. A second Ghost picked up a rock and put it on the mon-u-ment. Then they all settled down to wait.

Sharkey crawled forward, wondering if this was the last thing he'd ever do. Rain followed him. The branches thinned in front of them. The rays of the sun touched Sharkey's white skin.

He braced himself.

Somewhere behind him, a small, rough voice whispered, "Don't do it, shipmate. It's a trap."

CHAPTER 9

IF I LIVE

FOR THE BRIEFEST OF MOMENTS, SHARKEY THOUGHT THAT the trees themselves had spoken. But Rain's wide eyes told him that trees, like seaweed and coral, weren't supposed to talk.

"Who's there?" he whispered, trying to see past the twigs and branches.

"A friend, shipmate," replied the voice, "with a friendly warning. There's men hidin' over yonder. Got 'ere a couple of hours before you. You show yourself, you'll get an arrow in the guts. I'd creep away if I was you, quiet as a shrimp."

"*Quick* as a shrimp," said a second voice, more precise than the first.

"No," whispered Rain, grabbing Sharkey's arm. "You have to swap me! You said you would swap me!"

Sharkey glared at her. "Don't you make a sound!" he hissed. "Or I'll—I'll kill you. Just like I killed that Massy shark!"

He pulled her deeper into the thicket, searching for the

source of the two voices. He thought he saw a patch of fur, as small and gray as a rabbit.

Can't have been rabbits that warned me, though. I don't reckon rabbits can talk, any more than turtles can.

But if it wasn't rabbits, who was it? Why had they warned him? And most important of all, were they telling the truth?

He lifted the telling-scope and peered back at the group around the mon-u-ment. His mind raced. Surely, if the Ghosts had set a trap, Admiral Deeps would've given him a sign of some sort? All she had to do was shake her head, or—

Unless there was a reason why she couldn't, a reason why she stood so tight and stiff, as if she didn't want to be part of what was happening.

Sharkey shifted the telling-scope to the cart, trying to see past its wooden sides. Why hadn't the fourth Ghost climbed down? Why was he still sitting there, with his knife in his hand and his eyes fixed on something at his feet?

Some*thing* or some*one*?

A shiver ran down Sharkey's spine. "There's someone else hidden in that cart," he whispered. "Another Sunker, I bet, held at knifepoint so the adm'ral won't shout a warning."

He shifted the telling-scope again and scanned the bushes along the side of the road. He knew what he was looking for now, and it wasn't long before he saw it. A twitch of leaves. The curve of a shoulder, half-hidden by a branch.

The mysterious voices were right. It was a trap.

It crossed his mind then that Rain might be part of it, that this might've been what she had wanted from the very start.

To make her way onto the *Claw* and bring him here, where he could be killed.

But they weren't going to kill Sharkey, not if he could help it! He was as sorry as he could be for Admiral Deeps, stuck in the Up Above. But he wasn't going to risk his life to save her.

He grabbed Rain's arm, tight as a lobster claw. "You're going to get me back to the skiff," he hissed in her ear, "and no nasty tricks. You hear me?"

The girl looked at him sadly. "Will you not let me go?"

Sharkey shook his head, impatient. He wasn't sure if he could find the skiff without her. And if things got bad, at least he'd have his own hostage.

"No tricks!" he said again.

They crept back the way they had come. The going was too slow for Sharkey's liking—he wanted to be back home right now, with the Undersea closing around him and the familiar stink of the *Claw* calming his nerves. But he couldn't go faster. Tree branches threatened to snap in his face or poke out his good eye, and he had to push them aside with one hand while hanging on to Rain with the other.

And then they came to bare ground. They must have crossed it earlier, but Sharkey hadn't noticed, not in the dark.

He noticed it now. No cover, not for a hundred yards or so. Just earth and rock. And back down the road, the Ghosts waiting for him.

If we run, he thought, *they'll see us.*

Which meant they should crawl and hope not to be

spotted. But the thought of crawling across that wide-open space, with no kelp beds to hide in, gave Sharkey the horrors.

"We're going to run," he said. "Straight across to that next lot of trees."

"*Please* let me go," said Rain. "I will not tell them anything about the *Claw*. I promise I will not."

"Now!" said Sharkey. And he dashed out into the open, dragging the girl by her arm.

The light of the sun hit him like a hammer. It was so bright that Sharkey's good eye started watering again, and he could hardly see the ground in front of him. On his port side, he thought he glimpsed a flurry of gray fur.

They were no more than halfway across the bare ground when Sharkey heard a shout. "There! Brother Thrawn was right—there are more of them! Shoot! *Shoot!*"

And arrows began to fall about their ears.

Rain yelled with fright. Sharkey forgot about the rabbit, forgot about everything except the arrows. He wasn't used to running, but he was strong and lean from swimming long distances, and his body did what he asked of it. He let go of the girl's arm and dodged this way and that like a school of fish, all the while heading for the cover of the trees and fearing that he wasn't going to make it.

Something whacked into his starboard shoulder. He cried out and stumbled. To his surprise, Rain grabbed his hand and pulled him upright.

"Nearly there!" she panted. "Come on!"

It seemed to Sharkey that they ran and ran, and the arrows

fell and the trees came no closer. His shoulder was starting to hurt now, and he wanted to cry out again but didn't have the wind for it.

And then, to his relief, the trees were right there in front of him, and he was slipping between them.

The arrows stopped, and so did Sharkey and Rain. But only for a moment. Rain shook her head as if to clear it. "They could have *killed* me, shooting like that! They did not care!"

Sharkey put his hand to his shoulder and felt something poking through it. His clothes were sticky with blood.

Speared like a tunnyfish, he thought. *I never knew it'd hurt so much.*

He didn't feel like running any more. But Rain looked back again and said, "They are coming after us!"

They set off between the trees, and this time it was Rain who held Sharkey's arm, instead of the other way round. Sharkey didn't think he could've made it by himself. His shoulder felt as if it had been rammed up against a hot engine. He wanted to groan, but he jammed his mouth shut and gnawed his lip instead.

Every step hurt. But Rain wouldn't let him slow down. She kept looking over her shoulder, and once or twice she squeaked with fright. Sharkey stumbled along, half running, half walking. He had lost all sense of direction, and for all he knew, the Ghost girl was taking him in circles. There was no sign of the rabbit.

When they came to the rocks, Rain pulled him out into the open, shouting in his ear, "Keep going! We are nearly there!"

Sharkey didn't believe a word of it. *I'm going to get eaten,* he thought dizzily. *I'll never see the* Claw *again. I'll never be adm'ral.*

Behind them, someone shouted, "There they are!"

Sharkey gathered what little strength he had left and stumbled over the rocks, hanging on to Rain for dear life. Arrows hissed past them, sharp as knives.

If I live, I'll never spear another tunnyfish, thought Sharkey.

He was so close to the Undersea by now that he could almost taste it. It helped drag him forward when his shoulder was trying to stop him in his tracks. The rabbit was back, though now there seemed to be two of them. Or maybe it was just a couple of mud crabs, scuttling away from intruders.

Sharkey didn't care. He left a spatter of blood on every rock he passed, and he didn't care about that either. The strength was draining out of him, and all that mattered was getting back to the *Claw.*

"Where's the boat?" cried Rain.

"Boat?" Sharkey raised his numb head, wondering what she was talking about.

"The one you hid!"

She means the skiff, thought Sharkey, and he rubbed his eye and tried to remember what he'd done with it.

"Over there," he mumbled, pointing with his chin. "I think."

Rain dragged him towards a heap of kelp, and there was the skiff. Sharkey stood, swaying from side to side, while the girl pushed it into the water. Then he climbed in and picked up the paddle, wondering how on earth he was going to get them back to the *Claw*.

He dug the paddle into the water and almost blacked out with the pain. "Can't—do it!" he gasped. Except he was a Sunker, and Sunkers never gave up, not till they breathed their last. So he dug the paddle in again—

Rain scooted forward and knelt in front of him. She put her hands around his, and when the paddle went back into the water, she pushed at it with all her strength, so that Sharkey just had to guide it.

It still hurt. He couldn't hold the groans back now, no matter how hard he tried. But at least they were moving.

Rain was singing in a halting, breathless voice:

"Run run—run,
Do not stumble—or fall,
The race—is not done
Till you hear—the call . . ."

Her shoulders were up around her ears, and her eyes had that telltale whiteness about them. But her hands kept pushing at the paddle, one side, then the other.

Sharkey heard a *thunk* as an arrow hit the seat behind him.

Rain squeaked, "Where is the *Claw*?"

"Don't know." Sharkey was so full of pain that he couldn't see anything except a red blur, but he waved his hand vaguely. "Periscope depth. They'll be watching for us."

"Well, they had better hurry up," cried Rain as half a dozen arrows hissed past her. "Or they will be too late."

Sharkey thought he saw a swirling in the water, twenty or so yards to port. *Fish*, he thought. *A big one, going down.*

But it wasn't a fish, and it wasn't going down; it was coming up. The water churned and swirled as a gray conning tower poked out of the depths. The skiff rocked from side to side. The top of the conning tower flew open, and Gilly stuck her head out.

"There!" cried Rain, and she tried to make Sharkey paddle towards the tower, but his arms wouldn't do a thing and they spun in circles, around and around, while the arrows came closer and closer.

Sharkey thought Gilly threw something, and maybe Rain caught hold of it. Whatever it was, they started to move, even though his arms were hanging by his sides.

And then Cuttle was lying on the deck, clinging to the bow of the skiff while Rain and Gilly grabbed hold of Sharkey, and Gilly said, "Come on, sir!"

He staggered along the slippery deck, with the arrows still falling and Gilly shouting over her shoulder, "Leave it, Cuttle!"

Then somehow they were all scrambling down the ladder, with Rain in front of him and Gilly yelling, "Fasten the hatches! Open main vents! Dive! Dive!" and Sharkey hoping it wasn't *him* who was supposed to get the hatches or the vents, 'cos right now he wasn't even sure where they were.

His foot slipped on a rung. Air roared out of the ballast tanks. The *Claw* began to sink.

Somewhere nearby, Gilly shouted wordlessly, and Sharkey heard a *clunk* as the hatches were locked. The portholes darkened. He stood at the bottom of the ladder, swaying.

Then the last bit of strength drained out of him, and the lights were going . . . going . . . gone.

CHAPTER 10

IT'S THEM!

FOR ALL HER MISERY, PETREL HADN'T FORGOTTEN HOW TO make a good hidey-hole. This might not be the *Oyster*, but the idea was the same.

Make sure you've got at least two exits. Make the inside comfy and the outside ragged, as though no one's been there for months. Leave some peepholes so you can see danger on its way. Cover up your tracks when you come and go.

And so, while the captain bandaged Krill's sprained ankle with strips of bark, and the pigeon watched in exhausted silence, Petrel and Fin set to work lining the space under the vines with sticks and plaited reeds, and packing mud between them, to stop the rain coming in. They made sure it didn't look any different from the outside, and then they went back over their first hurried pathway, brushing away footprints.

Only when that was done did they go hunting for something to eat.

The first day, they found a few scraps of more-or-less

chewable seaweed. The second day, they came back with a handful of tiny nuts, which were better than seaweed, but not much.

By the fourth day, Petrel's hunger was raging so fiercely that all her other worries faded into insignificance. She knew that Krill must feel even worse, because he was so big and needed so much more to keep him going.

"Fish," she whispered as she and Fin crept through the scrub, watching out for danger. "That's what I want."

"We cannot light a fire," said Fin. "Someone would see it or smell it."

"Doesn't matter. I'll eat 'em raw." Petrel licked her lips. "Three of 'em. Raw and juicy. Then I'll take a dozen back to Krill."

"But we do not have a line," said Fin. "We do not have hooks."

"I *know* that. I'm not stupid."

"We will be lucky to find more taters."

"I know that too!"

"Then why do you pretend?" Fin's voice was harsh. "Why do you talk about finding things that we have no hope of finding? It just makes it worse."

Petrel stared at him. "Is this about your mam?"

"No."

"It is! Don't you want to look for her? I'm sure she's—"

"Stop it, Petrel! Please!" And his face was so unhappy that Petrel fell silent.

Despite their lack of fishing lines, they headed down to

the shore, where they managed to find some limpets. They wiggled a few out of their shells and ate them, then collected the rest for Krill.

They returned to the shelter a roundabout way, so as not to make a trail. As they came closer, they saw the captain waiting for them, his face streaked with mud. The pigeon, who had recovered her strength but showed no desire to leave, perched on his arm.

"The Devouts rode past again," said the captain.

"What?" said Petrel.

"When?" asked Fin.

"They came from the north, fourteen minutes and twenty-six seconds ago. One of their horses is going lame. They should not be riding it. It is not *right* to ride a lame horse."

From inside the shelter, Krill said, "Is that the bratlings back at last? Petrel, you've got to leave me here and keep going."

"Not without you," said Fin, crawling into the hidey-hole.

Petrel followed him. "Here, Krill, we brought you some limpets. What's this about the Devouts? I thought they were gone."

Hungry as he was, the big man brushed the food aside. "They were searching all over. Sheer luck they didn't find me and the cap'n. You've gotta go before that luck runs ou—"

He was interrupted by the chatter of the telegraph device. And this time, the message was not from the *Oyster*.

HAVE BOARDED SMALL UNDERWATER VESSEL *CLAW*. NEED YOUR POSITION. SIGNED, SLINK.

It was the most beautiful sound Petrel had ever heard. She put her hand over her mouth, hardly able to contain her relief, and when she took it away, she was smiling for the first time in days.

She poked her head out of the shelter. "Cap'n! Mister Smoke and Missus Slink have found an underwater vessel, and they're coming to get us! What's our position?"

"But we have not found the Song or the Singer yet," said the captain, crawling in to join them. The pigeon fluttered after him. "We cannot go."

Petrel sat back on her heels. The captain was smarter than all the rest of the *Oyster*'s crew put together, but once he settled on an idea, it was hard to shift him. And the search for the Song and the Singer seemed to have gripped him like nothing else.

It's that programming stuff, she thought. *Feels as if someone's reaching out from the long ago and moving us around to suit themselves. Which is all very clever, but what if it doesn't suit* us?

Aloud she said, "Song's not going to do anyone much good, Cap'n, if Albie overruns the bridge and takes the *Oyster* back south without us." Inspiration struck her. "And—and besides, maybe the Singer is on this underwater vessel!"

The captain nodded. "That is logical. Very well, our position is fifty degrees thirty minutes north, seven degrees twelve minutes west." He stroked the pigeon's feathers. "But according to my charts, the water on this coast is dangerously shallow. A large vessel will not be able to get anywhere near us."

"That's all right—it's small," said Petrel. "Missus Slink said so."

She tapped out the coordinates in general ship code and waited, breathless, for a reply. It came more quickly than she'd expected.

ESTIMATED TIME OF TRAVEL TWENTY-ONE HOURS FORTY-FOUR MINUTES.

"We'll have to help you down to the water, Krill," she said.

"I'm better than I was," said Krill. "I'll get there."

Petrel beamed at him. "And then we'll be heading back to the ship, and everything'll be all right. Folk won't want to follow Albie once they know how he lied to 'em. And Squid and Dolph'll be safe, and we'll—"

"Shhh!" Fin grabbed her arm.

"What?"

Very quietly, Fin said, "The Devouts have returned. I think they heard us."

Petrel shot up so fast that she almost fell over. "Where?"

Fin pointed. And there were the same two men, sitting very still on their horses and staring in the direction of the shelter.

"Blizzards!" whispered Petrel. "We've got to get out of here! Krill—"

The Head Cook picked up a rock and hefted it in his hand. "You three go. Creep out the back way. I'll keep 'em busy for as long as I can."

"No," whispered Petrel, coming to a rapid decision. "Fin and I'll draw 'em off. Cap'n, will you stay here with Krill?"

The captain looked as if he were about to argue. Petrel said quickly, "You can't run as fast as Fin and me. It's logical, right?"

The captain nodded. "It is logical." Then he looked out one of the peepholes and said, "They are coming this way."

Petrel grabbed the telegraph device, worried that it might start clattering again and give away the position of the hidey-hole. "Fin, let's go," she whispered. And the two of them crawled out the back exit.

The horses were snorting like whales and stamping their hooves. The children crept away from the shelter, still hidden by the bushes and rocks.

Can't jump up too soon, thought Petrel, *or they'll figure out where we came from. Can't go too late or they'll find Krill and the cap'n. A bit farther . . . A bit farther . . . Now!*

With a yelp, she leaped to her feet as if she'd been tucked up in the bushes and had only just noticed the Devouts. Fin was a heartbeat behind her, crying, "It is them! Run!"

And run they did.

WHEN SHARKEY WOKE UP AT LAST, HE WAS LYING ON THE berth above the batteries, with a rabbit stitching his shoulder.

Despite the sharp pain of the needle, he thought he must still be asleep. He thought it was a dream and that any minute now he'd see Admiral Deeps flying past in a cart, with an arrow in her hand. Because that was the sort of thing that happened in dreams.

But instead of the admiral, what he saw was Poddy,

leaning over him with an expression that was half-worried, half jumping out of her skin with excitement.

"Sir, you're awake!" she cried. She turned her head. "Gilly, Cuttle, he's awake!"

The needle bit into Sharkey's shoulder, and he winced and turned his head to peer at the rabbit. Its ears weren't as big as he remembered, and its tail was long and gray instead of short and white. It was poking the needle in and out of his flesh, right where the arrow had come through, and muttering to itself. Around its neck was a tattered green ribbon.

Sharkey winced again and croaked, "R-rabbit."

"It is a rat," said Rain, from his other side, in disapproving tones. "It sneaked onto the *Claw* with us. Or, rather, *they* did."

"That's right, shipmate," said a rough little voice. "There's two of us." And a long gray nose with whiskers sprouting from it poked over Sharkey's good shoulder.

He was glad of the distraction. He dragged his eyes away from the needle and said, "You—warned me. Back there. You—warned me about the trap. Why?"

Poddy leaned over him again and whispered, her eyes as bright as the sun, "'Cos it's them, sir! It's *them*!"

Sharkey had no idea what she was talking about, and his shoulder was hurting too much for him to work it out. With a groan, he closed his eye and went back to sleep.

WHEN HE WOKE THE SECOND TIME, THERE WAS AN ARGUMENT going on above his head.

"Rats cannot talk," said Rain. "I have never heard of such a thing."

"That's 'cos you're from the Up Above," retorted Poddy, "and there's plenty you haven't heard of. I bet you think turtles can't talk either, or dolphins. But they talk to Sharkey."

His nose was running. He sniffed, and both girls leaned over him. "Where are we?" he croaked.

"Heading sou'-sou'west, sir," said Poddy, "as ordered."

"Wha—?" Sharkey rubbed his eye, wondering if he'd misheard her. He hadn't given any orders, had he? "W-What's the time?"

Cuttle, who was at the helm, looked over his shoulder. "Seventy-five minutes till sunclimb, sir. You slept right through."

"You should've woken me," said Sharkey.

"You lost a lot of blood," said Rain. "The rats advised us—" She hesitated, as if she still didn't want to admit that rats could talk.

Poddy broke in. "They said we should let you sleep as long as you wanted, sir."

Sharkey rubbed his eye again. The rumble of diesels cut through his muddled thoughts, and he struggled up onto one elbow, grimacing with pain. "We're running on the surface?"

"Aye, sir," said Cuttle.

"Who's on watch?" Sharkey felt a surge of panic, remembering what had happened to the *Rampart*. "We *are* keeping a watch?"

"'Course we are, sir," said Poddy. "Don't worry, everything's good. Gilly's up above. And *he's* got the conn."

"Who's *he*? And why are we going sou'-sou'west? Did I give you the direction?"

"Nay," said Poddy. "It was *him*."

Sharkey felt as if he were going around in circles. *"Who?"*

Poddy beamed. "Great-Granfer, of course."

"Great-Gran— What are you talking about, Pod?"

Poddy edged back a little so Sharkey could see the two rats. "It's *them*, sir," she said proudly. "They've come to help us. It's Lin Lin and Adm'ral Cray!"

CHAPTER 11

LIN LIN AND ADM'RAL CRAY

I'm going mad, thought Sharkey. *The sun must've scorched my brain.*

He stared at the rat. "Adm'ral Cray," he said flatly.

The rat looked back at him, its fur scruffy, its silver eyes expressionless. "That's what they call me, shipmate."

"And Lin Lin," said Sharkey.

The second rat, the one with the green ribbon, bobbed its head. "At your service."

I need air, thought Sharkey. *I need—*

He grabbed hold of the periscope casing with one hand, dragged himself upright and hung on until his head stopped swimming. Then he said, "I have the conn. Poddy, stop both motors."

Poddy didn't move. "But sir, the adm'ral said—"

"I don't care what the adm'ral said. I'm in charge of this boat."

"Aye . . . sir," said Poddy, as if there were some doubt about it. "But we have to keep going."

"They've got friends who're stranded, sir," said Cuttle. "We have to get there as quick as we can."

Sharkey couldn't believe it. They were arguing with him! The middies were *arguing* with him!

He set his teeth in a snarl. "Who's your cap'n, Poddy?"

"You are, sir. But Adm'ral Cray said—"

"Stop. Both. Motors."

Rain looked pleased. Poddy looked as if someone had smacked her, but she trotted back to the big switches without further argument. The *Claw* slowed. The rats watched and listened, their heads swiveling back and forth like little gray rudders.

Sharkey didn't care what any of them thought. *He* was in charge, no one else. The submersible wasn't going anywhere without his orders, and he hadn't yet decided what those orders would be.

I need air.

Climbing up the conning tower was a challenge with only one good arm. He managed it without groaning, but by the time he stepped out onto the open deck, he was shaking with pain.

Gilly sprang to her feet when she saw him and said, "Sir, you shouldn't be up here. Go and rest. We're all right. We've got the adm'ral and Lin Lin to—"

"Shut up," said Sharkey. "Just—shut up. And go below."

"But I'm on watch, sir."

"Don't argue! I'll take the watch. Go below."

And then it was just him, sitting there with the stars above and the dark waves rising and falling around him, and his mind trying to tear itself in two.

Adm'ral Cray? Lin Lin? Really?

He shook his head. *Nay.*

But what if—?

Nay, I don't believe it.

The middies did, though, which he was going to have to change, quick smart.

They argued with me! Cuttle and Poddy ARGUED with me! They've never done that before.

Uncertainty hit him again. What if the rats really *were* Lin Lin and Admiral Cr—

NAY!

He wasn't thinking clearly; that was the problem. He hadn't been thinking clearly since the *Rampart* went down. That had torn something out of him, and now whatever he did seemed to make things worse.

What was it the Ghosts had shouted when they saw him? *Brother Thrawn was right—there are more of them!* Which meant they hadn't known for sure that there was another submersible. Not until Sharkey had turned up and proved it.

I shouldn't have gone, he thought. *I've put the* Claw *at risk. I've put ALL of us at risk.*

He wasn't used to being in the wrong, and it made him

angry. With himself, with the middies, with the pain in his shoulder, which was getting worse instead of better. With the rats.

Mustn't forget I'm on watch.

He glanced around the horizon, knowing he'd see nothing. The skimmers were never about this early. Suntime was when the Ghosts went hunting, and by then the *Claw*'d be deep in the Undersea. And Sharkey'd be laying down the law to his crew.

I'm in charge. No one else, no matter who they claim to be.

He heard a quick scuff of feet climbing the conning tower, and turned his back. He didn't want to talk to anyone, not yet. Not with this fizz of anger and confusion in his belly.

"Sir?" It was Poddy, right behind him.

"Go away, Pod."

"Sir, we thought you'd be pleased."

Sharkey stared at the eastern horizon. "Go away."

"But sir, they're the *ancestors*."

"Don't be a fool, Poddy."

"They *are*. I knew it as soon I saw them. And—and sir, if Adm'ral Deeps is alive then maybe Ma and Fa are too, and we can rescue all of 'em and get the *Rampart* watertight again, and everything'll be back the way it used to be!"

Sharkey's shoulder felt as if the arrow was still in there, jabbing away at him until he wanted to scream. And now here was Poddy jabbing away too.

"Can't we do what they say, sir? Can't we go and find their

friends who are in trouble? And then we could ask 'em for help."

He wanted to stop her but didn't know how. Not without admitting that the whole talking-to-the-ancestors business was a lie. And if he told her that, the middies would never listen to him again.

There was a bitter taste in his mouth. It had been there, he realized, ever since he saw Admiral Deeps through the telling-scope. Because Poddy was right—if the admiral was alive, then maybe everyone else was too. Maybe they were sitting in the Ghosts' camp, expecting Sharkey to rescue them.

Because he was a hero.

It was as if Poddy could read his thoughts. "They'll be waiting for us, sir. Ma and Fa and all the others. They know we'll come for 'em. And we will, won't we? 'Specially now we've got the ancestors."

It was too much for Sharkey. His guilt flared white-hot, and he whirled around so quick and nasty-faced that Poddy flinched backwards. "If it *was* the ancestors," he snarled, "you wouldn't hear 'em talk, 'cos you're just an ordinary little middy and why would they want to talk to a middy, eh? They talk to *me* 'cos I'm favored, I'm going to be adm'ral one day—"

It was like listening to someone else. He tried to stop but couldn't. The bitterness spilled out like poison, and Poddy copped every bit of it.

"—I'll be adm'ral one day and you'll *still* be nothing, so shut up, you don't know what you're talking about. Lin Lin and Adm'ral Cray don't care what happens to us, which means your ma and fa are lost and so's Adm'ral Deeps and the babies and the salties and everyone else, and you might as well get used to it."

Then he turned his back again and sat trembling with anger and indignation.

He heard a gulp behind him but didn't turn around. *I'm just telling her the truth,* he thought. *I'm doing her a favor.*

Another gulp, quickly covered up. Then Poddy said, in a small voice, "If we're not going anywhere just yet, may I—may I go for a swim, sir?"

Sharkey heaved a put-upon sigh. "I suppose so."

"Thank you, sir." And with that, she wriggled out of her jerkin and trousers and slid over the side, into a sea that was as gray as the predawn sky.

Sharkey knew he should call her back, but he was stuck in place, the poison in his blood turned to glue.

It had to be said, he told himself. *She's got to stop believing that we're going to get the others back. It's a stupid waste of time. We should be getting on with our lives.*

He wished it was *him* who'd gone for a swim instead of Poddy. Not that he could swim with his shoulder like this. Not that he could do anything. He was useless. One eye and one arm.

The bitterness filled him again, and he sat there feeling sorry for himself and wondering if Poddy'd get back before the sun roared up over the horizon. If she didn't, they'd have to stay Up Above and risk getting eaten by the Hungry Ghosts.

Except—Admiral Deeps hadn't got eaten. And Rain wasn't at all dangerous. In fact, she'd saved Sharkey's life. So was it true or wasn't it, what the Sunkers had always believed?

As Sharkey sat there, trying to make sense of it, the sky grew lighter and the nor'westerly wind picked up. It wasn't long before he began to worry. Poddy should've been back by now. Everyone knew how far you could swim before sunclimb, and everyone was careful.

"Where are you, Pod?" he muttered, not looking up. "What are you playing at? You get back here, quick smart."

Half of him thought she was probably no more than a few yards away, treading water. Playing a trick to get back at him for the things he'd said. But the other half knew that he shouldn't have let her go. It was risky swimming alone when your feelings were hurt.

"Poddy?" he called, over his shoulder. "You there?"

No answer. Sharkey climbed to his feet and turned around, feeling angry all over again for the worry she was causing him. He squinted at the edges of the boat to see if she was hiding. Then he raised his eye towards the west—and saw four skimmers bearing down on the *Claw*, with the first no more than half a sea mile away.

Sharkey's heart almost stopped beating. Skimmers before sunclimb? He'd never heard of such a thing. But there they were!

He leaped for the conning tower, with the word *Dive!* on his lips. Then he remembered Poddy. They *couldn't* dive, not while she was still out there.

"Poddy!" he shouted, scanning the water for that small, dark head. *"Poddy!"*

Gilly came scrambling up from below. "What's the matter, sir?"

"Skimmers!" cried Sharkey. "And Poddy's out there somewhere, and I *can't see her*!"

Gilly dived down the hatch again and came back with the telling-scope in her hand and Rain and the rats at her heels. Sharkey grabbed the telling-scope and jammed it to his good eye, but it didn't tell him a thing. He swept it north and south, east and west, right up to the approaching skimmers and back again, but he couldn't find Poddy anywhere. All he saw was gray light and gray water and the white sails closing in.

"Where *are* you, Poddy?" he muttered.

The rats stood on their hind legs, peering at the waves. "She ain't got much chance if she's still out there, shipmate," said the fake Admiral Cray.

"She *might* be all right," said Gilly uncertainly.

Sharkey shouted again, at the top of his lungs, *"Pooood-dyyyyy!"*

And then he saw her. In the growing light, halfway between the *Claw* and the skimmers. Swimming for her life.

"Gilly, Cuttle!" yelled Sharkey. "Due west, full speed!"

Gilly dashed below. Sharkey danced from foot to foot, afraid to take his eye off that bobbing head. He felt as if the telling-scope was a rope between them, and if he took it away from his eye, Poddy'd be lost.

"Hurry!" he cried.

"They need a hand down there, shipmate?" asked the fake admiral.

"Aye!" said Sharkey.

The rats dashed below again, and a moment later the submersible was under way. Sharkey groaned under his breath, knowing they weren't going to get there in time. The *Claw* wasn't made for going fast in the Up Above. She plunged through the waves like a wounded porpoise, up and down, up and down, with Rain clinging to the stay lines. Salt water spattered Sharkey's face, and he was soaked within seconds. His wounded shoulder throbbed, but he hardly noticed.

Poddy looked so tiny, even through the telling-scope. And the skimmers were so big.

"They're nearly on her," whispered Sharkey. He groaned aloud as one of the skimmers yawed to the side, its sails dropping. "They've seen her. No! *Poddyyyyy!*"

It was no use screaming. It was no use doing anything except watching, right up to the very last moment. Rain ran to the hatch and shouted something, and the motors slowed. Sharkey just watched, his heart almost bursting out of his chest, as his little cousin changed direction, still swimming strongly, still trying to get away from the Ghosts who had spotted her.

There was a bustling along the side of the skimmer, brown robes running hither and thither. Sharkey cursed them, cursed their parents and their grandparents and every single one of their ancestors—if they even *had* ancestors—right back to the dawn of time.

But it did no good. A sail billowed. The skimmer came around again. A dozen hands threw a net out over the water—

—and hauled it back in, with Poddy inside, kicking and fighting every inch of the way.

In a daze, Sharkey lowered the telling-scope. "They've got her," he said. He felt numb. "They'll be after us next."

He let Rain go through the hatch first, then he squeezed inside, shut both sets of clamps and half-fell down the ladder.

"Emerg—" His voice broke. He swallowed and tried again. "Emergency—deep."

A muscle in Cuttle's cheek clenched, but all he said was, "Emergency deep. Aye, sir."

The familiar sequence took over. Out of the corner of Sharkey's eye, he saw Gilly at the motors and the rats turning the big brass wheels.

The little submersible dived.

Without Poddy.

CHAPTER 12

WITHOUT PODDY

THEY DIVED WITHOUT PODDY.

I should be pleased, thought Rain. *One of them has been caught. I should be celebrating.*

But she was not. She had grown fond of the *Claw*'s youngest crew member. And besides, ever since the Devouts had sprung their trap and almost killed *her* in the process, she had realized that her original plan was not going to work.

In her first dreadful days on the submersible, she had managed to convince herself that if she could only smash its instruments and make the Sunkers surrender, the Devouts would be so pleased with her that they would let her little brother go.

But as the trap was sprung and the arrows fell around her, she had realized that the Devouts didn't care about her one way or the other. If she captured the Sunkers for them, they would be pleased, but they wouldn't release Bran. No, if she wanted to save him, she would have to be more devious.

That was why she had dragged Sharkey to safety. That was

why she was sitting on the bunk now, watching him and waiting for the right time to say her piece.

She was not the only one watching him. He had taken the *Claw* right down to the deep seabed, where the Devout ships could not find them. He had ordered the motors cut. Then he had slumped on the seat next to Cuttle, with his head in his hands.

Now everyone was waiting for him to speak. Even the rats were quiet, though they glanced at each other frequently.

At last Sharkey raised his head and said in a bleak, terrible voice, "Poddy's been caught."

Rain knew guilt when she saw it, and Sharkey was weighed down by it. *Something happened up on that deck,* she thought. *Something that made Poddy swim too far.*

But no one was asking, and Sharkey was not telling. Instead, he looked at Rain with his single eye. "You said the Ghosts don't really eat people. That the Sunkers'd be taken to a camp."

This was what Rain had been waiting for. "Yes. The reeducation camp."

Cuttle blinked. "Education? Well that doesn't sound so bad, sir, does it? Poddy's good at her letters."

"That's not the sort of education she's talkin' about, shipmate," said the rat who called himself Admiral Cray.

"You stay out of this," said Sharkey. "It's nothing to do with you."

Gilly said, "But it is, sir! They're our ancest—"

"Stop *arguing* with me!"

A strained silence fell over the little group. Rain listened to the sound of water pressing against the hull and wondered what would happen if it pressed too hard.

Sharkey rubbed the patch that covered his ruined eye. "Tell me about the camp," he said.

"Manners, boy," said the rat with the green ribbon.

Sharkey ignored her.

"It is not really reeducation," said Rain. "It is hard work. Breaking rocks and building roads."

Cuttle began, "Poddy doesn't mind hard w—"

But Sharkey held up his hand. "Go on."

Rain gnawed her lip as if she did not want to answer. Then she said, "I have not been inside the camp. But my brother is an Initiate, and they are supposed to help watch the prisoners. Bran is only little, and he is a kindhearted boy. Broth— Brother Thrawn set him to watch the prisoners in the quarry while they broke rocks, and told him that if someone stopped work, even for a moment, he must tell one of the guards. There was an old woman—Bran said she looked sick and hungry. So did the other prisoners, but she looked *really* sick. And she stopped work, and—and Bran told the guard, because he thought the old woman might be allowed to lie down for a while. Only—"

Sharkey seemed to be having trouble breathing. "Only— what?"

"Whippings," said the rat with the green ribbon. "Whippings and beatings and all sorts of nastiness, that's what *we* saw."

"That's right, shipmate," said the rat admiral. "Before we met up with you, we passed by the Citadel. Took a peek at the quarry while we was there. And I can tell you that the Devouts don't like folk who stop work. They don't like anythin' much, as far as we could tell. Don't reckon their prisoners last long. Couple of months at the most."

Gilly flinched. Cuttle stared at his hands.

"I asked Bro— Brother Thrawn if Bran could stay away from the quarry," said Rain. "I thought he might be able to just—just study or something." She sighed. "I should have known better. Broth— Brother Thrawn likes making people do things they do not want to do. He knew I was scared of the balloon— that is why he sent me up in it. And he knew Bran hated the whippings, so he made him watch them."

There were lies in there, which Rain did her best to make believable. But what she said next was completely honest. "I— I am afraid that Bran will get used to it. He is only little, and he wants to be a good Initiate, so he is doing his best not to mind so much. He is doing his best to despise the prisoners, like the Devouts do."

She stopped herself then, though she wanted to keep going, wanted to tell them the *real* truth. The *whole* truth. But she must not. There was too much at stake.

Sharkey sat very still, staring at the deck. The only movement came from his shoulders, which jerked several times, as if he were struggling with something inside himself.

Cuttle opened his mouth and shut it again. Gilly watched Sharkey, her own shoulders twitching in unison with his.

When Sharkey looked up at last, there was a light in his eye that Rain had never seen before. "We have to get her back," he whispered.

Cuttle sat up very straight. "How, sir?"

"Don't ask questions," said Sharkey. "I'll work it out."

"What if she's— What if she's been eaten already, sir?"

"The Ghosts didn't eat Adm'ral Deeps," said Sharkey.

Gilly leaned towards him. "Maybe the Ghosts haven't eaten any of 'em. Ma and Fa and Barnacle. And Blubber and Sprat—"

Sharkey laughed, though there was no humor in it. "If they're alive, we'll get 'em all back," he said recklessly. "Why not? The whole lot of 'em."

"How will you do it?" asked the rat Lin Lin.

"None of your business," said Sharkey.

"It might be our business, boy. You might need our help."

Sharkey shook his head. "You heard Rain. She knows about the camp."

"But can she slip into it and out again without being seen?" asked the rat. "Can she carry messages? Can she crawl under floors and over rafters and through pipes?"

The reckless gleam in Sharkey's eye turned to uncertainty and then to cunning. He stood up so that he towered over the rat.

"All right, *Great-Granmer*," he said. "Let's make a bargain."

"CAN YOU SEE THEM?" WHISPERED FIN.

"Hang on." Petrel wriggled forward and peered through

the bracken. "Nope. They're gone." She yawned. "Just as well too. Don't reckon I can run any more, not without something to eat. And a bit of sleep."

The two children had spent the afternoon and most of the night luring the horsemen away from Krill and the silver captain. They'd run, they'd crawled, they'd hidden. They'd scrambled over sharp rocks and through dense thickets, where the horses couldn't go. They would almost certainly have been caught in more open country. As it was, the growing lameness of one of the horses and the tangled nature of the bushland had worked to the children's advantage.

Now Petrel was so tired and hungry that she could hardly spit. But she was satisfied too, as if she had regained a bit of herself that was lost.

"There's no one knows how to run and hide as well as me," she said to Fin.

He nodded agreement. "But they will not give up, you know. They will send a pigeon for reinforcements."

"We'll be back on the *Oyster* by then," said Petrel, "eating Krill's best fish stew." She grinned, imagining the deck under her feet. "With grilled fish for pudding, and a nice bowl of fish soup to finish off. Albie'll be in chains, and everything'll be right again."

The thought of it made her want to dance. Despite her tiredness, she picked up the telegraph device and jumped to her feet. "We'd best get going. We've come a long way."

They didn't bother retracing the devious back-and-forth path that had brought them there—that would have taken the rest of the day. Instead, Petrel used the sun to guide them in an almost straight line, with Fin watching out for danger.

They were well under way when the telegraph device began to chatter out another message in general ship code.

Petrel gasped. "Oh!"

"What is it?" asked Fin.

"The *Claw*'s been delayed."

"When will they—"

Petrel held up her hand, still listening. "The *Claw*'s cap'n wants a bargain." Her voice rose in protest. "What? Blizzards, no! He says he'll only pick us up if we agree to help rescue his people from the Devouts."

"We could try. After we get back to the *Oyster*."

"No," said Petrel. "*Before* he takes us to the *Oyster*."

She and Fin looked at each other in dismay.

"What'll I tell 'em?" she whispered. "I thought we'd be back where we belong by first watch or sooner. And Squid and Dolph and everyone else who's trapped on the bridge'd be safe. But now— Who knows how long this'll take?"

"But we have no other way of returning to the ship," said Fin. "Which means—"

"Which means we ain't got a choice." And, feeling as lost and desolate as she ever had, Petrel began to tap out a reply.

"They agree," said the rat, taking her paw off the comm key. "They'll help get your friends back, and so will the adm'ral and I. And then you'll take us to our ship."

"So, where are they?" asked Sharkey, who didn't like all

these messages going back and forth in a code he didn't understand.

The rat gave him the coordinates, and he stiffened. "But that's—"

"That's what, shipmate?" asked the fake admiral, who was perched on top of the echo sounder.

"That's the Sealy Coast," said Sharkey, and the air around him seemed to grow colder. "Part of the Great Puddle."

Rain looked from one face to another, her forehead creased. "What is the Great Puddle?"

"It's a big stretch of shallow water," said Gilly. "Too shallow for submersibles, except for a couple of channels, and they're too narrow. Sunkers never go anywhere near the Great Puddle."

The rat admiral, up on his perch, went very still. "You're not backin' out of our agreement already, are you, shipmates?"

Cuttle and Gilly began to speak over each other.

"We can't go into the Great Puddle—"

"You *know* we can't, Adm'ral, not even for Poddy—"

"It's an old rule, never go into the Great Puddle—"

"It's too dangerous—"

"It's too *shallow!*"

The rat admiral took no notice of them. He was watching Sharkey.

"They're right," said Sharkey. "It'd be madness."

He realized as he said it that this was his way out. He'd made that stupid announcement—*We'll get 'em all back*—in the heat of the moment and was already regretting it. Now he could throw his hands in the air and say, "Well, we tried. But we can't go into the Great Puddle."

Except that wouldn't save Poddy, would it?

He thought of the reeducation camp, with its whippings and beatings. Thought of cheerful little Poddy getting sick and hungry, thought of her *dying*, all because of a bit of shallow water.

All because of *him*.

The recklessness took hold again. "The Puddle might be too shallow for the *Rampart*," he said. "That doesn't mean the *Claw* can't make it. Cuttle, find me a chart of the Sealy Coast."

When the chart came, he stared at it, making quick calculations in his head. "We'll need the tide with us. High water'll be just after eighteen hundred hours down that way. We'd better allow for delays—"

He spun around. "Send another message to your friends," he said to the rat Lin Lin. "Tell 'em—we've got no chance of getting there tonight. Tell 'em we'll pick 'em up tomorrow night. Seventeen hundred hours—that's an hour after sunfall. Tell 'em to be ready; we won't be able to contact 'em again, not till we're nearly there. If we have to go into the Great Puddle, we'll use one of the channels and run as deep and silent as we can. No periscope. No aerial. Nothing. Not till we have to."

He swung back to Gilly. "What's the charge on the batteries?"

"Full charge, sir."

"Air?"

"Air's clean, sir."

"Good," said Sharkey, though he didn't *feel* good. His belly was hollow, as if he hadn't eaten properly for days, and he could hardly believe he was doing this.

"Sir," whispered Cuttle, "are you sure? The Great *Puddle*?"

"'Course I'm sure," said Sharkey. "Don't worry, Cuttle. The batteries are charged, the air's topped up and we've got the ancestors on our side."

He bared his teeth at the rats. "What could possibly go wrong?"

CHAPTER 13

THE GREAT PUDDLE

As the sun rose the next morning, Petrel, Fin, Krill and the captain were tucked up in a rock cave, several feet above the high-tide mark. There was snow on the ground, and the pigeon's feathers were fluffed out with the cold.

"I don't like this," said Krill for the hundredth time. "We should be going straight back to the *Oyster*, not wasting our time on someone else's business. It's ten days since we left the ship, d'you realize that?"

"And we still have not found any trace of the Song," said the captain. "Or the Singer."

"Cap'n, with all due respect, it's getting harder and harder for me to worry about a song when my daughter's trapped on the bridge, along with Dolph and who knows else! Maybe today's the day Albie overruns 'em, and what are we doing? Going off to rescue a bunch of strangers!"

"Who might know the Song," said the captain in his sweet, determined voice. He put his hand on the ground, and the pigeon clambered onto it. "I do not think she wants to go back to the Devouts. I am going to call her Scroll."

With a sigh, Krill turned his frustration onto Petrel and Fin. "You should never have agreed to such a bargain, bratlings."

"We didn't have a choice," said Petrel. "I don't like it any more than you do, Krill, but we ain't seen another ship all this time, and you know it."

"She is right," said Fin. "This is our only chance of getting back to the *Oyster*."

"Hmph," the Head Cook rumbled deep in his throat. "I wish we'd never come north. Our troubles started when we left the ice." And he subsided into gloom.

Petrel gazed out at the water, thinking, *He's right. I don't care about changing the world, not anymore. It's too big and too nasty. I want to go back to the ice.*

She felt a brief flicker of guilt over Fin's mam. *He believes she's dead*, she reminded herself. *And maybe she is. No point staying in this horrible place for a dead woman.*

And for the rest of the morning she comforted herself with dreams of heading south, back to the ice, and of penguins and bergs and the sweet flesh of toothyfish.

It was past noon and the snow had melted away at last, when Scroll suddenly grew restless, bobbing up and down on the captain's wrist as if something was wrong.

Petrel shaded her eyes and stared at the horizon. "What's that, Cap'n? Looks like the sun coming up, only nowhere near as big and bright."

The captain was already on his feet. "It is a hot-air balloon with a basket underneath. And there is another one. Look, they are tethered to sailing ships!" He turned to Fin. "You did not tell us that the Devouts used hot-air balloons."

Fin's face was ashen. "But they do not! At least—they did not when *I* was with them. I have never seen such things before!"

"Those two men must have sent a pigeon for them," said the captain. "We will have to conceal the front of the cave, or the people in the baskets will see us."

"It's not just us they'll see," growled Krill, pushing himself up onto his elbows. "That water's a mite too clear for my liking. Petrel, send a message to Missus Slink, quick smart. Tell her about those balloon things and the Devout ships. The *Claw* mustn't come in, not yet. Not in daylight."

Petrel tapped out a warning on the telegraph device. But although she waited and waited, there was no reply.

"They said they would be traveling underwater," said the captain. "They will not receive our message until they surface."

"Then we'd best keep sending it," said Krill, "and hope like blazes they get it in time."

By the time the *Claw* came to the edge of the Great Puddle, the ocean floor was shelving upwards and there were reefs everywhere. Sharkey kept his eye on the dark green water outside the porthole and didn't share his thoughts with anyone.

At the helm, Gilly said, "Sir, we're coming up to the channel entrance."

"How long?" asked Sharkey.

"Ten minutes, sir."

"What's our depth?"

"Eighty-five feet, sir. And we've got forty feet of water under the keel."

"Steady as she goes."

"Aye, sir."

Sharkey glanced at the chronometer and raised his voice so that everyone could hear him. "We'll make the entrance to the channel at 13.20 hours. All stations!"

The two rats scurried to the diving-plane wheels. Cuttle stood by the motors, feet braced on the metal decking. Rain sat on the berth above the batteries, her eyes closed, her mouth moving silently.

At exactly 13.20 hours, Sharkey said, "Helm, make your heading due west. Two degrees up bubble. Dead slow ahead."

The voices came back to him in rapid fire.

"Due west. Aye, sir," cried Gilly.

"Dead slow ahead. Aye, sir," shouted Cuttle from the motors.

The rats stood on their hind legs and hauled at the diving-plane wheels. As the *Claw* swung around, her bow rose, and her running lights fell on the entrance to the channel.

It was like a gorge cut out of rock, and even narrower than Sharkey had expected. But other than trying to make it all the way across the Great Puddle in shallow water, and probably grounding themselves in the attempt, he could see no other way of getting close to the shore.

"Make your depth seventy-six feet," he said.

"Seventy-six feet. Aye, sir."

And when they reached seventy-six feet: "Ease your bubble."

"Ease bubble. Aye, sir."

As the *Claw* nosed forward between the rock walls, Rain began to sing, very quietly. The words whispered across the little cabin and curled around Sharkey's head.

"Hobgoblins tiptoe through the night
And imp and ghost and evil wight—"

Sharkey had no idea what a hobgoblin was, but he knew all about tiptoeing. That's what they were doing now, tiptoeing into dangerous waters.

"They do their best to give us fright," sang Rain.

"And fill us with dismay."

Outside the porthole, the sides of the channel were so close that seaweed and sponges wavered as they passed. The running lights touched clamshells and rocks and schools of fish. Sharkey saw a crab frantically kicking up sand to conceal itself, and bagtrout dashing into the weeds, as shy as oysters.

"But will we cower, will we hide?
Will we lock ourselves inside?"

As they approached the coast, the channel grew shallower, though nowhere near as shallow as the waters on either side of it. The skin on the back of Sharkey's neck tightened every time he gave the order to go up a few feet. He didn't *want* to go up. He wanted to hurry back to deep water and dive, down down down, so far that the Ghosts'd never find them.

He knew that Cuttle and Gilly wouldn't say a word against him, if that's what he decided. They'd just nod and keep on believing that he was a hero.

"Or will we hold ourselves with pride
And chase those ghouls away?"

Sharkey gritted his teeth and said, "Up five."

"Up five. Aye, sir."

At 15.40 hours, Sharkey took another look at the chart. If they kept following the channel, they'd end up too far north of the rendezvous. Which meant they had to leave its relative safety and go up into the *really* shallow water. The tide was on the rise, and sunfall wasn't far away, but still he didn't like it one bit.

Maybe we should wait till after sunfall. Except that'd make us late, and if anything slowed us down, we'd miss the tide.

He realized he was chewing his thumbnail and quickly glanced around to make sure no one had noticed. Rain was still singing. Gilly was tapping the gyroscope while Cuttle oiled the driveshaft. The rats were watching Sharkey with eyes that were too knowing for comfort.

He flushed and said, louder than he'd intended, "Take her up to twenty-five feet."

The rats turned the diving-plane wheels, and the *Claw* began to rise.

"Fifty-five feet," sang Gilly. "Fifty feet. Forty-five. Forty. Thirty-five. Thirty."

Outside the porthole, the water went from deep green to

pale blue. The sides of the channel gave way to a sandy bottom.

"Twenty-five—"

"Zero bubble," cried Sharkey. "Keep your trim."

The upward movement stopped. And there they were, easing into the sandy reaches of the Great Puddle, as quiet as a flounder, with no more than ten feet of water under them. And unknown dangers above.

THE DEVOUTS' SHIPS SAILED UP AND DOWN THE COAST ALL afternoon, with the balloons drifting high above them. Petrel and her friends crouched in the cave, hardly daring to move. The captain held Scroll in the palm of his hands, stroking her gently and occasionally whispering in her ear.

Late in the day, the wind turned. Now it blew offshore, and no matter how close to land the ships sailed, the balloons pulled out to sea.

It might have been funny if it weren't for the *Claw* on its way, and the water in the bay so clear and shallow that there was nowhere to hide.

"Go away, stupid Devouts," whispered Petrel. "Give up. Go *away!*"

Krill glowered at her. "How long since you sent that message, bratling? Send it again, and keep sending it."

She did. She tapped out warning after warning on the telegraph, her fingers slipping in their haste.

But then Fin groaned. "Listen!"

"Someone is shouting," said the captain. "I think it is the people in the baskets. They have seen something!"

And as Petrel watched in horror, the sailing ships turned away from the shore and headed out across the bay. Out across the clear shallow water, where there was nowhere to hide.

CHAPTER 14

NOWHERE TO HIDE

Sharkey had said that he wouldn't use periscope or aerial until he had to. But now the moment had come. If there was danger ahead, he needed to know about it.

The casings rattled as he cranked them upwards. Water gurgled past the hull. A shadow passed over the water.

Sharkey put his eye to the periscope and turned in a circle. It was one of those times when he wished he had two good eyes. He felt as if there were something creeping up on his blind side, something nasty that he needed to spot before it surprised him—

There was a clatter of sound from the comm behind him. "A message!" cried the rat Lin Lin. "Danger! Balloons! Devouts!"

At the same time, Sharkey roared at the top of his voice, "Hard astern!"

Cuttle threw himself at the switches, and the *Claw* shuddered into reverse. The words *Flood the quick-dive tank!* were burning on Sharkey's tongue, but he couldn't let them go, not yet, not until they were over the channel again.

He felt as if someone had glued him to the periscope. There were two skimmers coming straight at him, their sails growing bigger by the second. Behind him, Cuttle was coaxing the propeller to greater and greater speeds. The rats were poised beside the dive wheels, ready to throw themselves into action.

"What's happening, Sharkey?" cried Gilly, all formality forgotten.

"They're gaining on us. How far to the channel?"

"Nearly there."

The propeller rattled louder than Sharkey had ever heard it. "C'mon, *Claw*," he shouted to the little submersible. "Come *on*!"

He was afraid they wouldn't make it, but at last they were over the channel. He whipped the periscope back into its housing and shouted, "Half-ahead! Flood quick-dive tank, twenty degrees down angle!"

The rats threw themselves at the wheels, and Gilly's hands took them down to safety. Except they *weren't* safe, not yet, and they all knew it. The Ghosts wouldn't give up so easily.

As the *Claw* rumbled past seaweed and rock faces, Sharkey gnawed his thumbnail, no longer caring who saw him. "Not deep enough," he whispered through gritted teeth. "Not fast enough."

But they were already going too fast for such a narrow channel. Any faster and they'd run into one of the rock walls, and then nothing would save them.

Sharkey thought he saw another of those dreadful shadows pass overhead. The hairs on the back of his neck stood up. He could almost *feel* the skimmers gaining on them.

And then it happened, the thing he'd been dreading ever since the *Rampart* was attacked. Something clanged against the hull right above his head, so hard and loud that his ears rang. He yelped with the surprise of it, and so did Rain.

Gilly swore, "Blood of the ancestors!"

Another clang—and the thing that had hit them exploded.

The *Claw* bucked under their feet and slewed sideways. Gilly fought the helm, trying to get control. Rain fell off the berth. The rats clung to the dive wheels, their little paws skidding on the deck.

As the reverberations died away, Rain picked herself up and began to sing. *"H-H-H-Hobgoblins tiptoe through the n-n-night—"*

Sharkey wished he could sing with her. He'd never been so afraid, not even in the Up Above. But future admirals didn't sing. They didn't yelp either, and he would've taken that dreadful sound back if he could've. He clenched his teeth and gripped the overhead locker so tightly that his hands cramped.

Dodge? he thought. *But there's nowhere to dodge to, not until we get back to open water.*

Clangggg! Something else hit them. Sharkey waited for the explosion, but it didn't come. *Maybe they don't always work,* he thought. *All the same—*

"Cut running lights and switch to instruments," he said, trying to stop his voice cracking.

The lights went off, and the water outside turned dark green. "We need to get deeper," he said. "What's under us, Gilly?"

"Only five feet, Sharkey."

Which meant they were already running so close to the seabed that they risked tearing the submersible open from bow to stern. They couldn't *go* any deeper. They couldn't go faster either. Not with the lights off. Not with those rock walls looming on both sides.

"And imp and g-g-ghost and evil w-w-wight—" sang Rain.

Up to this point, the two rats had said nothing. But now Sharkey felt small claws scrabble from the chart table up onto his shoulder.

A rough voice in his ear said, "We ain't gunna lose 'em like this, shipmate. Water's too clear. Reckon it's time for a bit of clever thinkin'."

"What's Great-Granfer saying, Sharkey?" shouted Cuttle.

A third impact, somewhere near the stern. *Clanggggg!* This one *did* explode—*whoomp!* And despite Gilly's desperate grip on the helm, the *Claw* slewed sideways again.

"We've lost steering," cried Gilly.

"Hard astern!" shouted Sharkey.

Cuttle threw the motors into reverse. The submersible slowed, but not quickly enough.

Sharkey shouted again. "Grab hold!"

Small claws dug into his shoulder. Cuttle grabbed the nearest pipe while Gilly still clung to the helm. Rain hung on to the berth, and the rat Lin Lin hung on to Rain.

With an ugly crunch, the *Claw* rammed the channel wall.

Sharkey's bad shoulder hit the locker. The inside lanterns flickered. The bow bulkhead, right next to the porthole, crumpled inward.

We've been breached, thought Sharkey. *There'll be water pouring in any second!*

But the *Claw*, for all her great age, was a strong little vessel. Gradually, as the expected surge of water didn't come, Sharkey realized that although they were battered, they weren't yet holed. The pressure hull had survived the collision.

All the same, we're done for, he thought. *We can't go anywhere, not without steering. All the Ghosts have to do is sit up there and drop their explosives one by one until our hull gives way altogether.*

He couldn't bear it. The thought of the little submersible lying broken on the seabed, like the *Rampart*, made his throat hurt. The thought of Cuttle and Gilly dead or captured—

"Didn't you hear me, shipmate?" said a rough voice, and with a jolt Sharkey realized that the rat was still there on his shoulder.

"What?" he said.

"Clever thinkin', shipmate," said the rat. "That's what we need now."

Sharkey shook his head wordlessly. There wasn't a scrap of cleverness left in him. If he'd been a real hero, he might've been able to get them out of there. But he wasn't real. He was as fake as the rat Lin Lin and the rat Cray.

Behind him, Rain was trembling violently. Even Gilly and

Cuttle were shaking, which was something Sharkey had never thought he'd see.

"Can you sing a bit more, Rain?" asked Cuttle. "Sharkey'll c-come up with something, I know he will, but—"

Rain raised her voice. *"But d-do we cower, d-do we hide?"*

Gilly and Cuttle sang along with her. *"Do we l-lock our-selves inside?"*

But the rat admiral dug his claws deeper into Sharkey's shoulder, saying, "Clever, shipmate. That's what we want. Clever."

"Or do we hold ourselves with p-pride,
And chase those g-ghouls away?"

Sharkey felt sick. For all Cuttle's faith in him, he knew he was helpless. And Rain's song was wrong. Sometimes hiding was the only sensible thing to do. He'd hide the *Claw* like a shot if he could.

He thought of the crabs that had stirred up the sand as the little submersible passed. And the others that dropped a leg if they had to, if it gave them a chance of getting away.

Wish WE could drop a leg, thought Sharkey. *Make the Ghosts think they'd killed us already—*

The impossible idea and the next explosion hit at exactly the same moment. *Clannnnggggg! Whoooooomp!* The poor old *Claw* shuddered like a jellyfish, and Sharkey's mind shuddered with it. He gripped the locker, feeling stunned and fright-ened and hopeful all at once. Was it impossible? *Was* it?

There was only one way to find out.

He dragged himself upright. "Cuttle," he snapped, "drain

some oil off the diesel engines into a bucket. And find some bits of—of *stuff* that'll float to the surface. The berth—yes, the berth. Smash it. And take anything else you can think of. Anything we don't need. Rain, you help him. You too, Lin Lin. The more the better."

The boy, the girl and the rat hurried to do his bidding.

"Gilly, give me power to the little claw," said Sharkey.

As Gilly threw the switch, Sharkey slid into the retrieval seat and grabbed the lever. On his shoulder, the rat Cray was silent.

There was sand beneath them, for which Sharkey blessed his ancestors. *Lots* of sand. As soon as he dug the little claw into it, it swirled against the porthole. Behind him, Rain was banging away at the berth with a hammer.

"More," he mumbled to himself, and dug the claw into the seabed again and again, until there was sand everywhere, hanging in the water like a shroud.

Sharkey turned to the rat on his shoulder and said, through gritted teeth, "They won't be able to see us now."

"Mebbe not, shipmate," said the rat. "But sand won't stop bombs."

As if to prove his words, there was another *clannngggg* and the *whooomp!* that they had come to dread. A terrible grinding sound told Sharkey that part of the outer hull had gone.

"Quick, Cuttle!" he shouted, scanning the bulkhead for leaks. Nothing yet, but it was only a matter of time.

Cuttle dashed for'ard with a bucket half-full of oil. Rain and the rat Lin Lin trailed behind him, dragging the remains of the berth, a pile of clothes, the blades of a broken propeller, two plates and an ancient saucepan.

"Cuttle, give me the oil and take the little claw," snapped Sharkey, jumping up from his seat. "Keep stirring that sand up. Rain, come with me."

He climbed the ladder to the double hatch, ignoring the pain in his shoulder. Rain handed the bits of bunk up to him, and the propeller blades and everything else. Sharkey dumped it all above the inside hatch and rested the bucket in among the clothes.

"More sand," he cried to Cuttle.

He sealed the inside hatch and climbed down. Then, with everyone watching him expectantly, he waited.

His heart hammered against his ribs. His belly was hollow. If this didn't work, they were gone. *Everything* was gone.

Cllllaaaannngggg! Whooooooomp!

The *Claw* rocked sickeningly. Sharkey's ears rang.

"Last bit of sand," he shouted. Then, "Gilly, blow the top hatch."

There was a *whoosh* above their heads as oil, clothes, plates, saucepan, propeller, the remains of the bunk and a good chunk of their precious air were forced out of the hatch and up to the surface.

"Now quiet!" hissed Sharkey, holding up a warning hand. "Not a sound!"

It wasn't hard to picture what was happening Up Above. The air would get there first, boiling up in a great bubble. Then the bits of bunk and the propeller and the clothes. And finally the oil, spreading across the surface of the water in a telltale slick.

To any Sunker, it'd look like a fatally damaged submersible. If it was Sharkey up there, he'd be expecting bodies at any moment. And when they didn't come, he'd assume they were trapped below. Dying. Or already dead.

There was a fierce hope in Gilly's eyes and in Cuttle's too. But no one said anything.

Clannngggg on the *Claw*'s bow.

There was no explosion, which meant it must've been another dud. But still the sound pierced Sharkey's heart. The impossible idea hadn't worked. The one thing he had been able to think of, and it hadn't—

Now it was the rat Lin Lin who held up a paw. "Wait," she whispered. "That might just be a test. Or a fare-thee-well."

So they waited. With every moment that passed, Sharkey was expecting the next explosion, the one that would rip the damaged hull right open and kill them all.

But it didn't come.

And it didn't come.

And it didn't—

He glanced at the chronometer. How long had they been sitting there in silence? Half an hour? More? He thought night must be falling in the Up Above. Surely, if the Ghosts were going to keep bombarding them, it would have happened by now.

Except, if it were him up there, he'd hang around for a while, watching. Listening. Even when he thought his prey was dead. Make sure it wasn't a trick.

"Shhh!" he whispered, putting his finger to his lips. Then he cupped his hand over his ear to make sure everyone knew what he meant. Sound traveled easily through water. They mustn't do anything that would tell the listeners above that they were still alive.

Rain had no idea how long they sat there, as still as clods of earth. Her fingers hurt from clasping them so tight. But at last Sharkey yawned and said, in a more or less normal voice, "What's the charge on the batteries, Gilly?"

"Low," said Gilly, peering at her instruments. She copied his yawn. "Air's getting bad too, sir."

Rain stretched her legs cautiously. Her throat felt raw, as if she had been shouting.

"It'll be dark Up Above," said Sharkey. "Moon won't've risen yet. I say we go up and take a look. What do you reckon?"

In all the days that Rain had been on the submersible, she had never heard its captain ask anyone else's opinion. Cuttle looked surprised, and so did Gilly, but they nodded in agreement.

The rat who called herself Lin Lin pointed her nose at Rain and said, "You know more about the Devouts than anyone here, girl. What do *you* think?"

A dozen possibilities ran through Rain's head, but the only one that would help Bran was the truth. "I think they will be gone," she said. "They would not know you could trick them like that. I am sure they think they have killed us all."

Including me.

Sharkey nodded and declared, "We'll take her up, then."

"Without steering?" asked Rain.

"Don't need steering to go up and down," said Sharkey with surprising cheerfulness. "It's just handy if you want to go anywhere else."

To Sharkey's relief, the periscope was still working. He did a quick check to make sure that the Ghosts had indeed gone, and nodded to Gilly.

The *Claw* surfaced with what sounded like a shout of relief, though really it was just louder-than-usual gurgles and thumps. Sharkey scrambled up the ladder and forced open the hatches, and fresh air whistled into the cabin like a blessing.

It wasn't enough. He jumped out onto the deck, with the others close behind him.

Even in the dark, he could tell how battered the *Claw* was. Gone was the sleek outline that made the little submersible so agile underwater. Gone were the stay lines and the telegraph aerial. The deck plates were sprung and twisted, and part of the outer hull looked as if it had peeled away.

But for a while, at least, it hardly mattered. The sky was bright with stars, and the air was so clean and beautiful that Sharkey felt like weeping.

I'm alive, he thought. *They didn't get us. We're ALL alive.*

Gilly leaned against the conning tower, taking deep breaths. "Only good thing about the Up Above," she said. "It's got decent air."

"And stars," said Rain. She pointed to a cluster of bright points low in the sky. "That is Hope over there."

"Nay, that's the Lobster," said Cuttle. "You can navigate by him."

"That's no lobster," said the rat admiral, waving a small paw. "That's Solomon's Eye."

"No, it is *not*," said Rain. "Mama knew all about the stars. That is Hope, and the ones just past it are Truth Abandoned."

"Hope? Truth Abandoned?" said Gilly. "What sorts of names are those? The Truthy ones are the Lobster's Tail, which make up the beginning of the Great Reef. See, there's the rest of it, sprawled to the north."

"You're both wrong," said the rat Lin Lin. "What you're calling the Reef—"

Sharkey grinned at Rain. He knew he'd have to start being captain again soon. It was a fair way to shore, but he thought he could swim it, even with his bad shoulder. He'd take a line with him, one end tied to the *Claw*, in case the rats' friends couldn't swim. He'd find them and bring them back. Fix the steering and patch the worst of the damage. Check for leaks. Get out of here before sunclimb.

But for now—

For now he just stood there, smiling into the darkness. And breathing. *There are no words for this*, he thought.

And for the next few minutes, he gave himself up to letting the world spin in whatever direction it wanted, and not even trying to control it.

CHAPTER 15

"WHO'S YOUR CAPTAIN?"

PETREL WAS CRYING. She hadn't cried many times in her short hard life, but now the tears streamed down her cheeks, and she couldn't stop them.

"Coooo," said Scroll. "Cooooo."

None of them had moved since that awful moment when cheering and celebration had broken out on the sailing ships. Even the captain, a mechanical boy made of silver and wire, seemed stricken. Their best chance of getting back to the *Oyster* was gone. Folk who might have been allies were gone. Worst of all, Mister Smoke and Missus Slink were gone.

Petrel felt as if all the blood had drained from her body, leaving nothing but a shadow. Except shadows didn't grieve, not like this.

"They m-mightn't be dead," she said, though she knew they were.

No one answered her. They just sat, staring at their hands and feeling sick.

Out in the bay, something splashed. "Fish," said Krill sadly. "We should try and rig some sort of net."

Still no one moved.

The fish jumped again, closer.

And closer.

A pulse hammered in Petrel's throat. She stood up, her face wet, her hand pressed over her mouth.

A boy walked out of the water.

THERE WERE THREE OF THEM, STUMBLING OVER THE ROCKS towards Sharkey. Behind them limped a fourth, a huge man from the look of him, though it was too dark for details.

Sharkey stopped, with the sea swirling around his ankles and that odd feeling of contentment lingering in his veins. "Are you—"

"The *Claw*?" asked one of the dark figures. A girl.

"Aye," said Sharkey.

The girl took another step towards him, her voice fierce with hope. "Mister Smoke and Missus Slink—are they all right?"

"Who?"

"The rats!"

"Oh. Aye," said Sharkey. He was already walking up over the rocks, with the line in his hand, but he said over his shoulder, "Aye, they're alive and well."

The girl laughed, a ragged, hiccupy sound. "Alive and well, Fin!" she said to one of her companions. "Alive and well!"

Sharkey found a good, solid rock and knotted the line

around it. The other end ran out across the water, all the way to the *Claw*. "Can you swim?" he asked when he'd rejoined the four dark figures.

"No," said Fin.

"Not likely," said the girl.

"*None* of you?"

"None of us," said the girl. "Unless—Cap'n?"

Instantly, Sharkey's feeling of contentment vanished. Another captain? Another *captain*, coming onto his boat? He bristled at the outline of the big man. "You're in charge of this crew?"

"No, I am," said the fourth figure, a child no bigger than Poddy, with a hood concealing his face, and some sort of bird on his arm.

Sharkey snorted under his breath. "Well, don't expect to be captain of anything while you're on the *Claw*. You'll do what you're told on my boat. You all will, or you're not coming aboard."

There was a moment of silence, and then the girl said, "We're good at doing what we're told. Ain't we, Krill?"

"Hmph," said the big man, which might have meant anything. "About this bargain, lad—"

"Don't try to back out of it," said Sharkey quickly. "We're heading north as soon as we can. We get my people out first, and *then* I'll take you to your ship."

That silenced them again. Sharkey nodded towards the line. "Use that to drag yourselves out to the boat. But take off your outer clothes first, or there'll be nothing dry for you to change into."

The girl hesitated. "You waterproof, Cap'n?"

"I believe so," said the small figure, "though I have never tested it." He turned to Sharkey. "Do you know any songs?"

Sharkey didn't bother answering. *They're mad,* he thought. *Can't see how they'll be any help getting Poddy and the others back. But there's no one else.*

The strangers took off their outer clothes and put them in a pile next to him, along with a bag. Sharkey thought there was something odd about the little captain's face, though it was too dark to see properly.

I'll get a good look at him soon, he thought as the strangers slid into the water one by one, clinging to the line for dear life. The bird fluttered over their heads.

Sharkey took a smaller line from around his waist and tied the clothes in a ball, with the bag in the middle. When he heard a distant "Hoy!" from Gilly, he set about loosening the line that he had fastened around the rock.

It took much longer than he'd expected. The knot had jammed, probably because of the big man's weight, and although he dug at it until his fingers were bruised, it wouldn't budge.

Rope was too valuable to lose, so Sharkey didn't want to cut it. But there were urgent repairs to be done, and he had already wasted too much time. So in the end, he took out his knife and sliced through the knot.

He swam back out on his side, holding the clothes above the water with one hand. By the time he saw the battered bulk of the submersible half a dozen yards away, his shoulder felt as if it was on fire.

But he wasn't going to show any sort of weakness, not with another captain on board. He passed the bundle up to Gilly and hauled himself onto the deck, gritting his teeth against the pain.

"Are you all right, Sharkey?" whispered Gilly as he dried himself and put on his clothes. "You were gone so long! I was just getting ready to come after you."

Sharkey grunted. He was in no mood to be fussed over.

"Did you see the bird?" continued Gilly. "And the little cap'n? He asked me about songs—isn't that odd? Did you see that man Krill? He could hardly fit through the hatch. How're we going to feed someone that big?"

"We're not," muttered Sharkey. "He can find his own food. They all can. The bargain's for rescuing our people in exchange for taking 'em to their ship. No one said anything about feeding 'em."

"But that wouldn't be fair, and besides—"

"Are you arguing with me?"

"Nay, but Krill's alr—"

"Who's your cap'n?" Sharkey glowered at her.

"But he's—"

"*Who's* your cap'n, Gilly?"

He thought she pulled a face, but it was too dark to see, which was just as well for her.

"You are," she mumbled.

"Sir."

"You are. Sir."

"Glad to hear it."

Gilly didn't answer, but Sharkey knew he'd made his point.

The rats started this, he thought as he pulled on his eye patch and made his way down the ladder. *The middies never argued with me before the rats came. And it'll be worse now with so many strangers on board. I'll have to stamp on it before it gets out of hand.*

He stepped off the ladder, already issuing instructions. "Gilly's bringing your clothes down. Get 'em on and stow yourselves out of the way. And don't touch anything. Cuttle, bring me the big wrench. Then you and Gilly start work on the hull. I'm going to see what's wrong with the steer—"

His voice dried in his throat. Cuttle was standing by the chart table with the little captain . . . whose face was made of *silver.*

Cuttle looked up at Sharkey and beamed. "He's only small, but he knows all about navigation, sir. He says our chart's wrong in a few places, so we've been changing it. And then he's going to help us fix the hull in exchange for us telling him all the songs we know. And Fin and Rain and Petrel are making plans to get everyone out—"

"And Krill is cooking supper," added Rain. "Though he said he has never had to do it in his long underwear before."

Which was when Sharkey realized he'd been smelling fried fish ever since he came on board.

"I tried to tell you, sir," said Gilly, from somewhere above him. "But you wouldn't listen."

Sharkey had been hoping that the steering wouldn't be too difficult to fix. A problem with the linkages, maybe. But when he slid back over the side of the little submersible, into the cold water, he found that the rudder shaft was bent and could not be straightened.

Two-handed, replacing it would've been a hard job. One-handed and furious, it was wretched. But Sharkey wouldn't give up. He ducked below the surface to heave and tug and wrench at the stubborn metal, came up for a breath and then ducked down again, his teeth chattering, his shoulder aching.

Somewhere above him, the little silver captain was working alongside Gilly and Cuttle, hammering deck plates into place, patching the outer hull and checking the ballast tanks. The last time Sharkey had looked, Krill and Petrel were helping them, and so were the rats. Sharkey didn't like all these strangers touching his boat, but he didn't have much choice, not if he wanted the *Claw* back in working order before sunclimb.

By the time the new shaft was in place, he was exhausted, and so cold that he could no longer feel his fingers or toes. The sound of muffled hammering had stopped a quarter of an hour ago.

He dragged himself up onto the deck, where Gilly was waiting for him. "Well?" he croaked.

"It's not bad, sir," said Gilly. "That odd little cap'n of theirs knows what he's about. I reckon we're watertight, but we won't know for sure till we try it out."

With a great effort, Sharkey nodded. Then he pulled his clothes on and staggered below, shivering so badly that he could hardly speak.

"Breakfast, bratling?" asked Krill, looming out of the tiny galley and banging his head on a pipe. He rubbed his skull ruefully, as if the same thing had happened several times before, and said, "Rain and Fin caught a dozen pickle-heads while we were working. Never tried 'em myself, but Cuttle says they're tasty. Reckon you could do with a feed."

Sharkey ignored him. "You've got the conn," he croaked to Gilly, who'd come down the ladder behind him. "Take her down to periscope depth and watch the pressure. If it stays steady, head down the channel to deep water. Then set a course for ten miles or so south of the Citadel. And since *he* knows so much about everything"—he jerked his head at the child with the silver face—"let him find us a nice, safe bay where we can go ashore without being seen."

Then he turned his back on everyone, curled up under the chart table and was asleep before the dive siren sounded.

PETREL'S BELLY WAS FULL OF PICKLE-HEADS, SHE HAD A RAT on each knee, and her back rested against good, honest metal. It was the closest she'd come to being happy for days. Even the *Claw*'s crew seemed familiar, in a way that the Devouts and the starving villagers had not.

But deep inside, that lost feeling lingered. *I won't be right till I'm back on the* Oyster, she thought. *I wish I was there now.*

Beside her, Krill was trying unsuccessfully to make

himself smaller so he didn't take up so much of the tiny cabin. Cuttle and the captain shared a stool, with Scroll on the captain's arm. Gilly had the helm, and Fin and Rain were leaning against the dive wheels, talking quietly to each other.

Their hair's almost the same color, thought Petrel. *I wonder if she knows his mam. I wonder if that's what they're talking about.*

The *Claw* had reached deep water twenty minutes ago, and the hiss of it on the double hull was like a lullaby.

"Must be time for a story," boomed Krill.

"Or a Song," said the silver boy in a quiet voice. "We must not give up on our purpose."

Petrel didn't say anything, but she wished the captain *would* give up. It seemed to her that he was pulling one way, determined to find his Song, and she and Fin and Krill were pulling the other, trying to get back to the *Oyster*. And until they all pulled the same way, nothing good would happen.

She wriggled sideways until she was leaning against Krill's comforting bulk. She knew that the Head Cook missed the old icebreaker as much as she did. What's more, he must be half-mad with worry about Squid. But somehow he was still himself. He wasn't lost, not like Petrel.

"Stories? Songs?" Cuttle looked uncertainly at the sleeping Sharkey. "I'm not sure—"

"It's either that or dancing," said Krill, "and I don't reckon anyone except me'd survive the latter, not in a space like this."

Rain laughed, and Krill winked at her. "You volunteering to go first, bratling?"

"Me?" squeaked Rain. "No!"

Fin leaned forward. "Rain says the Devouts returned from the ice a month ago. And Brother Thrawn is still alive. I did not kill him after all! It was he who ordered the use of the balloons, and the throwers and bombs. That is right, is it not, Rain?"

The girl's laughter stopped abruptly. "Um—yes."

"If I had not seen them with my own eyes," continued Fin, "I would not have believed it. Brother Thrawn was always strictly against such things, even though they are not quite machines."

"He—he was changed by his injury," said Rain. "But—"

"That's not the sort of story I meant," said Krill, interrupting. "I want something with a happy ending. How about you, Mister Smoke? You got a story for us?"

"Why do you call him Mister Smoke?" asked Cuttle. "He's the adm'ral."

Krill raised his bushy eyebrows. "You been promoted, Mister Smoke?"

The rat ignored him. "When you've lived as long as I 'ave, shipmate," he said to Cuttle, "you accumulate names like barnacles on a ship's bottom. But they don't mean much. It's what's inside that counts."

Then, before anyone could ask another question, he leaped down from Petrel's knee, straightened his whiskers, struck a dramatic pose and cried, "I'll tell you a story, shipmates. A story about a place so cold that it can freeze the blood in your veins. So cold that your breath turns to ice as it comes out your mouth. I'll tell you the story of the *Oyster* . . ."

But Petrel was no longer listening. All she could hear were five words, ringing like a ship's bell in her ears. Like a message banged on the pipes, so loud that she couldn't ignore it.

It's what's inside that counts.

Ever since the shore party had walked towards that first village, Petrel had felt lost—as if the only time she could be happy, the only time she could be *herself*, was on the *Oyster*.

But now she wondered if that was right.

For the first time in weeks, she took herself back to that life-changing moment on the icebreaker's bridge, immediately after the battle with the Devouts, when she had finally had enough of being Nothing Girl. She remembered the heat inside her. The noise that wouldn't be silenced. The words that had burst out of her.

I'm not nothing. Never was, never will be! I'm Petrel! Quill's daughter. Seal's daughter too!

Surely those words still counted. Surely it was all still there inside her. The heat, the noise—and the *Oyster*, if only she could find it.

She closed her eyes and imagined herself walking those familiar passageways. Imagined it so hard and fierce that before long she could almost see the rivets and bolts and patches of rust and feel the clank of the engines beneath her feet.

It's all there, she thought. *It's inside me. I'm not nothing. Never was, never will be, no matter WHERE I am.*

It didn't entirely fix things, but it made her feel more solid, as if she could think about what was coming with a clear head and a clear heart.

And so as Mister Smoke's story wound around her, she set herself to working out how she could get a message to Squid and Dolph.

SHARKEY LAY UNDER THE CHART TABLE WITH HIS EYE CLOSED, pretending he was still asleep. He didn't believe half of what he heard. All that stuff about solid ocean and freezing blood was as false as his own stories.

They're just trying to impress the middies, he told himself.

He heard Cuttle laugh, and winced. None of his crew had laughed like that since the *Rampart* was lost. It should've made him happy to hear it, but it didn't. It made him feel left out and at odds with everyone.

He tried to summon the fury that had got him through the rudder change. *I should get up,* he thought. *Remind 'em who's cap'n of this boat.*

Except then the laughter would stop.

So in the end he didn't move. He just lay there, feeling useless and wondering who he was if he wasn't the most important person on board.

CHAPTER 16

I AM NOT LIKE
THE HUNGRY GHOSTS!

WHEN RAIN WAS LITTLE, HER MAMA USED TO SING A SONG about persistence. Rain thought she had forgotten the words years ago, but now a bit of the chorus came back to her.

. . . and wa–ter

Can wear away a stone.

Petrel was the water. She had been arguing with Sharkey ever since he got up, turning things this way and that, trying to convince him to send someone back to the *Oyster.*

"So when we get to this bay," she said, "the one the cap'n's picked out, Gilly and Cuttle ain't going ashore with us, right?"

Since Poddy had been captured, Sharkey had started changing for the better. Unfortunately, having these new people on board seemed to have changed him back again. He heaved one of those long-suffering sighs that made it sound as if he were the only person in the world with any sense, and said, "I *told* you. They're going to set out to sea, where they won't be caught." He nodded at the box in Petrel's hands. "And bring the *Claw* back in when we send 'em a comm."

Rain breathed in the stink of the little submersible, wondering if she was brave enough for what was coming.

I have to be, she thought, and she glanced sideways at Petrel. Mister Smoke's story last night had ended with a description of the Devouts' bloodthirsty attack on the *Oyster*, and how it was mostly Petrel who had foiled it.

I have to be as brave as she is, thought Rain.

"They're gunna sit out there doing nothing?" asked the girl she admired.

"There's still repair work to do," replied Sharkey.

Petrel screwed up her face as if she were thinking. "Tell you what, Cap'n Sharkey—how about one of us stays with 'em?"

Sharkey began to speak, but Petrel cut him off. "You see, we've worked out a good, solid plan for rescuing your friends, and I reckon it'll do the trick, especially if we can get the masks right and if Mister Smoke can smuggle 'em into the re-education camp. But no one's said anything about what we do with all these Sunkers *after* we rescue 'em."

"We can—"

"Now I'm sure you've thought about it long and hard, and you've prob'ly got something clever up your sleeve that you ain't told us about yet—"

Sharkey reddened.

He has nothing up his sleeve, thought Rain. *He has not thought any further than getting Poddy away from the whippings. But*

Petrel is right. He cannot take anyone else onto the Claw. *Even now there is hardly room to breathe.*

She squeezed closer to the chart table, pretending to study one of the maps. Cuttle was at the helm, and Fin and Krill were crammed next to the batteries. Behind them, the silver boy was asking Gilly about Sunker songs. But each time she sang a line or two, he shook his head and said, "No, that is not it. Try another one, if you please."

"Rain's the one you should talk to," said Gilly. "She knows lots of songs."

Petrel's voice rose above all the others. "—what you *really* need is a ship. A big one that'll take all your people and get 'em away nice and quick. And once that's done, you can think about getting the *Rampart* afloat again."

"We don't need—"

"And the good thing is, we've *got* a ship—or at least we *will* have, once we get it back from Albie. And all Cuttle and Gilly'd have to do is take a couple of us to where it's anchored. They could take Krill and the cap'n, maybe—"

This time it was Sharkey who broke in. "I need Krill."

"His ankle—"

"His ankle's nearly better."

"Perhaps you could sprain it again," Fin murmured to Krill. "It would be worth it if it would get us back to the *Oyster*."

Rain did not know quite what to make of Fin. The demon-hunting expedition had left the Citadel before she and Bran had come to live there, so all she knew of the boy was the stories she had overheard. At first he had been famous for his courage, for being the Initiate who would risk his life on the ice. Then, when the battered expedition had returned, he became known as the worst of all possible traitors.

Rain wished he would not quiz her about what was happening in the Citadel—she was afraid he might stumble upon the truth.

"I need your cap'n too," said Sharkey, ignoring everyone but Petrel. "I need *all* of you. That was the bargain, and you agreed to it."

"How about a rat? One little rat? That wouldn't make much difference to you, but it'd help us a *lot*. Missus Slink could run up the *Oyster*'s anchor chain, creep onto the bridge and tell Dolph and Squid that we're alive. She could fix the telegraph too, so we could talk to 'em—"

"Nay!" said Sharkey very loudly, as if that were the last word on the matter.

Petrel looked hard at him, and he reddened again. Neither of them said anything for more than a minute.

Someone tapped Rain's arm, and she turned, startled. It was the silver boy. "According to Gilly, you know many songs," he said. "Will you sing them to me?"

Rain knew she should be afraid of him. After all, this was the demon the Devouts feared and hated. But she had seen how easy Petrel and Fin were with him; and besides, there was something about him that reminded her of Bran. "What sort of songs?" she asked.

"Every sort. I will not know what I am looking for until I hear it."

Behind them, Petrel was speaking again, her voice no more than a murmur. "I know you're top high brass of this vessel, Cap'n Sharkey, and everyone does what you tell 'em. And I know that's the Sunker way. But we do things differently on the *Oyster*. We try to bend a bit if we can, to help our friends."

Rain peeped over her shoulder to see how Sharkey would respond.

But Petrel was still talking. "'Course, you don't *have* to bend. 'Cos you're right—we *did* agree to the bargain. But I gotta tell you that you're reminding me more and more of Fin's stories about the Devouts. They're the ones you call Hungry Ghosts. *They* don't bend either."

And with that, she walked away, though she couldn't go far, not on the *Claw*.

Sharkey's face went from red to white. He raised his hand, as if to summon her back, then lowered it again.

As brave as Petrel AND as clever, thought Rain. Then she turned to the silver boy and said, "Yes, I will sing to you."

SHARKEY RAISED THE HAMMER AND BROUGHT IT DOWN WITH a whack on the sheet of tin. *I am nothing like the Hungry Ghosts.*

He raised it again. Brought it down harder. *I'm NOTH-ING like the Ghosts. She doesn't know what she's talking about. None of 'em do. I shouldn't take any notice.*

But still Petrel's quiet words clung to him like a suckerfish.

He tightened his grip on the hammer. Beside him, at the bench of the minuscule workshop, the silver child was tapping at a second sheet, persuading it into the right shape for the masks Petrel had suggested. The pigeon, which seemed to follow him everywhere, was perched on the lathe, its head turning back and forth with every swing of the hammer.

At the far end of the bench, Rain was singing.

"Would you walk into the jaws of a tiger?

Would you pat a hungry bear on the snout—"

The silver child interrupted her, just as he had done with the last twenty songs. "That is not it. Another one, please."

Sharkey gritted his teeth. "I am nothing." *Whack.* "Like." *Whack.* "The Hungry Ghosts!" *Whack.*

He didn't realize he'd spoken aloud until the silver child looked up and said, "Of course you are not. You love machines, and the Devouts hate them. You are pale from lack of sunlight, whereas their skin has a little color, like Rain's."

The pigeon cooed in agreement.

"It's more than that!" said Sharkey.

The silver child regarded him thoughtfully. "They are not kind to their horses, but I have not seen you with a horse, so I cannot make a comparison." And he went back to his task, shaping the tin masks and placing them in the sealskin bag that held the comm, while Rain sang to him.

Sharkey was speechless. He told himself that he should be angry, but somehow the anger would not come. Instead, his mind wavered. Petrel was one of the most annoying people he'd ever known, and yet there was something about her—

"I went wandering," sang Rain,

"Over the hills so bright—"

"No," said the captain. "Another one, please."

Sharkey put down his hammer and said abruptly, "The rat with the green ribbon. Lin Lin, Missus Slink, whatever she calls herself. Could she ride one of our turtles? The mechanical ones? You've seen 'em, haven't you?"

"What is their range?" asked the silver child.

"Several hundred miles if the sea's calm. But their direction finders won't work over that distance."

"She could steer by the stars."

"Right," said Sharkey. And he went out to issue new orders.

THE FOLLOWING NIGHT, THE *CLAW* SIDLED INTO A DEEPWATER bay, nine and a half miles sou'west of the Citadel. The weather was clear, the moon was rising, and Missus Slink was long gone, riding her mechanical turtle across the waves towards the last known position of the *Oyster*.

One by one, everyone except Gilly and Cuttle climbed the ladder to the deck and jumped across the gap onto a disused stone pier. Then as the little submersible slid away, with orders to stand well out to sea until summoned, they set their course nor'-nor'east.

This is the third time I've been on terra, thought Sharkey. *There's nothing to be afraid of . . . except for the Hungry Ghosts.*

"They are not ghosts," murmured Fin in his ear.

"What?" Sharkey turned to stare at the other boy.

"You keep muttering about ghosts, and that is wrong. They are the Devouts. They are as human as you and I. You need to know that if you wish to fight them."

Sharkey was about to laugh out loud at the notion, when

he realized that Fin was right. After all, there was no denying that Rain was human, though Sharkey wasn't sure when he had started to see her that way. And the men who had brought Admiral Deeps to the rendezvous had looked human enough. Which meant that all the old stories were wrong.

"How do you know about 'em?" he asked Fin.

"I used to be one of them."

Sharkey had half realized it, from the conversations and stories he'd overheard. But hearing it said so plainly was a different thing altogether. "No—"

"They sent me south to destroy the *Oyster* and its captain. But I met Petrel—and I changed." A smile transformed Fin's rather serious face. "She has that effect on people."

That was too much for Sharkey. "Not on me, she doesn't," he said. And he sped up until he was right at the front of the little group, like a proper captain, with no one and nothing to distract him except his own thoughts.

They had been walking for a bit more than two hours when the silver child stopped. The road they'd been following was potholed and rutted, with ditches on either side. Now enormous piles of stone loomed out of the darkness like silent messengers from three hundred years ago.

"That was the university," said the silver child. "That is where the man who made me, Serran Coe, had his laboratory."

Sharkey tried to picture it but couldn't.

Krill growled, "The world's changed since you saw it last, Cap'n, and not for the better."

There was no sign of Hungry Ghosts in the ruined

university, but a little way past it was a clump of houses—at least, that's what Rain told Sharkey they were. He couldn't imagine living inside such poor-looking things. They just sat motionless on the side of the road, tiny boxes of mud and straw with square portholes.

"And not a fish to be seen," he whispered to Rain as they crept past. "What a miserable life!"

Rain's eyes crinkled at the corners, and they walked together for another hour, occasionally whispering to each other about the things they saw, which helped Sharkey forget his fears.

"What happened to your songs?" he asked at one point. "The ones you were singing for the little captain? Did he find what he was looking for?"

"No," said Rain. "I sang everything I could remember, but—" She stopped, jerking to a halt. "There," she breathed. "Can you see it?"

"See what?" Sharkey peered into the darkness, his heart thumping like a badly tuned engine. Ahead of him, pretty much due north, the land rose up in a sort of seamount.

"It is the Citadel," said Fin, coming up behind them. Like Sharkey, he sounded as if he'd rather be somewhere else.

Petrel joined them, shifting the bag that held the comm and the masks from one hand to the other. "That whole hill?"

"Nah," said Mister Smoke, teetering on her shoulder. "Citadel's just the bit at the top. The rest of it's a rubbishy sort of town called Tower of Strength. Used to be a nice little city—"

"Three hundred years ago it was called Gouty Head," said the silver child.

"That's right," said the rat. "But it looks like the Devouts tore down anythin' that'd been built with machines, and re-made it. It's all rammed earth and misery these days, 'cept for the Citadel, which is made of hand-cut marble and self-righteousness."

"The Citadel is where B-Brother Thrawn lives," whispered Rain.

There was no crinkle at the corners of her eyes now, and the way she said "B-Brother Thrawn," each time with that fearful hesitation, was starting to worry Sharkey. It reminded him of the time a Massy shark had swum right up to one of the *Claw*'s portholes and looked in.

It'd been bigger than the submersible, with monstrous jaws and an eye like stone, and Gilly and Cuttle had had night-mares for weeks afterwards. Sharkey too, though he'd never admitted it.

Brother Thrawn sounded a bit like that Massy shark. Cruel by nature. Too big to fight. Made you want to crawl under a rock until it went away.

But he's human, according to Fin, Sharkey told himself. *And if he's human, he can be fooled.*

"Come on," muttered Krill. "Let's get to the quarry and find somewhere to hide for the day."

The hill grew bigger as they approached it, until at last it squatted above them like a toadfish waiting for its prey. Moonlight touched the town's earthen walls, and Sharkey shuddered and looked away. Scroll cooed softly into the darkness.

"There is the Devouts' dovecote," whispered Fin, pointing to a shape set well back from the road. "The goats are next to it, and horses next to the goats—that is, if they have not changed things."

Sharkey turned to Rain, trusting she wouldn't mock him for his ignorance. "Goats?"

"Um—a bit like horses, only smaller. And trickier." Rain smiled anxiously. "Bran likes them."

"Where's the reeducation camp?"

"It is farther up the road. About a mile beyond the quarry."

They passed the mouth of the quarry and climbed its northern edge, with Mister Smoke issuing directions. "Straight ahead, shipmates. Now turn the wheel to starboard—no, you've overcorrected. Port half a degree and up the rise. That's it—hold that bearing."

The ground was rough and covered in dense prickly bushes that came up to Sharkey's chin and made it hard going, despite the moonlight. He put one foot in front of the other, wondering if he was about to tumble off the edge or get grabbed by something he couldn't see.

"Starboard twelve degrees," said Mister Smoke. "Past that outcrop. Now swing the wheel half a turn—and drop anchor."

Sharkey found himself in a narrow clearing with trees and bushes on one side and the rim of the quarry on the other. He sank to his knees, with Rain beside him. Behind them, Krill sat down with a hiss of relief.

The silver child said, "Is your ankle hurting? Would you like me to bind it again?"

"No, Cap'n, it'll be all right," said Krill. "I just need to sit for a bit."

Above their heads, Scroll flew in a wide circle, then settled onto a tree branch and tucked her head under her wing. Petrel put the sealskin bag down, slid forward to the edge of the cliff and peered over. After a while she crept back and said, "Fin, what are those big posts for, in the middle of the quarry?"

"They are whipping posts," said Fin quietly.

"*Whipping* posts?"

"For prisoners who stop work without permission."

Krill, Petrel and Sharkey stared at him. Rain said, "I told you."

The silver child shook his head. "They should not whip people. It is not right."

"Of course it is not," said Fin. "But—" He hunched his shoulders, as if there were things he didn't want to remember. "But when you are in the middle of it, you somehow persuade yourself that it *is* right. That it is the best thing to do."

"That is why they take children so young," said Rain. "So they can twist their thinking."

Petrel sighed. "What time do they come to work?"

"An hour after sunrise," said Fin.

"Well, I'm gunna sleep till then," said Petrel. "Mister Smoke, will you wake me up when it's time?"

"I will, shipmate. I'll stand guard too, though I doubt anyone but us'll set their course in this direction."

Like Petrel, Sharkey was used to sleeping when and where he could. But tonight he was too restless. He lay there in the darkness, thinking about friendship, the sort that Petrel and Fin had. *He* had never had a friendship like that. He'd been respected and obeyed, but that was all based on a lie. Petrel and Fin wouldn't lie to each other; he was sure of it.

He wondered if he was changing, as Fin had said. He wondered if he and Rain were friends.

Maybe . . .

Beside him, Rain was singing quietly.

"How tall the tree
The first to fall,
How wise to flee—"

She was interrupted by a flurry of movement from the silver child. "You did not sing me *that* song," he said, his eyes fixed on Rain's face.

"I only just remembered it," said Rain. "It is from a circus that came to our village when I was seven. I have not sung it for years."

"A circus?"

"There was a girl called Grim who could fold herself into a tiny box and slow down her heart until we all thought she was dead, and a blind boy who could hear the world breathing, and fortune-telling ducks, and that song, which the girl sang at the end."

"Will you sing it again?" asked the silver child. "Mister Smoke, come and listen."

The rat joined them, and Rain began to sing in a sweet, true voice.

"How tall the tree
The first to fall,
How wise to flee,
The worst of all.
But hear the song
The singer gives,
The trunk is gone,
The root still lives."

By the time she finished, Petrel, Fin and Krill were there too, crouched in front of her with expressions of astonishment on their faces.

"Is that *it*?" asked Krill.

"It is," said the silver child.

Krill shook his head. "What are the chances you'd stumble on the Song and the Singer, Cap'n, just like that?"

"Rain is *a* singer," said the silver child, "not *the* Singer. She is not the one I am looking for."

"Many people know that song," said Rain, "not just me. They sing it secretly, where the Devouts will not hear them— or at least they used to. There was another verse, about the sun and the moon, but I cannot remember it."

"I have never heard it," said Fin. "What does it mean?"

"It is about hope," replied Rain. "Terrible things happen, but underneath there is still hope."

Petrel's eyebrows pinched together. "I s'pose I should be glad. But to be honest, Cap'n, it's a bit of a letdown. All that fuss for a song about hope? I thought it was gunna be something big and important. A song with teeth. Something we could use against the Devouts."

"The Song is not about hope," said the silver child. "It is about something else, but I do not know what, not yet. It is like a code, and I need more information before I can solve it. I must find the Singer."

Krill nodded slowly. "Fair enough, Cap'n. But first we've gotta free the Sunkers and get the *Oyster* back from Albie. What d'you say to that?"

"I agree," said the silver child. "If the Sunkers are free and the *Oyster* is ours, we will have more resources to search for the Singer."

"Good," said Krill. He turned to the children. "It's only a couple of hours till dawn, bratlings, but I suggest we all try to get some sleep."

Sharkey lay down again, with his head on his arm. Rain sang the song quietly once more, and then she lay down too, with her back to Sharkey.

I like her, he thought. *She's braver than she thinks.*

And he closed his eyes and didn't move until Mister Smoke tapped him on the shoulder, whispering, "Rise and shine, shipmate. Keep your head low and your voice quiet. They're on their way, comin' down the road from the camp."

CHAPTER 17

HOPE . . . AND DESPAIR

DOLPH HADN'T HAD SO MUCH AS A SIP OF WATER FOR TWO days. None of them had. And that was a serious problem.

When the food ran out five days ago, Squid had crossed her arms and said, "We're all used to going hungry. An empty belly won't hurt us, not for a while."

But water was a different matter. Even in the leanest winters down south, when shipfolk had died by the dozens, there'd been plenty of water.

To make it worse, for the last few days there'd been a constant rattling in the ship's pipes—not proper messages, just nonsense to stop them communicating with the rest of the crew. Dolph *thought* that a few of the Cooks were still holding out, and maybe one other lot of Officers, but she couldn't be sure.

And now Skua had taken to mocking them from the other side of the barricade. "Water, sweet water," he shouted, every few hours. "All you can drink! What, you don't want any? Then I'll have to drink it all myself." He made loud glugging sounds. "Ooooh, that is *so* good."

Dolph and Squid stood firm. But for Minke and her friends, Skua's mockery was the last straw. Hard-faced and dry-tongued, they advanced on the two young women.

"Move aside," said Minke over the rattling of the pipes. "We're taking the barricade down."

"No," said Dolph, though it hurt her throat to speak.

"Krill's not coming back," said Minke. "He's dead."

"I don't believe it," said Squid.

"The barricade stays," said Dolph with as much authority as she could muster.

"You can't keep us here," said Minke.

Dolph shrugged. "If you want to go, then go. But Squid and I ain't joining Albie, not for anything."

At that, Minke and her friends backed off, whispering among themselves. But then they came forward again, their faces harder than ever.

"You two can stay here and die," said Minke, "but we're going. Let us through."

Dolph and Squid looked at each other—and nodded.

They had to take part of the barricade down to let the others out. They worked quickly and silently, hoping that Albie and Skua were off somewhere else, bullying folk, and wouldn't take this moment to launch an attack.

They had just removed one of the largest bits of driftwood,

which had been braced hard against the base of the bulkhead, when Dolph thought she heard a scraping sound, like something being dragged.

She held up her hand. "Wait." And despite everything, there was still enough of Orca in her to make Minke hesitate.

Next to Dolph's foot, right where the driftwood had been jammed in place, a screw turned. A patch of bulkhead was lifted out of the way by small paws. Dolph thought she saw the flash of a tiny screwdriver. Then that disappeared, and Missus Slink came into sight, with a sealskin harness around her chest and a large water flask dragging behind her.

If Albie had attacked at that moment, no one would have been capable of stopping him. They couldn't move. They couldn't speak. They just stood there, open-mouthed and staring.

"And about time, too," said Missus Slink, stepping crossly out of the harness. "I've been banging out messages to you for hours but couldn't make myself heard over that stupid rattling." She peered up at their stunned faces, then pointed to the water flask. "Well? I thought you were thirsty."

Sharkey almost didn't recognize the sunkers. They stumbled into the quarry like sleepwalkers, a hundred or so of them, their faces as gray as the rags they wore. The babies were crying. The middies and the old salts looked as if they didn't have a hope in the world.

"What's the *matter* with 'em?" whispered Sharkey.

"Don't reckon they're getting enough to eat, poor things,"

replied Petrel. "They look worse than shipfolk after a long, hard winter."

"Nay." Sharkey shook his head. "Sunkers don't despair just 'cos they're hungry. Sunkers are as tough as sharkskin, as strong as iron. They never give up—"

Fin interrupted him. "They will have been told about the attack on the *Claw*. The guards like to gloat over such things. They probably believe that you and Cuttle and Gilly are dead."

Sharkey must have made a noise of some sort, because Rain touched his shoulder. "Do not worry. We will get them out."

But that wasn't enough for Sharkey. He stared down into the quarry with a sick feeling in his belly. It was a mixture of anger and helplessness, and when he spotted Poddy, looking as gray and beaten as the rest of the Sunkers, it grew even worse.

He hated feeling helpless. He wanted to *do* something, like—like stand up, right there and then, and shout, "I'm here, Pod! I'm alive, and so're Gilly and Cuttle! And the *Claw*'s just a couple of hours away, a bit battered but still watertight. Don't despair! *Don't despair!*"

He didn't do it, of course. There was a score of Ghosts below, most of them with cudgels. *Not Ghosts. Devouts,* he reminded himself. *Humans.*

There were beasts down there too, as big as turtles—nay, bigger. More like small dolphins, only with four legs and wicked teeth.

"Dogs," whispered Rain, beside him. "Vicious dogs."

Sharkey lay on the rim of the quarry, watching the dogs

and the Devouts, seeing where they walked and what they did and whom they took notice of. After a few minutes, he whispered, "Mister Smoke, you see Poddy down there? Could you sneak close to her and tell her we're all alive still, and no serious damage to the *Claw*?"

"I'm not sure that's wise, lad," said Krill.

Sharkey suspected that the big man was right. But he still had that desperate need to *do* something, so he ignored his misgivings and said to the rat, "Tell Poddy we're here to get 'em out."

"Aye, shipmate," said Mister Smoke, and he dashed away.

In the sky above the Citadel, an enormous flock of pigeons wheeled and turned in silence. But down in the quarry, the noise was rising. The stronger prisoners used saws and chisels to cut blocks out of the quarry wall. The middies and the weaker adults gathered smaller bits of stone and hammered them to chips. Before long, everyone was so covered in rock dust that Sharkey struggled to recognize them.

Still, he managed to pick out Poddy's parents, and Cuttle's and Gilly's, and all his aunts and uncles and cousins. With a flood of relief, he realized that almost everyone had survived. The feeling of helplessness lessened.

Can't wait to see Gilly's face, he told himself, *and Cuttle's too, when they find out their ma and fa are alive.*

He heard a gasp from Rain. "There is Bran! Over there!"

Rain's brother stood beside one of the Gho— beside one of the Devouts, wearing brown robes that were too big for him.

His shoulders were hunched, and his feet scuffed the dirt. As Sharkey watched, the Devout leaned over and said something, and Bran immediately stood up straight and stiff, as if he were trying to be something he wasn't.

"Where's Mister Smoke?" whispered Petrel. "Cap'n, can you see him?"

"He is approaching a girl," said the silver child. He indicated a spot not far from Bran. "Is that Poddy?"

"Aye," said Sharkey grimly.

His cousin was pounding stones to chips, her head bowed, her spine a curve of grief. Her arm rose and fell as if it weighed a ton.

Sharkey saw the exact moment when she spotted the rat. For a split second, her hammer hesitated in midair—then it fell, exactly as it had done so many times before. Her head was still bowed. The curve of her spine looked as heartbroken as ever.

But now, beneath that heartbreak there was something else.

Hope.

She shuffled to one side and bent her head, as if she were trying to come at the stones from a different angle. Or as if she were listening to a small, rough voice and hearing the truth about what had happened to the *Claw*.

And then the hammer was lying idle in her hands, and *she* was talking, very quickly and quietly. Sharkey could see her lips moving, and the urgency of it, and the way her eyes flickered from side to side, watching the guards, checking to see that *they* weren't watching *her*.

Sharkey held his breath. There was something happening over at the other side of the quarry. One of the Sunkers had blood running down his arm. A Devout was standing over him, ordering him back to work.

"That is not right," said the silver child, half rising to his feet. "He is injured. He needs medical treatment—"

"Shh, Cap'n!" said Krill, pulling him down again.

The other guards were scanning the prisoners, in case they took this as an excuse to stop work. No one seemed to have spotted Poddy—no one except Bran, who ducked his head and stared at the ground. Beside Sharkey, Rain was singing under her breath, her eyes fixed on her little brother.

At last Poddy raised her hammer and went back to bashing at the stone. At the same time, she whispered something to the person next to her, who passed it on to the next person and the next and the next.

It was like the turning of a tide, subtle but strong. Folk still stumbled from one rock to the other. Their shoulders still sagged. Their faces still *seemed* hopeless and defeated.

But Sharkey knew better. The Sunkers had woken up.

Poddy, at the center of it, was pounding away with her hammer as if the crumbling rock was Brother Thrawn's head. She must have thought she'd got away with that brief stoppage. No one had shouted at her. No one had dragged her to the whipping posts.

All the same, the sick feeling in Sharkey's gut suddenly grew worse. *It was a mistake,* he thought, *sending Mister Smoke down into the quarry. I should've listened to Krill.*

He was right. The guard next to Bran grabbed the boy's shoulder and said something.

Bran shook his head. *No. No!*

But the guard was nodding. *Yes!* And pointing at Poddy. He *had* seen her stop work; he must've been watching out of the corner of his eye, waiting for Bran to report her.

Except Bran *hadn't* reported her. Now both he and Poddy were in trouble, and it was Sharkey's fault.

"No," he whispered.

"No," breathed Rain, her eyes fixed on her little brother.

"Steady," growled Krill. "Remember the plan."

The guard hustled Bran over to where Poddy was smashing rocks. When she saw them, her hammer faltered and her shoulders hunched, as if she were trying to hide. The guard shouted at her. His voice was drowned out by the wind and the hammering, but his meaning was clear. He hauled Poddy to her feet and began to drag the two children towards the whipping posts.

Behind him, every single prisoner laid down his or her hammer and chisel.

The sudden silence was like a blow. Sharkey's ears rang with it. And they rang again when the guards began yelling and lashing out with their cudgels.

Still, no one picked up a tool. The prisoners stood, ragged

and stubborn, their faces as hard as the rock behind them, their eyes fixed on Poddy and the guard who held her.

Sharkey felt a moment of intense pride. But then the guard shouted again. And this time his voice carried right up to the lip of the quarry.

"She is to be punished for stopping work. Fifteen lashes of the whip. The boy will be punished for not reporting her. He has been warned before. Five lashes of the whip."

"No," said Rain, and a sob caught in her throat. "That is too cruel!"

The guard continued. "And if you lot do not get back to work, the punishment will be doubled. For both of them."

For a long moment, no one moved. Then, down in the quarry, Admiral Deeps stepped forward, her voice strong. "She's too young for fifteen lashes. I'll take her punishment. I'll take it for both of 'em."

It just about tore the breath out of Sharkey's lungs to hear those words. Shook him from head to toe. Made him realize for the first time ever what being an admiral was about. It *wasn't* just the respect and the admiration. It wasn't just the power either. Admiral Deeps was looking after her people. She was stepping in to save them.

Except it wasn't going to work. The guard sneered at her. "You can be whipped *as well*, if that is your fancy," he cried, and his fellow guards laughed. "Or you can have this for free."

And he raised his cudgel and knocked her down.

Sharkey was on his feet in an instant. He wasn't the only one. Rain scrambled up too, saying, "We must stop them!"

Petrel and Fin pulled them down. "We *can't*, not till to-night! That's the plan, remember?" Petrel said.

"We cannot wait till tonight," cried Rain. "We must do something *now*, before they are hurt!"

"She is right," said the silver captain. "They should not be whipped."

"Shhh!" said Krill. "Keep your voices down!"

It was then that Mister Smoke returned, trotting towards them with his ragged coat covered in rock dust. "Poddy says there's a secret tunnel, shipmates—"

"She's going to be whipped," said Sharkey. "They saw her stop work. I shouldn't have sent you."

"—up the road at the camp where they sleep. The prisoners've dug it as far as the shoreline—"

"Didn't you *hear* me?" said Sharkey.

"—but they can't use it, 'cos the guards are out there all night and every night with their dogs. They need a diversion, something that'll give 'em time to—"

"A diversion," cried Rain. "That is what we want *now*!"

Sharkey wanted to save Rain's little brother almost as much as he wanted to save Poddy. But for all his anger and guilt, his clever mind would not stop working. "No, we'd be caught in an instant. And that wouldn't do anyone any good."

"But we have to do *something*!"

"*Shhh!*" warned Krill.

Too late. One of the guards raised his head and stared up at the cliff top. Then he began to shout.

There was no time for discussion. Mister Smoke dived into

the undergrowth, and Petrel threw the bag of masks after him. Krill leaped to his feet with amazing agility for such a big man. Sharkey grabbed Rain's hand, and they ran for their lives.

It wasn't until they were a hundred yards away that he realized the others weren't with them.

CHAPTER 18

CAPTURED

KRILL STARTED OUT STRONGLY. But the ground between the trees was pitted with rabbit holes, and by the time they'd gone twenty yards, his ankle had given way again. Petrel and Fin grabbed his elbows and tried to haul him along, but that just made things worse.

"Leave me!" he gasped, leaning against the base of an enormous rocky outcrop. "Save the cap'n! They'll smash him if they catch him."

Petrel could hear the Devouts crashing up the hill towards them. A dog barked, and ten more answered it. Scroll fluttered above the captain's head in agitation.

"They will smash you too," said the captain. "I will not leave you here, Krill. It would not be right. A captain does not desert his crew."

The Head Cook hissed through his teeth, "You *must* go. You're the one who matters, not me. Get out of here!"

"I will not," said the captain.

The dogs were howling now—a deep, hungry sound that made Petrel's skin tighten. She wanted to keep running—every fiber in her body urged her to escape while she still could. But the captain was right. They couldn't leave Krill behind.

She swallowed. "Looks like we're staying. Can you fight, Krill?"

"Reckon so, bratling, as long as it doesn't involve walking."

"Fin?" said Petrel.

Fin looked as if he wanted to run as much as she did. But he nodded at Petrel, and they began snatching up good, solid branches they could use as weapons.

"This way!" shouted a man from in among the bushes. "They have not got far!"

Petrel, Fin and Krill backed into a semicircle around the rock face, with the captain behind them. They were only just in time. Four men burst out of the bushes with dogs straining at their leashes. Two of them saw Sharkey and Rain disappearing into the distance, and kept running. The other two stopped and shouted over their shoulders, "We have them!"

The dogs drew their lips back from their teeth and snarled. Petrel shivered. Beside her, Fin gripped his branch with white knuckles.

"We've fought worse than this," said Krill in a quiet rumble. His face was gray with pain, but his eyes were determined, and the bones in his beard rattled ferociously.

"Aye," whispered Petrel, though her legs trembled, and she couldn't imagine fighting anyone. Fin's shoulder nudged hers, and she nudged him back. Scroll's wings churned the air above the captain's head.

"Here we go," said Krill. "Here come the rest of 'em."

Men and dogs milled out of the bushes, shouting and barking so loudly that Petrel could hardly hear herself think. She held her branch in both hands, copying Krill, and braced her legs as if she were on the deck of the *Oyster* with a storm coming.

She thought the men would rush them. That's what she'd have done, with so many against so few. Instead, they stopped some distance away and held their dogs back. The shouting was replaced by a low murmur.

"They are still afraid of him," whispered Fin. "Listen!"

"Demon," murmured the men.

"Demon!"

"Demon!"

Petrel drew in her breath and shouted across the gap, "He'll kill you if you come any closer!"

"I will not," said the captain in her ear. "I cannot."

"Shhh!" whispered Petrel. "It's what they think that counts."

Fin took a half step forward. "It is true," he cried. "I have seen it myself. You will be dead before you can blink."

The Devouts glowered at him. One of them, his beaky nose shining with suspicion, turned to his fellows and said, "Who is that boy? I have seen him before."

Someone else said, "Is he not the Initiate who went south with us? The one who attacked Brother Thrawn? Is he not *the traitor*?"

For a few seconds, the words seemed to hang in the early-morning air like icicles. Then the Devouts erupted with hatred. "Traitor!" they screamed. "Consorter with demons! You will pay for your crimes. You *and* your mother!"

Petrel felt Fin go rigid beside her. His mouth opened and shut, but nothing came out.

Krill's steady rumble broke the spell. "It's words, lad, that's all. They're trying to divide us. It's all part of the fight, just as much as the cudgels and the dogs. Don't let 'em see that they've got to you."

"They have not," Fin said quickly. "They have not got to me." And he raised his voice again. "The demon will boil the blood in your veins, men and dogs. You will all die."

To Petrel's surprise, the captain stepped forward then. "If your blood boils, you will certainly die," he said in a high, clear voice. "But first I think you will swell up and leak through the skin. You might even burst from the pressure."

He sounded horribly convincing. Petrel watched the men whisper to one another, heads nodding and shaking in argument. One of them pointed down the hill, and three men ran back the way they had come.

The man with the sharp nose turned to the small, defiant group and shouted, "You are lying, demon. If you were going to kill us, you would have done so already."

All the same, he and his fellows seemed in no hurry to advance. The dogs strained at their leashes, and the men held them back.

The captain whispered in Petrel's ear. "I did *not* lie. I did not say that *I* would make those things happen."

The Devouts had clearly taken it that way, however. Petrel felt a flicker of hope. This was a nasty trap, but she'd spent her whole life escaping from nasty traps. Maybe she and her friends could escape from this one.

What we need is a back door, she thought. *Except we ain't got one, not here, not unless we could climb up on top of this outcrop. But if we could do it, so could . . .*

The realization hit her as hard as any cudgel. Those three men who had been sent away!

She swung around, shouting a warning, "Cap'n, watch out above!"

But she was too late. The three men were already up there, with an enormous rock in their hands. As the words left Petrel's mouth, the rock fell, plummeting through the air like a thunderbolt.

The captain looked up . . . and the rock hit him.

He took three ungainly steps, then fell to the ground with half of his beautiful face crushed. At the same time, the Devouts rushed in.

The next few minutes were among the most dreadful Petrel had ever known. Dogs and men flew at her, and she did her best to hold them off, ducking away from cudgels and teeth, then leaping back in with her branch flailing.

Beside her, Krill roared with fury and lashed out at anyone who came within reach. Two men fell under his fearsome blows, and then another. A dog yelped with pain. Another dog threw itself at Krill's legs, and he scooped it up and tossed it away.

On Petrel's other side, Fin was straddling the captain's body and smashing his branch in a wide arc that no one could get past. Scroll pecked wildly at dogs and men. And all the time, the captain lay still and silent, and Petrel's heart was breaking.

In the end, it was a question of numbers. There were so many Devouts that even Krill's great strength couldn't hold them off for long. It took seven men and three dogs to bring him down, but bring him down they did. One moment, he was fighting; the next, he too lay silent on the ground, with blood trickling from his scalp.

With Krill gone, Petrel and Fin didn't have a hope. They fought on, trying to protect the captain's body, but it wasn't long before their weapons were knocked from their hands, and they were thrown to the ground.

Scroll gave a mournful *coo* and flew away.

Petrel knew what was going to happen next, and had no idea how to stop it. She could see the men's feet shuffling past as they gathered around the captain, hefting their cudgels and murmuring to one another.

"Do you think it is still dangerous? Might it wake up and boil our blood?"

"I do not know."

"We must make sure it is truly dead."

"Yes. We will crush it completely. Tear it apart."

For all Petrel knew, the captain *was* truly dead. She had no idea how he worked or whether he could be mended after that crushing blow to the face. *She* couldn't do it—that was for sure—and neither could Fin or Krill. But maybe Mister Smoke and Missus Slink could fix him, if they could only get him back to the *Oyster*.

There's still a chance, she told herself fiercely. *We might still get out of this. I might be able to save my friends.*

But if the Devouts tore the captain apart, if they crushed him completely, there'd be nothing left to save.

She tried to wriggle away from the man who held her. He snarled, as vicious as the dogs, and twisted her arm until she yelped. Behind her, the other Devouts were raising their cudgels—

"Wait!" shrieked Petrel. "Wait or we'll all die!"

She saw the cudgels hesitate and plowed on, not knowing what she was going to say until the words were out of her mouth. "If you smash the rest of him, a—a *gas*'ll come out."

She hoped they knew what a gas was. But maybe they didn't. After all, they had turned their back on every sort of knowledge except superstition. "A *poisonous* gas," she shouted.

"A miasma," said Fin in a muffled voice.

"Aye, a miasma, that's right. A nasty one. It'll kill everyone here and—and then it'll spread and kill everyone in the Citadel. Including Brother Thrawn."

Her words were greeted by a deathly silence. The men who had been looming over the captain took a step backwards.

Someone said, "She is lying."

189

Someone else said, "Perhaps. We must seek Brother Thrawn's advice."

"What shall we do with them in the meantime?"

"Tie them to the whipping posts. Then when we kill them, we can make a show of it. Let the peasants see what happens to those who defy us."

And with no further ado, the Devouts picked up Petrel, Fin and the captain and carried them down the hill towards the quarry.

Krill they dragged.

SHARKEY AND RAIN REACHED THE BOTTOM OF THE HILL without being stopped. Sharkey wasn't sure where they were going—he just wanted somewhere to hide for the rest of the day, somewhere safe and familiar, where he could think about what to do next.

"The sea," he said. "Set course for the sea, quick."

And so they headed towards the coast, with Rain leading the way. It was easier in daylight than it had been in darkness, but Sharkey didn't like it any better. *Wish I had good, solid metal around me,* he thought as his bare feet squelched through the mud. *Instead of all this—this earth.*

Tower of Strength and the Citadel were behind them now, but there were people everywhere, poor, hungry-looking creatures carrying bundles of sticks or leading scrawny animals. The two children ducked from cover to cover until at last they left the fields and the trees behind and stood on a rise with a little crescent beach below them and no sign of Devouts or anyone else.

And there was the sea, sighing and swelling like an old friend.

Sharkey couldn't take his eyes off it. He wanted to dive in, right there and then. He wanted to swim and swim until the Devouts and Brother Thrawn and the whipping posts were far behind him.

But that wouldn't help Poddy.

He turned to Rain and said, "We need a good hiding pl—"

"*There they are!*"

The shout, from the trees behind them, was like a blow to the belly. Sharkey grabbed Rain's hand again and tried to drag her towards the beach, crying "Run!"

But instead of running, Rain dug in her heels. And when Sharkey let go of her hand, she grabbed his arm. Then, to his horror, she turned towards the approaching Devouts and shouted, "I have him! Come quickly! Do not let him get away!"

Sharkey was so shocked that for a moment he couldn't move. He just stood there, staring at Rain. She shouted again, "Come quickly!"

That was enough for Sharkey. With a cry of disgust, he tore himself loose and ran. His legs pumped. His arms swung to keep his balance. His bare feet leaped over clods of earth and rocks and anything else that got in his way.

Behind him, the men egged each other on with great shouts. Sharkey couldn't hear the dogs. *They* ran in silence, and so did he, heaving the salty air in and out of his lungs, thinking of Poddy and how he *had* to remain free, had to save her.

When he came to the beach, he tore across the sand and into the water with gouts of spray splashing up around him. As soon as it was deep enough, he began to swim.

He'd taken no more than three strokes when the dogs were upon him, a writhing mass of coarse hair and sharp teeth and paws. They bit him and pushed him under and tried to drag him back towards the shore.

But Sharkey was a Sunker, and Sunkers fought to the very end, even when they'd been betrayed. He squirmed and wriggled and punched until he was free of the teeth and the scrabbling paws. His head shot to the surface, and he took a quick breath and dived under again. He couldn't see a thing, but he knew where open water lay, he could feel it in his bones, and he dragged himself towards it, with his heart and soul bent on escape.

He thought he'd made it. He gave one last kick and thought he was free. But then a hand grabbed hold of his leg. Another hand seized his foot and hauled it upwards. Sharkey's head hit the sand and bounced off. He took in a mouthful of water—and was dragged to the surface, spluttering and choking.

Before he could catch his breath, the men had his hands tied behind his back, and he was trussed up like a crab ready for the pot.

CHAPTER 19

BROTHER THRAWN

THE DEVOUTS DRAGGED SHARKEY ALONG THE BEACH, JERKING the rope this way and that and laughing when he fell to his knees on the sand. He tried to catch Rain's eye, but she wouldn't look at him.

Instead, she said, "He is the last of the underwater savages. I am glad you caught him. Thank you for saving me."

One of the men, whose brown robe was hitched up over his trousers so he could run, looked down at her. "Brother Thrawn thought you were dead."

Rain shuddered. "At times I *wished* I was dead."

"Well, you are safe now, and Brother Thrawn will be wanting to see you as soon as possible. He will want to see the savage too, no doubt." The man tipped his head towards Sharkey. "Is he really the last of them?"

"Yes," said Rain. "There are a couple of small children somewhere, but they will die soon enough without anyone to look after them."

Sharkey stared at her in disbelief. *I thought we were friends. How could I've been so stupid?*

The man jerked at the rope, and Sharkey stumbled up over the rise and into the trees, with the dogs nipping at his heels. He kept his head down, trying to act as if he were beaten. But all the while he was thinking.

If I can get away, where can I run to? Can I use the tunnel to get Poddy and the others out? And what if I can't get away?

He was scared of what was coming, but he was angry too. Angry at Rain, angry at Brother Thrawn, angry at every single person in the Up Above. What had the Sunkers ever done to them? Nothing, that's what. Sunkers just wanted to be left alone, to live their lives the way they'd done for three hundred years.

But the Devouts wouldn't let them.

By the time they came to Tower of Strength, Sharkey was fuming. Which was just as well, because otherwise his courage might have failed him. There was the Citadel high above him, more toadlike than ever, and he was being dragged up the busy road towards it, with the Devouts discussing his fate.

"What do you think Brother Thrawn will do to him?"

"Hang him. That is what I would do. Hang the lot of them."

Four men on horses overtook them. Another three strode down the hill with purposeful faces. The Devouts hauled Sharkey out of the way, still talking.

"Break his bones."

"Drown him."

They both laughed at that, and Rain said, "It would serve him right to drown. If he loves water so much, give it to him."

"You *are* a fierce one," said the man with the hitched-up robes, in admiring tones. "I always thought you were meek as a mouse."

"I have had to fight for my life," said Rain, "and it has changed me. No more meekness."

Sharkey saw her throat move as if she were singing under her breath. *A treachery song,* he thought, and looked away.

The road that ran up through Tower of Strength was made of tiny stone chips, like the ones Poddy had been pounding in the quarry. It was a neat road, despite the comings and goings of men and horses. But all around it was squalor.

For as long as Sharkey could remember, the *Claw* and the *Rampart* had stunk of sweat, engine oil and fish. Occasionally, if the recyclers broke down, the reek of sewage was added to the mix for a day or so.

But this was different. The houses on either side of the road were crumbling, their walls propped up with sticks and stones, their roofs half-caved in. There was no glass in their portholes, just flaps of filthy cloth, and the stink of hopelessness that rose from them made Sharkey recoil.

Pale-haired children played in some of the doorways, their faces gaunt with hunger, their limbs so thin that they looked as if they might snap. Others drooped in their mothers' laps. But as the horsemen trotted past, holding their robes over their noses, the women and children scuttled back inside.

Like fish, thought Sharkey, *hiding from a predator.*

At first it was a relief to come to the top of the hill and leave the houses behind. The smell lessened, the road flattened out, and there was even a bush or two growing beside it. But then Sharkey saw the Citadel.

From below, he had thought it looked like a squatting toad, but now he could see that there was another part to it, a tall, pointed thing that rose above it, white and hard. In fact, the whole thing was white and hard, like a bird skeleton lying on its back with its beak in the air.

Dead, he thought. *It looks dead.*

"Feast your eyes, savage," said one of the Devouts. "That is the spire of our Citadel, and the center of the civilized world. People can see it from a hundred miles away on a clear day. You poor ignorant savages never had anything so fine."

We had better things than dead-bird houses, thought Sharkey. *We had the* Rampart. *We had the* Resilience *and the* Rogue *and the* Rumbustious. *And the* Claw, *which is still out there somewhere. Least, I hope it is.*

The road took them to a high stone wall with a well-guarded wooden gate, and the gate took them to a world of neatness and order. Sharkey had never seen so many straight lines. Even the pebbles seemed to line up one behind another, as if they were too scared to do anything else.

There were Devouts everywhere, in the same brown robes as Sharkey's captors'. They were all men—there was not a woman among them, which to Sharkey was as strange as the straight lines. He looked around and realized that there were no middies either, or babies, which probably accounted for the neatness.

It's mean, he thought suddenly. *It's mean and hollow, and it's got nothing to do with real life.*

The new Devouts had an air of excitement about them, and one of them, a big man with scratches on his face, stopped and said, "Have you heard? We captured the demon and its helpers."

"*And* the boy traitor," said a second man, "the one who injured Brother Thrawn so grievously. What a thumping we gave *him*."

"Tomorrow morning they will be put to death, all four of them. It will be quite a spectacle."

Sharkey's anger slid away like dirty water, and he was almost knocked down by a wave of horror. Because of him and his rescue expedition, the others had been caught, every one of them. And now they were going to die.

The man with the scratched face peered at him. "Is this another of the demon's cohort?"

"No, he is one of the underwater lot," said the hitched-robe man. "The last, thankfully."

The other men spat on the ground, and as Sharkey was dragged away, one of them said, "They are as hard to get rid of as cockroaches."

Up close, the Citadel looked bigger and more corpse-like than ever. Everything about it was white and bleak, and the only sounds were footsteps and the mutterings of passersby.

Sharkey felt as if he were dead already, and lost in some terrible afterworld where the Hungry Ghosts would torment him for the rest of time.

"Punishment cells," asked one of his captors, "or Brother Thrawn? What do you think?"

"Brother Thrawn, definitely."

"Poosk will be there, of course."

They both snorted, as if Poosk was someone they enjoyed despising. "Pathetic little man," said one of them. "I do not know how Brother Thrawn puts up with him."

"He is well named. Poosk. Flea. Parasite."

"Have you heard him going on and on about what an honor it is to serve our leader?"

"Well, he is right. It *is* an honor to serve. As a member of the Circle, or a hunter of demons, or a warrior. But as a *nursemaid*?"

They snorted again. Then they became very serious and hustled Sharkey and Rain though a hatch— *Nay*. Sharkey made himself concentrate. Made himself find the right word. They went through a *door*—and into the Citadel itself.

And now at last he saw the workings of the empire that had eaten the world. The wide passages were packed with men, all of them bustling back and forth with scrolls in their hands and important expressions on their faces.

Every now and then, a couple of them would stop and talk to each other in low voices before hurrying about their business.

As Sharkey was dragged past, he overheard snatches of conversation.

"—have *five* fields? They reported only three. Find out the truth, and then—"

"—news from the Northern Zone suggests that—"

"—someone trying to teach the peasants to read in District Four. I have ordered a purge, and I think we should also—"

There was no crowing over the new prisoners here, and no one so much as glanced at Sharkey and his captors. They were too busy, and the crowded passages seemed to go on forever. But at last Sharkey was shoved into a long line of men that was creeping, bit by bit, through a doorway.

It took them nearly half an hour to shuffle from the end of the line to the door. Plenty of time to think about the tunnel. Plenty of time to think about Petrel and her friends and to wonder if they were expecting him to come to their rescue.

I can't, he thought. *I'll be lucky to save myself. And if by some miracle I manage that, the next thing'll be Poddy. And then Adm'ral Deeps and the rest of the Sunkers. That's why I'm here.*

He felt as if he were standing in front of Petrel, trying to excuse himself and not doing a very good job of it. The despair threatened to grab him again, and he fought it with all his Sunker strength.

I'm sorry, he said to the imaginary Petrel, *but I can't afford to worry about anyone else. I hope you escape—I really do. But I can't help you.*

It was an ugly thing to say, especially after they'd come

here to help *him*. But he knew it was sensible. *No distractions,* he said to himself. And with that resolution, he turned his mind away from the other four captives and focused on what was in front of him.

As soon as he passed through the doorway, Sharkey knew where he was. *This is the control room,* he thought. *This is center of everything.*

It was ten times as big as the whole of the *Claw*. The ceiling was carved in intricate patterns, and the walls were draped with silver-gray cloth that looked even finer than sea silk. Spaced out along the base of the walls were cavities, and in each cavity was an enormous fire, so that, despite the stone underfoot, the room was as warm as a summer's night.

At the far end was a wheeled chair with a man sitting in it.

And that, thought Sharkey, *is the high adm'ral. Brother Thrawn.*

The man in the wheeled chair was thin and angry-looking, with lines on his face that might've been carved with a knife. There was a coldness to him, and a heat as well, and his eyes were so full of hatred that Sharkey took an involuntary step backwards, and Rain went very still, as if she didn't want to be noticed.

Ahead of them, the long line of men made their reports.

"Brother Thrawn, the grain harvest from Subdistrict Seven, Village Number Four, was only half of last year's harvest. The peasants claim they are starving and have asked for their tithe to be halved as well."

"Brother Thrawn, I am pleased to report that the factional

rebellion in the Northern Zone has been squashed, and the ringleaders hanged. This *does* leave us with a temporary problem of leadership—"

"Brother Thrawn, three of our informers in District Nine have died in the last six months. Their deaths appear to be accidental—"

The horrible thing about it, thought Sharkey, was that it was all so ordinary. The Devouts spoke in dry, level voices, as if they were talking about marks on paper rather than people's lives and, after a pause, Brother Thrawn answered in an equally dry voice.

"The tithe will not be halved. They are not starving but lazy."

"Send Brother Trounce to assume leadership of the Northern Zone. He will come down hard—"

"Of course the deaths are not accidental. Hang twenty peasants from each village."

Sharkey and his captors moved forward step-by-step. Rain's face was so stiff that she might have been made of coral. The line in front of them grew shorter—

And suddenly Sharkey realized that it wasn't Brother Thrawn speaking, after all. It was his nursemaid, Brother Poosk.

Rain's uncle was such a nondescript little man that Sharkey hadn't even noticed him. Like the other Devouts, he wore brown robes, but his were made of rougher cloth, and although they were neat, they were also old and threadbare.

Whenever someone asked Brother Thrawn a question,

Poosk would bend a respectful ear to his leader, listen to the answer, and pass it on in that arid voice. Between questions he held a cup to Brother Thrawn's lips, then wiped them gently with a cloth.

When it was Sharkey's turn, the hitched-robe man shoved him forward and said, "Brother Thrawn, I am pleased to report that we have caught the last of the underwater savages. He was with the demon but ran off separately. I do not know how he escaped the attack of three days ago."

The figure in the wheeled chair mumbled something. Poosk bent closer. "What is that you say, dear leader? They are crowding you?"

The two men holding Sharkey quickly shuffled back a few steps. Sharkey glanced at Rain. Her eyes were fixed on Brother Thrawn. Her throat moved.

Brother Thrawn said something else, though Sharkey couldn't pick out the words, not from where he was. He wondered what was wrong with the man and whether he could be healed.

I bet Surgeon Blue could fix him, he thought. *And Thrawn'll never know, because I'll never tell him.*

Poosk raised his voice and passed Brother Thrawn's message on. "The day's audience is finished. Our dear leader is tired. You may leave the prisoner here, roped to a chair, so he cannot escape."

The dozens of men who had been waiting in line behind Sharkey left without a murmur, their sandaled feet slapping on the marble floor. But the hitched-robe man said, "The prisoner is slippery, Brother, and violent. Perhaps we should stay."

Poosk drew himself up to his not-very-impressive height. "Are you doubting our leader's wisdom?"

"No," said the man. "I just thought—"

Poosk held up a hand for silence. Then he bent his head closer to Brother Thrawn's lips. "It is not your place—to think," he relayed. "Tie him up and leave us. The girl can stay too."

At that, Poosk looked up with a surprised expression, as if he'd been so busy passing on Brother Thrawn's instructions that he'd hardly noticed who else was in the room. "Niece," he said, "is that *you*? Are you alive after all?"

"She helped catch the boy," said the hitched-robe man. "He was trying to drag her away, and she grabbed hold of him. She is a hero, she is."

"Oh," said Poosk, "I am so relieved, so proud—"

There was a sound from Brother Thrawn, and Poosk broke off, his plump cheeks flushed. "Yes, of course," he said. "My apologies, Brother."

Through most of this, Sharkey was looking for ways out. Looking for things he could use. He hadn't found anything yet, but his gaze kept coming back to Brother Thrawn's frozen figure. To the hatred that radiated from him, so powerful that Sharkey could almost touch it.

No wonder everyone jumps to obey him. He might be stuck in that chair, but he's got enough nastiness in him for a dozen Massy sharks.

Brother Poosk, on the other hand, was like one of the tiny fish that cleaned the teeth of those sharks, ducking in and out of their dreadful jaws day and night. The little fish were necessary, but no one liked them or took any notice of them. Not even the Massy sharks.

If I could get loose, thought Sharkey, *I could shove Poosk out of the way as easy as a baby. He'd probably cry as soon as I touched him. But not Thrawn. He's the one to watch, even though he can't move. I bet he's got a few tricks up his sleeve.*

Unfortunately, getting loose was about to become even harder. Sharkey's captors tied him to a heavy chair, then placed it a couple of yards away from their leader.

Before he left, the hitched-robe man whispered, "You keep a polite tongue in your head, savage, when you speak to Brother Thrawn. Or else." Then he and his friend left the room, closing the door quietly behind them.

And that's when Sharkey discovered where the *real* danger lay.

CHAPTER 20

UNCLE POOSK

IT WAS SUBTLE AT FIRST. Brother Poosk still bent to listen to his leader. Still mopped the helpless man's face and bobbed and ducked around him, attending to this and that.

"Brother Thrawn wants to know," he said, as the door closed, "how you escaped from the underwater machine. He was sure his men had destroyed it."

Sharkey didn't answer. Something had changed, and he was trying to work out what it was.

He looked at Rain, but she was staring at the floor. He looked at Brother Thrawn, at the mad glint in his eyes, at the rage and the viciousness and the nastiness. From this close, Sharkey could see that it was directed at—

—at Brother Poosk.

Sharkey blinked. Hang on, that wasn't right. What had Poosk done except run around being helpful and passing on messages? Look at him—even now he was moving Brother

Thrawn's left arm so it didn't rub against the edge of the chair, then trotting around to the other side.

In the end, it was the spring in Poosk's step that gave him away. Everyone else probably thought it was eagerness to serve. But to Sharkey, with his history of deception, it looked like something else.

A subtle glee.

Sharkey's eyes widened involuntarily. Everyone seemed to think of Brother Poosk as nothing more than an irritating servant. They despised him. They laughed behind his back.

But what if *he* was the one laughing? What if *he* was in charge?

Sharkey looked again, and listened, and knew he was right. It wasn't *instructions* coming out of Brother Thrawn's mouth. It was meaningless mumbles. *He* hadn't condemned sixty villagers to hanging. It was Poosk!

Which meant it was Poosk who had sent Sharkey's captors out of the room. It was probably Poosk who had caused the *Rampart* to be bombarded, and the *Claw* too. The handover trap, the catapults, the balloons—they were all Brother Poosk.

And Rain knew it.

Sharkey didn't look at the girl. He didn't look at Poosk either. He kept his face blank and his eyes fixed on Brother Thrawn, as if he still believed the masquerade. Because if Rain's uncle was clever enough to snatch this sort of power, to keep this sort of secret, then he was far more dangerous than he appeared to be. And if Sharkey wanted to save his own skin, and Poddy's too, he'd better keep quiet about it.

"Well?" said Brother Poosk in his humble, I'm-just-passing-on-the-question voice. "You must not keep Brother Thrawn waiting, savage. How did you escape?"

Sharkey had no intention of answering any questions. But it made no difference. Rain answered for him.

With lowered eyes, she told her uncle how Sharkey had tricked their pursuers. She told him about the oil and the broken-up berth and the expelled air. She even told him about the little claw and how it had been used to stir the sand.

The only thing she didn't mention was the part *she* had played. In *her* story, she'd been a helpless prisoner the whole time, unable to do anything except watch in terror.

If Sharkey hadn't hated her so much, he would've admired her. This was a side of Rain he'd never seen before. But he should've guessed it was there. After all, just about everything she'd ever said to him was a lie.

At the end of Rain's story, Poosk put his ear to Brother Thrawn's mouth and nodded several times. Then he said, in a surprised voice, "Really? You want *me* to question the savage boy? I am not at all sure, dear leader. I do not have your intellect—"

He really was astonishingly clever, thought Sharkey. His words, his voice, the look on his face—it was so convincing.

And all the time, Brother Thrawn's eyes burned with hatred.

"Very well," said Brother Poosk. "I will do my best." He turned his nondescript expression to Sharkey. "What is your name, boy?"

Rain murmured, "It is Sharkey."

"A savage name for a savage boy," said Poosk. "Dear me, how I hate to think of my niece in his company." Those mild eyes inspected Rain. "I hope none of the savagery rubbed off on her. Her little brother would be so upset."

"No, Uncle," said Rain, staring at her hands. "It did not rub off."

"Good," said Brother Poosk. "Now"—he turned back to Sharkey—"Brother Thrawn would like to know what you and the demon were doing above the quarry. You might as well tell him. If you do not, my niece will. Family is so important, is it not, Sharkey? Hmm?"

He stepped closer, his head tilted to one side. "Where is *your* family, by the way? Were they in the quarry? Did you see them cutting rocks, I wonder? It looks like hard work, I know, but really it builds character, and no one can argue with that. Mind you, Admiral Deeps does not need any character building. Such a *fine* leader. It must have been hard to lose her. Dear me, yes. And harder still to carry on without her. Such a responsibility . . ."

Sharkey wasn't sure how it happened, but there was something about that quiet voice that sidled past his defenses. He found himself nodding. After all, Admiral Deeps *was* a fine leader. And it *had* been hard to lose her. Where was the harm in admitting such a thing?

But once he had agreed with that, it was difficult to stop. And when Brother Poosk said kindly, "I suppose you came to the quarry with some thought of rescuing your fellows, did you not?" Sharkey croaked, "Aye."

"Of course you did," cried Poosk. "Any loyal person would have done the same. But loyalty is not enough, is it? It takes courage to walk into the lion's den."

Sharkey didn't know what a lion's den was, but he agreed with the rest of it. "Aye," he said again.

"I expect you had a plan," said Poosk. He looked over his shoulder to where Brother Thrawn seethed in his chair. "A brave, clever boy like this would have had a plan, dear leader."

Sharkey saw the trap and knew without a doubt that he mustn't say another word, no matter how harmless it seemed. But there was that quiet voice again, sneaking into the cracks, crawling into the spaces between who Sharkey was and who he wanted to be.

"Or perhaps there was no plan when you got here," murmured Poosk. "But then something came to you. Some little weakness you saw? Something you could exploit? Why, all those people are relying on you, Sharkey. Waiting for you to save them. And you are not going to let them down. That is not the sort of boy you are; I can see it in your face. The determination. The courage. The cleverness—"

It's true, thought Sharkey. *I'm NOT going to let them down. I'm going to get out of here, and then—*

"Then what?" asked Poosk.

To his horror, Sharkey realized he'd spoken his thoughts aloud. "And then—and then—" he stuttered.

"There *is* a plan, is there not?" asked Poosk. "Or perhaps just the beginnings of one? A loose end that we have not caught? A hole in the careful fabric that Brother Thrawn has woven? I wonder what it is, hmm?"

Sharkey clamped his lips together, determined not to give anything away. But the nondescript little man kept talking at him, and talking and talking, and before long he found himself nodding again.

He felt like a fish on the end of a line, being dragged along with a hook in its mouth, and no way of saving itself. He was sure he'd eventually let something slip. Something important. Or else Rain would do it. She'd told her uncle pretty much everything else. It was only a matter of time before she remembered Poddy's message about the tunnel.

I have to stop this, thought Sharkey. *I have to stop it in its tracks. Now!*

Except he could think of only one way to stop that mild voice, and he didn't want to do it. He opened his mouth—and shut it again. *Say it,* he told himself. But he couldn't. His whole life had been about self-preservation, and the habit was too strong to break.

But then Rain said, "Uncle—" and Sharkey was *sure* she was going to say something about the tunnel. In desperation, he thought, *What would Petrel do?*

The answer was obvious. Sharkey dragged in a ragged

breath and, before he could change his mind, said, "And then I'm going to kill you."

He saw the shock in Rain's eyes as he stammered, "I—I didn't realize at first. I thought Brother Thrawn was running things. But he's not. It's you. So it's you I have to kill. Then everything will fall apart, and my people'll be able to escape."

Brother Poosk folded his hands on his chest and twiddled his thumbs. All pretense was gone now, and his hard little eyes bored into Sharkey's. "My, my," he said. "What a clever little savage it is. Or did *you* tell him, Rain?"

The girl's face grew white with horror. "No, Uncle! I said nothing, I promise. He is just—clever."

"I see. And do you admire this clever boy, niece? Have you developed a *fondness* for him?"

"No, Uncle."

"Good, good. Because we cannot keep him, can we? Not when he goes around saying this sort of thing." He smiled. "What do you suggest we do with him?"

Rain ducked her head and whispered, "I am sure you will think of something, Uncle."

"I am sure I will," said Poosk. "Now, let me see—"

He bustled across the room, mumbling to himself. Sharkey wondered if the little man was going to kill him now or later. He hoped it was later. He hoped that Poosk wouldn't question Rain any further, wouldn't find out about the tunnel. If it remained a secret, the Sunkers might eventually find their own way of distracting the guards and the dogs. They might escape without Sharkey's help.

They'd better be able to, he thought. *I haven't been much use so far. I haven't saved Poddy. I haven't saved anyone, not even myself.*

But he hadn't betrayed anyone either, and that was something to cling to.

He took a deep breath, wishing he could say good-bye to Poddy. *I'm scared,* he thought.

Behind him, Poosk said, "Ah, here we are. A nice bit of silk left over from Brother Thrawn's undershirt. Just the thing."

And before Sharkey knew it, a piece of cloth had been thrust into his mouth, and another piece tied tight around it.

"Now, how is he going to die, I wonder?" Poosk scratched his chin and turned to Brother Thrawn. "Dear leader, I await your advice."

Thrawn glared. But Poosk nodded vigorously, as if his leader had replied, and said, "An excellent idea. Killed while attempting to escape! What could be more appropriate? The boy gets one pathetic chance at freedom and dies in the attempt."

He swung around. "What do you think, niece? You helped capture him, after all. You should have a say in his exit. Killed while escaping, yes?"

"Yes, Uncle," whispered Rain.

Sharkey thought he heard a quiet *hmmm*, and Poosk's eyes narrowed. "You are not *singing*, are you?"

"N-no, Uncle."

"You know Brother Thrawn cannot abide singing."

"Yes, Uncle."

"Now, where were we? Ah, the escape attempt—"

"Uncle," whispered Rain.

Sharkey's heart jolted. Had his sacrifice been for nothing? Had Rain remembered the tunnel at last?

But if she had, she wasn't saying so. "Uncle. I was wondering about Br— about my brother."

"What about him? He is to be whipped tomorrow morning, after the demon and its fellows are executed."

"Yes, I—I know. But since I helped capture the savage boy"—Rain didn't so much as look at Sharkey—"I thought maybe Brother Thrawn might let my brother off. Just this once."

Poosk sniffed. "A dangerous precedent. What do you think, Brother Thrawn? Are we feeling merciful? Are we feeling kind?"

A low growl escaped from Thrawn's lips. Poosk smiled delightedly. "We are? Well then, Rain, your request is granted. Consider yourself and your brother exceptionally lucky."

"I do, Uncle. And thank you."

"Well, don't just stand there simpering, girl. Go and tell those guards to come back. Brother Thrawn wants a word with them."

As Rain hurried to the door, Sharkey braced himself. Behind the gag, his breath came in short, painful gasps. *Now? Will they kill me now?*

But when the guards shuffled back into the room, Poosk merely said, "Brother Thrawn wants the savage thrown into the punishment hole. And you are to release the young Initiate while you are there. Our dear leader has forgiven him because of the heroism of his sister."

Sharkey trembled with relief. But as the men untied him from the chair and marched him out of the room, he knew that the relief would not last. Sooner or later they would come for him. And then they would kill him.

CHAPTER 21

THE PUNISHMENT HOLE

SOMETHING WAS HAUNTING THE *OYSTER*.

It started as a whisper, seeping out of the bulkheads whenever the rattling in the pipes died down for a moment or two. *"Albie's lying . . . Albie's lying . . ."*

From Braid to Grease Alley it went, and back again, the same words over and over.

"Albie's lying . . ."

It was more effective than any pipe message, and more puzzling. No one could tell where it came from or who it was. Some folk, listening carefully, swore that the voice belonged to First Officer Orca, which was a frightening thing, considering how long Orca had been dead.

Others said it was Dolph, Orca's daughter. But that was impossible, because Dolph and a few others were still barricaded on the bridge and refusing to come out.

Soon the same conversation was springing up all over the ship.

"So if it's not Orca and it's not Dolph, who is it?"

"Must be a haunt."

"Or maybe it's the ship itself, growing a voice!"

No one speculated on the message itself—at least not out loud, not where one of Albie's cronies might hear. But they all wondered what the whisper would say next. And before long, they had an answer.

"Albie's lying," said the whisper. *"The cap'n's alive, and so's Krill."*

That set the crew abuzz! They'd heard more or less the same thing from the bridge, before Albie's folk had started the constant rattling in the pipes. But this wasn't just Dolph or Squid banging out a message. This was a haunt—or the ship itself! And while it was true that folk wanted strong leadership, they didn't like being lied to, not one bit. In every corner of the *Oyster*, they started asking the questions that should have been asked two weeks ago.

An infuriated Albie tried to find the source of the whispers but was no more successful than anyone else. So he summoned most of his mutineers down to Grease Alley for new orders.

It was his first and only mistake, but it was enough. In Braid, a large group of young Officers took advantage of the situation to demand that First Officer Hump and Second Officer Weddell be released, along with the other ranking prisoners. And when the few remaining mutineers refused, the Officers overpowered them and threw them down the Commons ladderway with their jackets tied over their heads.

In Dufftown, the Cooks who had blockaded themselves

in the galley gathered round the burners with hope in their eyes for the first time in days. And before ten minutes had passed, they'd rolled up their sleeves and agreed that if Krill truly was alive, they were going to do something about it.

Even in Grease Alley, which was the center of Albie's power, folk began to question whether they wanted him running the *whole* ship, which is what would happen if they headed south without the captain or Krill.

"He's the best possible Chief Engineer," they whispered, looking over their shoulders to make sure they couldn't be overheard. "But he's a bit too quick with his fists to make a good cap'n."

By this time, Albie and his mutineers were cracking heads as enthusiastically as they'd done in the old days. But they were too late. The whispers had done their damage.

And there was more to come. In the secret tunnels that ran throughout the ship, previously known only to Mister Smoke, Missus Slink and Petrel, Third Officer Dolph wiped the rust from her face, took a swig of water from a lidded cup and started whispering again.

"Alive . . . they're alive . . . Petrel and Fin too . . . they're all alive, north of here . . ."

THE PUNISHMENT HOLE WAS SET IN THE MIDDLE OF A courtyard, with a solid wooden cover on top of it and an iron grating beneath the cover. The guards raised the grating and pushed Sharkey down a set of narrow stone steps. The smell that rose to meet him was old and terrible.

"Hey, Initiate!" shouted one of the guards from the top of the steps. "Get up here. Thanks to your sister, you have escaped punishment."

There was a scuffling sound from one corner, and Bran appeared, blinking in the light. His robes were crumpled and filthy, and his face was streaked with tears.

"Hurry up," said the man. "And do not get into trouble again. I doubt Brother Thrawn will be so merciful a second time."

Bran scrambled up the steps. The grating clanged shut, and the wooden cover was drawn over it. Total darkness descended.

Sharkey stood at the bottom of the steps, listening. He was used to confined spaces and darkness, and although the punishment hole was obviously meant to frighten him, it didn't. Or at least, it didn't make him any more afraid than he already was.

He heard the slow trickle of water and a skittering sound that made him think of small animals. And something else. A movement. A breath.

Poddy.

He couldn't speak because of the gag, and his hands were still tied behind his back. But he managed to grunt.

"Sharkey, is that you?" came a whisper.

He grunted again, and next thing he knew, a familiar hand was pulling the gag away from his mouth. He drew the foul air into his lungs and whispered, "Poddy! You all right?"

"Aye, mostly."

"Can you untie my hands?"

It took Poddy a while to get the knots undone, but Sharkey stood patiently while she fumbled at them. Except for the stink, he could almost imagine they were in the *Claw*, with the lights off and Cuttle napping under the chart table.

Sunkers weren't much given to shows of emotion, but when the ropes fell from Sharkey's wrists at last, he threw his arms around Poddy, and they hugged each other fiercely. Then they felt their way along the wall, running their hands over damp stones, until they came to a corner. The skittering sound grew louder.

"Careful," said Poddy. "Don't tread on the rats."

"Rats?" said Sharkey. "Not Mister Smo—" He paused, realizing that his cousin wouldn't know who he was talking about. "I mean—not Adm'ral Cray?"

"Nay, these ones don't talk. Bran was scared of 'em at first, but he got used to 'em. Sharkey, what's happening? Where's the *Claw*? They told us you were dead, and we believed 'em until I talked to Adm'ral Cray."

Sharkey let out a breath and began to tell Poddy everything that had happened since she'd been captured. He left out nothing except his own death sentence.

When he finished, Poddy hissed through her teeth. "I never thought Rain'd do something so nasty."

"I reckon she did it to save Bran from a whipping," said Sharkey.

"Still, she shouldn't have. This is all her fault."

The old Sharkey would have agreed with Poddy so he'd

come out of it looking nice and shiny. The new one said, "Nay, Poddy. I mucked things up. I should've thought more carefully before I sent Mister—Adm'ral Cray with that message."

The foul air moved as Poddy shook her head. "It gave us hope, knowing you were out there. And we need a bit of hope. 'Specially me, right now. With this—" For the first time, her voice wobbled. "With this whipping on its way."

"You don't want to be whipped, Pod? I can hardly believe it!"

The wobble turned to a snort of reluctant laughter.

"We'd best work out how we're going to escape, then," continued Sharkey. "I suppose you've tried that grate."

"It's bolted from above. Bran and I both tried it. He didn't want to, not at first. He thought he deserved to be down here. But I talked to him, and after a bit he changed his mind."

"What about the walls?"

"They're solid all around. There's a waste hole in the floor, right in the middle, but it's too small to climb through."

"Hmm," said Sharkey, trying to sound as if he had a few ideas. But the only ideas he had were bad ones, about what was coming. *Killed while escaping.* He couldn't tell Poddy about it—if she knew the guards were going to kill him, she'd try to stop them. And then she'd be killed too.

What would Petrel do?

"Tell you what," he said. "Those guards're gunna come back for me at some stage. Don't know when, but old Thrawn wants to—to ask me some more questions, because he didn't have time earlier. So when they come for me, I'm gunna kick up a fuss, and you're gunna make a run for it."

"Not without you."

"Aye, without me. 'Cos, you see—" Sharkey was thinking on his feet, twisting things around, the way he had done so often in the past. But it wasn't to make himself look good, not this time. "'Cos you see, it's—it's easier for me to escape if I know you're away already. If I have to think about you, that'll hold me back."

Silence from Poddy. Then slowly she said, "I suppose that makes sense."

"'Course it does, Pod. And once you're out of here, head south—"

As best he could, he described the bay where Cuttle and Gilly were waiting with the *Claw*. With any luck, Missus Slink would've reached the *Oyster* and fixed the telegraph, in which case the ship might be there too. With a bit more luck, Petrel, Fin, Krill and the silver child would've escaped, and maybe even the rest of the Sunkers. And they'd all head south and meet up. All except Sharkey.

"You'll join us, won't you?" asked Poddy. "Soon as you can get away?"

"'Course I will. Keep your eyes open and you'll see me skipping along behind you, glad to be getting back to the Undersea." He yawned. "I'm a bit short of sleep, Pod. It's still daylight out there, and I don't reckon they'll come for me till tonight sometime."

And when they do, he thought, *I'll kick up such a fuss that Poddy'll be out of here and away before they even notice she's gone. And once that's done—*

But he didn't want to think about what was going to happen after that. He wanted to think about the *Claw,* and the Undersea and maybe a couple of dolphins swimming past the porthole.

And freedom.

THE DEVOUTS WEREN'T TAKING ANY CHANCES WITH THEIR dangerous new prisoners. Once they'd marched the Sunkers back to the reeducation camp, they trussed Petrel, Fin, Krill and the captain to the whipping posts in the middle of the quarry and surrounded them with armed guards.

Petrel had tried to count the guards several times, but there were too many. A group of them was hammering away at something behind her, but the rest were watching her and her friends. If she so much as twitched, scores of eyes focused on her, glaring and suspicious, as if she were an army of warriors rather than one small, dusty girl.

It might have been funny if it weren't so terrible.

Krill had regained consciousness some time ago, and he glared back at the guards with such ferocity that Petrel half expected to see smoke rising from them. Fin had retreated to somewhere deep inside himself, and the captain—the poor, broken captain—slumped in his ropes as if he would never move again.

He found his Song, thought Petrel, *but it didn't do him any*

222

good. And again she thought of that mysterious someone reaching out from the past and moving things around to suit themselves. *Bet they didn't expect things to end up like this.*

She knew that Sharkey had been captured and that Rain had betrayed him. The guards had taken great pleasure in telling them so. She knew too that she and Krill and Fin were to be hanged tomorrow morning, right here in the quarry, and that the captain was to be burned on the hottest fire possible, to destroy the poison miasma.

She licked her parched lips and tried to think, but hunger, thirst and the fear of what was coming made it almost impossible.

Got to get us out of here.

As darkness fell, the Devouts fetched dozens of flaming torches and set them in a ring around the whipping posts, so that the prisoners were lit almost as brightly as day. There were shadows, of course, that danced and moved with the flickering of the flames, and the hammering continued behind Petrel's back. But the rest of the guards still watched so keenly that she couldn't even blink the quarry dust out of her eyes without attracting their attention.

Got to make 'em look away, she thought. *Got to make 'em think I'm so useless there's no reason to watch me anymore.*

She knew how to do it. Up until a few months ago, it had been her only weapon against the crew that had rejected her. She hadn't dared do it since then, because she'd been afraid of losing everything she'd gained.

But now there was nothing left to lose.

Slowly—infinitesimally slowly—she let her head droop. She thought of defeat and misery and loss. She hunched her shoulders and made her eyes blank and stupid.

It shouldn't have worked. After all, some of the guards had heard her talk and seen her fight. They knew she wasn't stupid.

But as Petrel's face grew dull, the men nearest to her began to shuffle their feet as if they'd lost interest in her, as if Krill, Fin and the captain were the real threat, and Petrel was just someone who'd been swept up in the excitement. They'd still hang her, of course, but there was no reason to watch her so closely.

It wasn't long before Krill caught on to what Petrel was doing, and turned his ferocious gaze upon her. "This is your fault, witless girl," he hissed, just loud enough for the guards to hear. "If you had half a brain, we'd never have been caught. We should've known better than to let you tag along."

His words shouldn't have hurt—after all, he was pretending, just like Petrel. But they did hurt a little, and so did the sniggering from the guards. For a moment Petrel felt dreadfully alone—

She glanced sideways at Fin and saw his eye close in a barely perceptible wink. *He HASN'T retreated inside himself,* she realized. *He's pretending too!*

That gave her courage. She wasn't alone. She was with her friends, her fierce, clever friends.

She made her face stupider than ever. She didn't have a plan. She didn't even have much hope, not if she was being honest with herself. But she couldn't just stand there and wait for the end.

And so, as the shadows from the torches flickered, and the guards turned their attention to Fin, Krill and the captain, Petrel began to work on the ropes that tied her wrists.

CHAPTER 22

"ARE WE FRIENDS, YOU AND ME?"

WHEN PODDY WOKE SHARKEY, WITH A HAND OVER HIS mouth, he knew the moment had come. He nodded, to show he was properly awake, and sat up, his heart beating as fast and rackety as the *Claw*'s pistons.

At first he could hear nothing except the scurrying of rats. But then there came a sound from above them, a scraping noise, as if someone was trying to drag the wooden cover off the grating and not quite managing it.

Sharkey braced himself, ready to start shouting and hitting anyone who tried to grab him. *I'll give 'em a black eye or two*, he promised himself. *I'll give 'em something to remember me by.*

There was a *thunk*, and fresh air wafted down to them from where the wooden cover had shifted a little. Another *thunk*. Sharkey had expected to see daylight, but the darkness of the punishment hole hardly changed.

He gripped Poddy's hand, his nails biting into her palm.

"It's nighttime," he whispered. "I didn't mean to sleep so long. You be ready to run."

She nodded.

Bit by bit, the wooden cover was dragged away from the grating. Sharkey couldn't work out why it was taking so long. The men who had brought him here had picked it up with no trouble at all. Had Poosk sent a weakling to kill him? Or were they just teasing him, drawing out the moment so he'd suffer more?

He tried to make himself relax, but he was wound too tight and couldn't let any of it go.

It seemed like forever before the cover was removed. Sharkey heard the bolt being dragged back. Then someone leaned over the grating and whispered, "Poddy!"

Before Sharkey could stop her, Pod had replied, "Bran?"

"I cannot lift this by myself," said Bran. "Can you and Sharkey help me?"

Poddy was already on her feet, but Sharkey pulled her back. "No," he whispered.

"But Sharkey, it's Bran. He's come to free us!"

"It's a trap," said Sharkey, knowing that *this* was the escape attempt, *this* was where he would be killed. "Bran might think he's helping us. But he's not alone up there."

"I can't hear anyone else."

"Doesn't matter," said Sharkey. "They're there somewhere."

He knew he had to move. If he wanted to give Poddy a chance of getting away safely, he had to climb out of the hole.

Had to distract whoever was waiting to kill him. Trouble was, he wasn't sure he could do it. Life had never seemed more precious.

"*Poddy!*" whispered Bran again.

"I'm coming," said Sharkey, raising his voice so the boy could hear him. "I'll help you." To Poddy he whispered, "Stay where you are until you hear shouting. Then run for your life."

"But Sharkey—"

He could've snapped out an order, and she would've obeyed him. But he was sick of orders. And besides, he didn't want her last memory of him to be a bad one. So instead he said, "Are we friends, you and me, Pod?"

"Friends?" She sounded startled, as if she'd never even considered such a thing. But then she said, "Aye, Sharkey!"

"Then out of friendship, I'm asking you to do this." He nodded towards the grate. "It's a trap, and I know how to deal with it. So I want you stay here till the shouting starts. Then run. Understand?"

He could feel her staring at him in the darkness. But in the end she whispered, "All right. But you be careful."

He squeezed her hand one last time, then crept towards the stone stairs.

Going up them nearly broke his nerve. With every step, he expected to see Bran shoved to one side by half a dozen men. He wondered how his death would come. A knife? An arrow? A crack over the head with one of those cudgels?

Don't think about it, he told himself. *Think about giving*

Poddy a chance. Think about causing as much trouble as I can before they get me.

He reached the top of the stairs without anything bad happening, and crouched there, looking up at Bran through the bars of the grate. He couldn't see the boy's face, but he could hear his breath coming quick and shallow, as if he were frightened half to death.

Me too, thought Sharkey.

Aloud, he said, "Have you got the bolt pulled right back?"

"Y-yes," said Bran.

Once unbolted, the grating wasn't hard to lift, not for someone of Sharkey's size and strength. He lowered it carefully to the ground.

"Where is Poddy?" whispered Bran. His breath was a cloud on the night air, and the pebbles at his feet were white with frost.

"She's coming in a minute," said Sharkey, and he made himself straighten up. "Thanks for helping us. You'd better run along now, back to your bed. Don't want you to get into trouble."

Bran nodded. But before he went, he whispered, "Nearly everyone is at the quarry. Rain said there will be a diversion just before dawn." Then he turned and ran into the darkness.

Sharkey stood there, waiting for death to arrive. Bran's words lingered in his ears, but they made no sense. Every inch of his skin prickled with tension. He wished he were ironclad and double-hulled. He wished there were two hundred feet of good, clean seawater between him and the Devouts.

Beside him, someone whispered, "What'd he say?"

Sharkey almost jumped out of his skin. "I told you to stay below!"

"I *did* stay below. And now I'm here. What'd he *say*?" asked Poddy.

But Sharkey couldn't answer, he was so afraid for her. "Get out of here, Pod," he whispered. "Right now. Run!"

He pushed her, but she stood her ground. "We're friends—that's what you said. I'll run when you run."

Sharkey could've screamed with frustration. "Just go!"

"Not without you."

Which meant that Sharkey had to grab her hand and drag her across the cobblestones towards the wall, all the time expecting someone to leap out and grab them—and how would he save Poddy then?

But no one leaped at them. The night remained quiet—and Sharkey didn't trust it, not one bit.

It's one of Poosk's games, he thought. *He wants us to think we've escaped. That's when he'll take us.*

To Poddy he whispered, "Same rules as before, Pod. If I start shouting, you run."

There was no point even trying the well-guarded gate. The two children crept along the base of the wall, keeping to the deep shadows and running their hands over the stone.

"Here," breathed Sharkey.

The cracks he had found were tiny, but they were enough for Poddy, who dug in her fingers and toes and scrambled right to the top, quick and silent, as if she were scaling a tier of bunks in the belly of the old *Rampart*. Sharkey scanned the shadows one more time, then followed her, his fingers clutching at the crevices, his bad shoulder hurting all the way up and all the way down the other side.

With the wall behind them, they crept onto the road that wound down the hill. The moon was up, which meant it must be past midnight. But it was still too low to give much light, and they made their way by instinct as much as anything. They slipped and skidded on patches of ice, and a couple of times they almost ran headfirst into one of those stinking hovels, but they caught themselves just in time.

Sharkey's skin prickled worse than ever, but they saw no one. And—as far as Sharkey could tell—no one saw them.

They were at the bottom of the road before he remembered Bran's words. *Nearly everyone is at the quarry. Rain said there will be a diversion just before dawn.*

Sharkey didn't want to think about Rain, who had been her uncle's tool all along. But maybe she was telling the truth this time. Maybe nearly everyone *was* at the quarry. Maybe he was supposed to wait until just before dawn for the diversion, then try to get the Sunkers out through the tunnel. Maybe *that* was the trap.

It didn't make sense. But then, nothing the Devouts did made sense, not to Sharkey. And Rain was a Devout, whatever she said.

He peered south and saw a glow, like the beginnings of sunclimb, in the direction of the quarry. Petrel and Fin were down there somewhere, waiting for their deaths, and so were Krill and the silver child.

I can't help 'em, he reminded himself. *I've got to get the Sunkers out. No distractions!*

"Pod," he whispered. "The camp where you sleep, it's just up the road from here, right?"

"Aye, no more than a mile."

"And the guards bring you to the quarry an hour or so after sunclimb?"

"That's right. The rest of the time they're patrolling outside—there's always a dozen or more of 'em. With dogs. They go all the way down to the shore and back."

"Can you see 'em from inside the camp?"

"Nay. But sometimes we hear 'em. And we've been told they're always out there. *Always*. A few of the older middies wanted to try the tunnel anyway, but the adm'ral wouldn't let 'em. She says we'll never get the chance to dig another one, if this one's discovered. And the dogs've got noses so keen, they'd smell us as soon as we came out the other end. We've been trying to come up with a way of getting rid of 'em, and of *knowing* we've got rid of 'em."

"Well, tonight might be the night, Pod. Can you take us to this camp, nice and quiet?"

"What about the dogs?"

"We'll stay downwind, just in case."

"Aye, Sharkey!"

They set off again, with the wind in their faces. Poddy guided Sharkey off the road and across plowed fields that were capped with white, like storm waves. Their bare feet made no sound, and they didn't speak until they reached the camp.

It was as dark as the rest of the countryside, except for a single fire. In its glow, Sharkey saw walls higher than those around the Citadel, and a gate that was bolted so firmly that it looked as if it would stand forever.

"Can't climb *those* walls," whispered Poddy. "We tried, but there's not a crack in 'em."

As the children crouched in the darkness, two men walked into the light of the fire. They stopped and talked briefly, then went in opposite directions.

"What are we going to do?" whispered Poddy.

"Wait. Let's see how many of 'em there are."

They waited for at least half an hour, clenching their teeth against the cold. In that time, the same men came back again, greeted each other in the light of the fire, and kept walking. The moon was a bulge of silver, halfway up the sky.

"There's only the two of 'em," whispered Poddy. "And *no dogs*!"

"Aye. They must all be at the quarry. Adm'ral Deeps could bring everyone out now, and the Devouts'd be none the wiser."

"But she won't *know*, Sharkey! She's got no way of telling!"

Sharkey chewed his thumbnail. *Rain thinks I'm going to wait till just before dawn. All the more reason to do it now!*

"Where does this tunnel come out?" he asked.

"Near the shore. In a bunch of trees. I reckon I could find it."

"Let's go and see."

They crept away from the camp as silently as they had come, and headed for the shore. It was no more than three hundred yards away at that point, and Sharkey could hardly wait to get there, to smell the salt water and the seaweed, to hear the murmur of the waves.

Still, he didn't take any risks, and neither did Poddy. For the last hundred yards, they crawled on their bellies through the frosty grass, stopping frequently to listen for the sound of footsteps or voices. But they heard nothing.

It took them another forty minutes or so to find the end of the tunnel, which was so well hidden that they crept past it a dozen times without seeing it. But at last Sharkey pulled a pile of brambles to one side, and there it was.

Poddy's eyes gleamed with excitement. "Are we going in?"

"I am," said Sharkey. "You're going to wait here."

"Nay, Sharkey. You won't be able to find your way around. It's not just Sunkers in the camp—there's other prisoners too. And Adm'ral Deeps reckons a couple of 'em aren't really prisoners—they're there to keep an eye on us and tell the guards what we're up to. You wouldn't believe the tricks we had to pull to stop 'em finding out about the tunnel."

Sharkey didn't want to send Poddy back into danger, not now that she was free. But he didn't want to blunder around the camp and mess everything up either.

Besides, dawn was still some way off. If Poddy went into the camp, *he* could sneak back to the top of the quarry and search for the portable comm device. With that, they could signal the *Claw*.

"All right," he said. "But you be extra-careful, Pod!"

"Aye, Sharkey!" And she wriggled headfirst into the tunnel.

Sharkey pulled the brambles across the entrance. Then, with a quick glance at the stars to make sure he was going in the right direction, he set off, back towards the quarry.

WHEN THE MESSAGE CAME THROUGH, DOLPH WAS DOWN IN Grease Alley. She had an iron rod in her left hand and a knife in her right, and Chief Engineer Albie was trying to kill her.

"Haaa!" roared Albie, and his wrench swung through the air with deadly accuracy.

But Dolph ducked under the blow, the way her mam had taught her, and jabbed the iron rod towards Albie's ribs. With her other hand, she sliced at his bare arm and drew blood.

The Chief Engineer didn't even flinch. He swung hard and low at Dolph's knees, and she leaped out of the way just in time, her heart racing. In the background, she could hear the rest of the fighting, like a muffled roar, as the core of the mutineers battled to keep the crew away from the engines.

"Give—up—Albie," she panted.

His lips parted in a vicious grin. "*You*—give—up, Orca's girl."

"Never." And Dolph's knife darted in and out again, so quick that Albie couldn't guard against it.

More blood, though not enough to slow the Chief Engineer down. Dolph bounced on her toes, trying to look as if she still had all the energy in the world. But she was tiring, and she knew it.

Albie's next swing clipped her right arm, so that she nearly dropped the knife. She didn't make a sound, but Albie laughed and swung again. Dolph stepped backwards—and found herself wedged into a corner next to the digester.

The stink of the ship's waste. The greasy floor. Nowhere to jump. For the first time, she understood that she might lose this fight. Albie's grin spread as he realized the same thing.

Mam, thought Dolph. *Help me!* And she surged out of the corner, using her knife to drive Albie back.

He grunted with surprise—and all around them, the pipes began to rattle out a message from First Officer Hump on the bridge.

SHORE PARTY DUE TO BE EXECUTED IN MORNING, said the pipes, in general ship code. THEY NEED US NOW!

It was impossible not to be distracted by it. Dolph's first thought was that Missus Slink must have fixed the telegraph. Her second thought was that Albie was still taking in the message and that she could kill him right now if she wanted to. It was probably the best thing to do—otherwise he'd always be a problem. Her mam, Orca, would have killed him without hesitation. And Dolph was as loyal as she could be to Orca's memory.

But at the same time, she was trying to do things differently. And so, instead of using her knife, she raised the iron rod and whacked Albie across the skull. And as he fell to the deck, unconscious, she leaped over his body, shouting, "Put him in the Dufftown brig. And get those engines going. We're heading north, full speed!"

CHAPTER 23

WE KNEW YOU'D COME FOR US

SHARKEY CREPT UP THE NORTH SIDE OF THE QUARRY, AS quickly and silently as he could. The moon was high now, and he could almost see where he was going, which was just as well. Prickly bushes jabbed at him from all sides. Stones and pebbles turned under his feet. Below him, in the heart of the quarry, a hundred small fires burned, and the sound of hammering filled the night air.

No distractions, Sharkey told himself. *I can't help 'em, so it's a waste of time even thinking about it.*

He heard something moving up ahead and froze. It was a dragging sound, a rustling of grass and twigs, and for a moment he wished Rain were there with him—*she'd* know what it was.

But then he remembered. Rain was the enemy. *If she was here, she'd just betray me again.*

He waited. The dragging sound stopped. Somewhere near Sharkey's foot, a small, rough voice said, "Come to 'elp, 'ave you, shipmate?"

Sharkey almost fell off the edge of the quarry, he was so startled. "Mister Smoke," he whispered. "What are you doing here?"

"Been sendin' a message to the *Oyster*. Givin' 'em our position. Lettin' 'em know what's happenin' down yonder." He twitched his long nose towards the quarry.

Sharkey swallowed. "What's happening?"

"Ain't you looked?"

"Not yet."

The rat beckoned him. Sharkey didn't want to go, but he found himself dropping to his hands and knees and crawling to the edge.

What he saw was like a scene from a nightmare. A hundred or more crude torches were arranged in a circle, so they lit up the quarry like sunclimb. No one was chipping at the rocks, however. There were no prisoners at all, just the Devouts and their dogs, standing beside the torches, with anticipation rising from them as hot and hungry as a diesel engine.

No. Wait. There *were* prisoners. In the middle of the circle, like the eye of a storm, the whipping posts held four sagging figures. Petrel. Fin. Krill. The silver child.

The hammering stopped, then started again. With an effort, Sharkey dragged his eyes away from the four figures to where a score or so of Devouts were building a platform, with three posts on it.

Sharkey's guts tried to tie themselves in a knot. "What's that for?" he whispered.

"That's a gibbet, shipmate. They're gunna hang Petrel, Fin

and Krill at dawn. And over yonder you'll see a bonfire. That's for the cap'n. They're gunna burn what can be burned, and melt the rest."

Sharkey stared at him. "Will the *Oyster* get here in time? To save 'em?"

"Not a chance, shipmate."

I can't help 'em, thought Sharkey. *I've got to rescue my people. No distractions.*

Except if their positions were reversed, if it were Sharkey down there in the quarry, he couldn't imagine Petrel walking away. She'd be up here plotting, and so would Krill and Fin. And the little silver captain would be wanting to help, and Rain would—

No. Don't think about Rain.

"I could come back," whispered Sharkey, his eyes fixed on the gibbet. "I've got to get the Sunkers out and send 'em down the coast, but then I could come back. I don't know what I can—"

"I knew you wouldn't let us down, shipmate," said the rat. "'Ere, do you want this?" And he dragged a sack out of the bushes and dumped it in front of Sharkey.

"The comm," said Sharkey. "Adm'ral Deeps'll need it to signal the *Claw*." He opened the sack, and his fingers brushed against tin.

The masks.

The original plan, thought up by Petrel and added to by everyone else, had involved Mister Smoke smuggling the masks into the reeducation camp, along with enough wood and rags to make several flaming torches, and a note to explain how terrified the Devouts were of the "demon."

Because of the tunnel, the masks were no longer needed. But it struck Sharkey that maybe he could use them for a different purpose . . .

"I'll take the whole thing," he said, tying the mouth of the sack shut and slinging it over his shoulder. "I don't know if I can help, but I'll do my best. What about you, Mister Smoke?"

"Don't worry about me, shipmate. I got me own plans. Gotta find Scroll, for a start. I'm 'opin' she can 'elp me with somethin'."

"Well then," said Sharkey. "Fair tides and clear water."

"Same to you, shipmate." Mister Smoke turned away.

Sharkey whispered, "Wait!"

"Aye? What is it?"

"You're not—you're not really the adm'ral, are you? You're not really one of the ancestors?"

He heard a whisper of sound, like rat laughter. "What do you think, shipmate?" said Mister Smoke. And, with a twitch of his nose, he was gone.

RAIN WAS CURLED UP ON HER BED IN THE LITTLE CLOSET, waiting for the night to pass. Now that she was back, it was hard to believe that the last two weeks with the Sunker children had happened. Everything was exactly as it had been before. She had managed to speak briefly to Bran after he was released from the punishment hole, but apart from that, all her time had been spent acting as her uncle's unpaid servant.

After supper he had locked her in her room and would not let her out until an hour or so before dawn. Her job then would be to feed Brother Thrawn spoonfuls of gruel while Uncle Poosk tucked into a breakfast of eggs, black pudding, crab cakes, roast goose and pastries—all of it meant for his "dear leader."

Once breakfast was finished, the day's audience would begin, with Devouts from all over the world bringing their reports and questions. At least, that was the normal order of things. Today would be different because of the executions.

Rain turned her face to her wooden pillow, trying not to think about anything except Bran. She had managed to save him from a whipping, but she was not sure she could save him from turning into a proper Devout. Not unless she got him away from here.

"And that is why," she sang, under her breath,
"I WILL do this.
No matter how
Afraid I am—"

A sharp rap on her door made her flinch. She heard the key turn in the lock, and dressed quickly, throwing on a skirt and a vest and pulling on her boots. Then she crept out the door.

Uncle Poosk was already seated at the dining table, his face pink with pleasure at the sight of the crab cakes. "Executions give me an appetite," he said to Rain. "Hurry up and feed our dear leader, and we will be on our way."

Brother Thrawn was sitting in his wheeled chair in the

next room, dressed in clean robes. His mad eyes stared at Rain as she draped a rug over his knees. "Gurr—" he mumbled. "Gurr-lll."

Rain froze. Was that a word? A *proper* word? She licked her lips. "Did—did you say 'girl,' Brother?" she whispered.

There it was, the slightest nod, and sweat breaking out on the man's gaunt forehead, as if the movement had taken nearly all his strength.

"Are you—are you getting better?"

Another infinitesimal nod.

Rain stood there, gaping. What did this mean? Should she tell her uncle? Did it change things?

No.

"Brother Thrawn," she whispered, "do you want to get your revenge on Uncle Poosk? Do you want your people to know the truth about what he is doing?"

She could see the answer in Thrawn's eyes. It was like a shout, and she almost fell backwards with the force of it.

But she sang a quick, silent song for courage, then said, "I will help you. But you will have to help me too. Can you pretend, just for the next little while, that you are *not* getting better?"

A third nod.

"Good. This is what we are going to do," said Rain.

She bent closer and whispered hurriedly in his ear. Then she grabbed the back of the chair and wheeled it into the dining room, where Uncle Poosk was stuffing himself, as if he could not get enough of the rich food—which was probably true.

Like Rain's mama, Poosk had grown up in poverty and had struggled all his life to climb out of it. He was not the sort of man who would ever rise to wealth and power on his own. But in the weeks since the disastrous expedition had returned from the icy south, he had done it through Brother Thrawn.

"Greetings, revered leader," he murmured as Rain pushed the chair to the other end of the table. "What a day we have ahead of us, beginning with an execution at dawn. You must be there, of course. How would we manage without your wise presence?"

His words were humble, but the sarcastic tone gave him away. He never bothered pretending when it was just Rain and Brother Thrawn in the room with him. Brother Thrawn couldn't betray him, and Rain wouldn't. Not when he could so easily hurt Bran.

She fed Brother Thrawn as quickly as she could, which was not very quickly at all. He hated the gruel, and she hated spooning it into him. But at last, with a quarter of the bowl still full, he clenched his teeth and refused to eat any more.

Rain picked up the bowl and stood there as if she weren't sure what to do next.

"What is the matter?" asked her uncle, looking up from his plate, with a crumb of pastry clinging to his lip. "Have you forgotten your duties?"

"No, Uncle."

"Then put the bowl next to mine, here." He rapped the table with his knuckles. "I have nearly finished."

"Yes, Uncle." Rain walked towards him, singing under her breath, *"But will we cower, will we hide . . ."*

And then, somehow, in the middle of her song, she tripped, and the bowl flew out of her hand and spilled gruel all over her uncle's clean robe.

"Oh! I am sorry!" she gasped, backing away with her hand over her mouth.

Apologies were never enough for Uncle Poosk. He leaped to his feet with a cry of anger and slapped her across the face. "Useless girl! Now I will have to change."

"I am sorry," whispered Rain again. She dared not touch her stinging cheek. "Can I help? Tell me what to do, and I will do it."

She ran ahead of him, opening the door of his room and hovering there anxiously.

"Bah!" said her uncle, elbowing her to one side. "Make sure Thrawn's hands are clean. I do not want to waste another minute."

And he slammed the door in her face.

With trembling fingers, Rain turned the key in the lock. Uncle Poosk was too busy cursing to hear it, but she knew she didn't have long. She ran back to the table, grabbed Brother Thrawn's chair and, without a word, wheeled it towards the audience chamber.

They were not quite there when the door handle rattled behind them. Rain flinched.

"What is this?" cried her uncle. "What have you done, stupid girl? Let me out at once!"

Quickly, Rain pushed Brother Thrawn through the empty audience chamber and shut the heavy doors behind them. Her uncle's cries grew muffled.

The Initiates' dormitory was four long corridors away, just past the door that led to the underground storerooms. To Rain, every step seemed like an eternity. Her hands were clammy and cold, and she was having trouble breathing. She kept expecting Uncle Poosk to break free from his prison and come after her.

But then she saw Bran waiting outside the dormitory, as she had instructed. She hugged him with all her strength. "Are you ready?" she whispered.

The little boy nodded.

Rain dredged her memory for the bravest song she knew. To her surprise, it was one of her own.

"I tried to break the depth gauge
To save my brother's life—"

She nodded to herself. She had been terrified then, just as she was now. But she would do what had to be done.

With her heart beating wildly, she went over the words she had prepared for the guards at the gate. *Brother Thrawn is going to oversee the execution of the demon and its followers. Let us through.*

Then she and her little brother pushed the leader of the world out the door of the Citadel.

By the time Sharkey made it back to the mouth of the tunnel, with the sack over his shoulder, Admiral Deeps was already crawling out.

She was filthy and bruised, but when she saw Sharkey, she pulled herself up to her full height and gripped his arm. "Well done," she murmured. "*Very* well done. We had no idea the guard dogs were gone! Without you, we'd never have tried the tunnel tonight."

"It was Poddy, Adm'ral, as much as me," said Sharkey.

Deeps laughed under her breath. "Modest as usual, eh? Here, give me a hand."

More people were coming out of the tunnel by then, some of them so weak they had to be dragged along. There were two of them, then three, then a dozen. Sharkey and Admiral Deeps stood on either side of the entrance, helping the Sunkers to their feet and propping them up until they were steady.

Out came Sharkey's uncles and aunts and cousins, and Cuttle's ma, and Gilly's fa and all the other people he had been so relieved to see in the quarry. Only now it was even better, because they were right there in front of him, and he could grip their hands and clasp their shoulders without even trying to wipe away his tears.

Nearly everyone who emerged whispered, "We knew you'd come for us, Sharkey."

"It wasn't just me," he said over and over again. "There's others, and they're in trouble." But no one seemed to hear that last bit, no matter how often he said it.

At last the whole of the *Rampart*'s crew was gathered under the trees, a filthy, ragged, whispering crowd, as familiar and dear to Sharkey as his own two hands. With a quick signal, Admiral Deeps called the senior salties to her side and said, "We're heading sou'west, keeping well away from the road. No stragglers. Stickle, Pike, Scale, you three bring up the rear. Sharkey and I'll lead the way. Come!"

Sharkey started to obey her. It was automatic, and besides, he *wanted* to go with her; he really did. After all the confusion and fear of the last fortnight, he was back with his people. What's more, he was a hero, a *real* one this time. Everyone loved him. He could go with them, and no one would know he'd deserted Petrel and her friends, just when they needed him most.

No one except him and Mister Smoke.

Before he could change his mind, he stopped and took the comm device out of the bag. "Adm'ral, you can use this to signal Gilly on the *Claw*. She'll only be able to take four or five, and the rest of the crew'll have to hide. Did Poddy tell you about the *Oyster*?"

"She did," said the Admiral, accepting the comm. "Will they pick us up?"

"I reckon so, though not straightaway. Some of their people are in trouble. Ship's coming to the rescue, but they're too far away to help. Which is why I have to go back."

"Go back?" Deeps stared at him, the bruises on her face as dark as ink. "Nay, Sharkey, you're coming with us."

"But I want—"

"It's not what you *want*, Sharkey. It's what you *must do*." The Admiral's voice hardened. "I thought you understood that. Your duty is to your people. And if we have to manage without the *Oyster*, we will."

"But I—"

"Nay, I'll have no argument. What if you get caught again? We can't take such a risk. Who else among us can hear the ancestors?"

Sharkey stared at her, his heart sinking. "But—"

"Poddy told us about the talking rats, but I don't believe they're Lin Lin and Adm'ral Cray, any more than you do. You're the only one the ancestors have ever spoken to. And right now, we need their wisdom more than ever. Which means we need *you*."

Her hand gripped Sharkey's wrist. He tried to pull away, but even half-starved, she was stronger than he was, and he found himself being hauled through the trees, towards the shore.

He knew that Admiral Deeps was right in one way. The Sunkers *did* need him. Not to talk to the ancestors but to guide the Sunkers across strange country and make sure they found the bay where the *Claw* was waiting.

Trouble was, Petrel and her friends needed him more.

He didn't have to ask himself what she would do, not this time. He knew what was right. And he knew the exact words that would make Admiral Deeps let him go. But he didn't think he could get them out. Because once they were said, there'd be no more *hero*. There'd be no more back patting and *Well done* and *We knew you'd come for us*.

In fact, he'd be lucky if any of the Sunkers ever spoke to him again. Especially Admiral Deeps.

He dug in his heels. The admiral jolted to a stop, saying, "What *is* the matter?"

"It was—" The words stuck like a fish bone in Sharkey's throat.

All around him, Sunkers were heading to the shore as quickly and quietly as they could. Anyone too weak to hobble was carried. Surgeon Blue was limping from one small group to another. And there was Poddy, trotting towards Sharkey, her face bright with joy. Which made it even harder.

But not as hard as walking away, with the gibbet and the bonfire behind him.

"It was a lie," he said.

"What?" Admiral Deeps was losing patience with him, hero or not. "What are you talking about?"

Sharkey took a jagged breath. Then he looked straight at the admiral and said, "The ancestors never spoke to me. *Never.* I lied. I'm sorry."

The joy in Poddy's face went out like a light. At the same time, the admiral's fingers loosened with shock.

"I'm sorry!" said Sharkey again, more to Poddy than to anyone else. And he pulled his hand free and ran back the way he had come.

ONE HAND, THOUGHT PETREL. *All this time, and I've only got one hand free.*

But one hand was better than none. And no one had noticed, not yet, which meant she could start work on the other hand. Her head still bowed. Her face still dull with stupidity. And in her heart, the desperate need to save her friends.

She'd hoped the Devouts might grow careless, standing

guard all night, but they showed no signs of it. If anything, they watched Krill, Fin and the captain more closely than ever. The only one they ignored was Petrel.

Her left hand was easier to untie than her right. Carefully, she flexed her wrists, keeping the rope around them and watching the guards out of the corner of her eye. Something was happening. What was it? The hammering behind her had stopped, and the Devouts were milling around purposefully.

They went for Krill first, a mob of them with cudgels at the ready. They untied the ropes that held him to the whipping post, then dragged him bodily past Petrel, with the Head Cook struggling all the way. But his hands were bound, and his ankle was useless, and all he could do was bruise a few of them, getting worse bruises in return.

Petrel turned her head and saw the platform behind her. With its ropes. And its nooses. And Krill being dragged towards it.

Her heart almost tore itself from her body in fright. They were going to hang him. They weren't going to wait for dawn; they were going to do it now. What's more, another group of Devouts was advancing on Fin and the captain. And on *her*. Her hands might be free, but that wasn't nearly enough. It was time for the executions, and she couldn't do a thing to stop them.

CHAPTER 24

EXECUTION

SHARKEY RAN SOUTH ALONG THE ROAD, FEELING AS IF HE had a fever. His face burned at the thought of what he had just done. His chest ached. He knew there was a good chance he'd never see the *Claw* again. And if he did, it certainly wouldn't be as captain.

Maybe the Oyster*'ll take me,* he thought bleakly. *I could work in the engine room and pretend I'm still in the Undersea.*

He tightened his grip on the sack and looked up at the stars. By the position of the Lobster, it was less than an hour till dawn, which meant he had to be extra careful. Rain's trap was about to be sprung, and he was determined not to get caught in it.

He'd just passed the road that led up to the Citadel when he heard something coming down the hill towards him. A cart maybe, its wheels rattling on the icy pebbles. Sharkey slid into the ditch and crouched there in the mud and the weeds, trying to quiet his breathing.

The rattling sound came closer. And there in the moonlight was Brother Thrawn, hunched in his wheeled chair, with Rain and Bran pushing him towards the quarry.

If Sharkey could've killed them with a look, he would've done it, and danced around their dead bodies. He shrank down as they passed, his face inches above the freezing mud, his eye half-closed so as not to catch the moonlight. A frog croaked nearby. The rattle of the wheeled chair grew louder and louder, and then it passed him and continued down the road.

Sharkey didn't move. Poosk'd be along any second, keeping an eye on Brother Thrawn. There'd be guards too, ready to spring the trap.

Which I'm not going to fall into.

He waited, with the cold seeping through his clothes. But there were no more footsteps. Brother Poosk and the guards did not come.

Sharkey's pulse hammered in his ears. Where were they? Had they gone to the reeducation camp instead of the quarry? Was that part of the trap?

No. Poosk wouldn't let Brother Thrawn go anywhere without him! It'd be too easy for things to go wrong, for the whole pretend-nursemaid thing to fall apart. So if he's not here, where is he?

Sharkey inched his way out of the ditch, staring after the chair. This didn't make any sense. What was Rain doing? She had betrayed him, so she *must* be against him. She *must* be working with Poosk. But if that was the case, where *was* Poosk? Where were the guar—

The realization hit him like a flood tide. If Poosk wasn't

here, maybe he didn't know what was happening. Maybe it *wasn't* a trap after all!

And suddenly Sharkey saw the sense in Rain's betrayal.

Those two guards and their dogs would've caught him in the end—he knew that now. For all his determination, he'd been lost from the moment they came out of the trees. He hadn't understood it at the time. But Rain had.

And she'd understood too that she was more useful free than as a prisoner. Free, she could send Bran to let Sharkey and Poddy out of the punishment hole. Free, she could set up a diversion.

Sharkey felt as if the weight of the oceans had lifted off his shoulders. She hadn't betrayed him after all! She'd just been clever.

He almost laughed out loud at the beauty of it. She'd fooled him as effectively as he'd ever fooled the Sunkers. What's more, she'd fooled Poosk.

He raced after the wheeled chair, leaving a trail of mud behind him. *Hope I'm right*, he thought. *Hope this isn't the stupidest thing I ever did.*

And he hissed, "Rain!"

She stopped dead but didn't turn around. Sharkey thought he heard a whisper of song, trembling on the night air. He tried again. "Rain! It's me, Sharkey!"

Rain spun around, her hand to her mouth. Her little brother leaned against her, his face concealed by his hood.

"Sharkey," whispered Rain. "You got away."

"Aye, and Poddy too, and all the rest of the Sunkers—"

There was a grunt of protest from the man in the wheeled chair, and a barely formed word. "Nnno-o."

Rain bent over him and said, "If you want, I can always give you back to Brother Poosk. I do not mind."

At which Brother Thrawn fell silent.

"Are you taking him to the quarry?" asked Sharkey. "Is he your diversion?"

"Yes."

"It's a good start, but I don't think it'll be enough."

"I know," said Rain. "But it was all I could think of."

"Mister Smoke's around somewhere—he's got plans too, though he didn't say what. And I've got these." Sharkey tapped the sack. "You start things off, and I'll come in when they're already shaken up a bit."

He was trying to sound confident, and it must have worked, because Rain beamed at him and said, "We are going to save them!"

"Aye," said Sharkey, "'course we are. Bran, do you know much about goats?"

The little boy pushed his hood out of his eyes and nodded.

"He is good with animals," said Rain.

"Then he'd best come with me," said Sharkey. "Because all I know is fish, and I suspect goats are a bit different."

The noose around Petrel's neck was coarse and scratchy. The stool she balanced on had a wobbly leg. One of the Devouts stood ready to kick it out from under her.

Where are you, Mister Smoke? she thought. *I wish you'd come!*

But even if Mister Smoke *did* come, it could only be to say good-bye. Because Fin had a stool beneath *his* feet and a noose around *his* neck too. So did Krill. And on the other side of the quarry, three men waited for the signal to plunge their flaming torches into the wood stacked around the silver captain.

Petrel's hands were loose inside their ropes, but what good was that? Even if she could grab the noose as she fell, the Devouts would be upon her in an instant. She'd still die. It'd just take a bit longer.

This is the end, she thought. *I wish Krill and Fin weren't so far away. I wish I could hug 'em. I wish I could talk to the cap'n one last time, tell him I'm sorry we never found his Singer.*

She wondered what the Devouts were waiting for. Someone important, maybe? Whoever it was, she hoped they never came! She hoped—

A movement near the quarry entrance caught her attention. The ranks of Devouts were parting to let someone through. Someone important.

A chill of horror ran down Petrel's back. The waiting was over.

The doves in their cote fluttered restlessly as the two boys crept past. Next door to them, the goats were quiet. Sharkey followed Bran into the pen and closed the gate behind them. Under his feet, the ground was chopped, and frosted with ice.

"Du-usk!" called Bran softly. "Mee-eek!"

Sharkey heard a crying sound, like a baby wanting its ma,

and a patter of hooves. Next moment, he found himself sur-rounded by a dozen or more hairy bodies, all butting up against him and trying to nibble his fingers, as excitable as a bunch of middies and twice as smelly.

He stood very still and tall, trying to keep his hands away from the curious mouths. But Bran rubbed the goats' heads and scratched their ears and chatted to them as if they were old friends.

"What are we going to do with them?" he asked.

Sharkey undid the neck of the sack and showed Bran the contents. "I want to tie these to 'em, and send 'em running into the quarry."

"Where the Brothers are?" Bran's eyes were enormous.

"Aye. Can we do that?"

The little boy thought for a minute, scratching his lip with his finger, then said, "If I take a bucket of grain, they will fol-low me up the road, and then I could throw the bucket—except I cannot throw very far."

"I can," said Sharkey.

And they set to work.

THE LAST PERSON PETREL EXPECTED TO SEE WAS RAIN. But there she was, her face white in the torchlight, pushing a stooped figure in a wheeled chair. A murmuring rose all across the quarry, and the Devouts edged forward.

Petrel turned her head carefully to look at Fin and Krill, and they looked back at her with desperate eyes. Rain might have pretended to be their friend on the *Claw*, but she had shown her true colors when she betrayed Sharkey. She wasn't here to help them. She was here to watch them die.

The wheeled chair stopped halfway between the platform and the unlit bonfire. Rain bent over the stooped figure, listened—and moved the chair back ten yards towards the quarry entrance, as if to get a better view.

The Devouts made way for her, nudging one another into position with their elbows, and the three men on the platform, waiting to kick away the stools, straightened up expectantly. The guards with the flaming torches moved closer to the silver captain.

Petrel heard a flurry of wings overhead, and the torches guttered, then sprang high again. She stared at the figure in the wheeled chair. It was Brother Thrawn. She'd seen him only once, but the harsh lines of his face had stuck in her mind.

The man nearest the chair held up his hand for silence. Rain said something to him, and he repeated her words. "Before the executions are carried out, our dear leader wishes to make an announcement," he bellowed.

His voice reached every corner of the quarry and bounced off the rough stone in a wave of echoes. *Announcement . . . announcement . . . announcement . . .*

"He has important news that he particularly wishes to convey to us. In person." *Person . . . person . . .*

"He cannot speak above a whisper, but—"

Rain gestured an invitation. The man with the loud voice puffed out his chest with importance. "But *I* will listen and pass on his words."

And he bent over Brother Thrawn.

For half a minute or more, nothing happened. The man shifted uncomfortably, waiting for his leader to say something.

Petrel thought she heard a grunting sound. And suddenly, she felt a spark of hope. She wasn't sure why. Nothing had changed—or had it? She flexed her fingers, trying to get the blood flowing.

"What was that, Brother?" asked the man.

Another grunt, like someone trying—and failing—to speak. The man straightened up, his face red. He whispered to Rain, and she whispered back.

"*What?*" cried the man, his eyes bulging. "I do not believe it!"

Somehow, quiet Rain found her voice. "It is true!" *True . . . true . . . true . . .* "He cannot talk." *Talk . . . talk . . .*

Disbelief rippled from one side of the quarry to the other. Voices rose in protest.

"Of course he can talk. He has been giving us orders."

"You are not listening carefully enough."

"Where is Brother Poosk? The man is a fool, but at least he knows how to listen."

One voice could be heard above them all—the man who had first spoken. "His condition has grown suddenly worse, yes? Is *that* what he wanted to tell us?"

Petrel had to make herself breathe. The hope that they might not be going to die after all was almost as painful as the despair.

"No," said Rain. "He has *not* suddenly grown worse." Then

she cleared her throat and began to sing, softly at first, then more strongly.

"He has been like this
Since he came back from the south.
He cannot say a word.
Brother Poosk has taken you all
For fools."

The Devouts stared at one another. "Fools?" they said. "No, I do not believe it!"

Within seconds, both Rain and the man with the loud voice were pushed aside by a dozen brothers, who pressed as close as they could to Thrawn's chair, begging him to speak.

But all Brother Thrawn did was grunt.

The men stepped back in horror. "The girl was right," said one of them in a low voice. Then he raised his head and shouted it. "The girl was right! He cannot speak! Poosk has taken us for *fools*!"

Fools . . . fools . . . FOOLS . . . The word echoed around the quarry, bouncing off stone and growing in volume as the Devouts repeated it in outraged voices.

"Fools? Us?"

Those disciplined ranks disappeared as if they had never existed. Torches waved this way and that. Some of them fell to the ground and were extinguished by the mud. The three men on the platform jumped down and joined their fellows, surging towards Brother Thrawn in a shouting throng.

Petrel eased her wrists out of the ropes and hopped off the stool. No one tried to stop her. They were too wrapped up in their own anger, bellowing at Rain, who cowered behind the wheeled chair. "Where is he?" they screamed. "Where is Poosk? *Where is he?*"

Petrel slipped the noose from Fin's neck and untied his ropes with quick fingers. "You do Krill," she whispered. "I'll do the cap'n."

The ropes that pinioned the captain's arms and legs were too tight, and she couldn't untie them, not with time so short. But the rope that tied him to the stake was looser. Petrel dug at it with her broken nails until it came free, then looked around for Fin to help her carry the captain. But Fin was beckoning *her*—

Which was when Petrel remembered Krill's ankle.

The blood roared in her ears. *We can't carry both of 'em. But we can't leave one of 'em behind either.*

She began to drag the captain towards the platform, thinking that maybe Krill could carry him while she and Fin supported the Head Cook.

Somewhere in the shouting crowd, the man with the loud voice bellowed, "Quiet! *Quiet!* We will find Poosk and bring him to justice. But we cannot all go."

Petrel froze.

"Some of us must stay here and guard the prisoners."

NO!

But the brown-robed men at the back of the crowd were already remembering their duty, and turning around . . .

In the sudden shocked silence, as the Devouts saw that the

platform was empty and their prisoners loose, Petrel thought she heard three things.

Wings overhead.

A baby crying.

A grunt of effort, as if someone had thrown something with all their strength.

The next minute, that *something* came hurtling over the heads of the Devouts. It was a wooden bucket, and it hit the empty platform with a *thud*. A man shouted. A dog barked. Another man, closer to the quarry mouth, screamed. Echoes bounced off the rock walls, and heads turned in every direction, trying to work out what was happening.

More screams. Then someone cried, "Demons! *Demons!* A *horde* of them!" And the Devouts scattered in every direction.

But not all of them were panicking, not yet. Two men ran, grim-faced, towards Petrel and the captain. Four more closed in on Fin and Krill. Petrel lowered the captain to the ground and stood over him with clenched fists, determined to defend him to the last. She heard the wings again but dared not look up.

The first man knocked her aside with a single blow. The second one raised his cudgel to smash the captain—

"*No!*" shrieked Petrel, scrambling to her feet and throwing herself at him. But he was more than twice her size, and he shrugged her off as if she hardly existed, then raised his cudgel again. Ten yards away, Fin and Krill were taking a battering.

Petrel looked around frantically. She couldn't believe this was the end. There must be a weapon or—or *something*—

And then she saw it. She threw herself at the man a second time, with such ferocity that she spoiled his aim. The cudgel smashed into the ground, an inch from the captain's head. The man cursed and began to lift it once more.

But before he could strike, Petrel pointed to a spot behind him and screamed, *"Demons!"*

Fin's head jerked up, his cheek dark with blood. He saw what Petrel had seen. *"Demons!"* he shouted.

And *"DEMONS!"* bellowed Krill. *"COMING THIS WAY!"*

For men whose whole lives had been built on superstition and fear, those words were impossible to ignore. All six of the Devouts glanced over their shoulders—and then *they* were screaming too, everything else forgotten as a horde of hairy demons raced towards them. Or, rather, a flock of goats with shiny tin masks tied between their horns—masks that, in the torchlight, looked exactly like the captain's silver face.

The six men fled without a backward glance. A single captured demon, half-dead and trussed up, was one thing. But a *horde* of the creatures, free to wreak their terrible revenge, was another.

Petrel was breathing hard, as if she'd just run the length of the *Oyster* and back. She bent down and grabbed the captain under his arms.

A familiar voice said, "Stand aside, shipmate!"

"Mister Smoke!" cried Petrel, and there was the rat, grinning up at her, with his fur filthy and a feather tucked behind his ear.

"You 'elp Krill," said Mister Smoke. "We'll take the cap'n."

He whistled. And suddenly Petrel heard the wings again, directly overhead, and found herself in the midst of hundreds of pigeons.

But before they could land, the goats dashed past a second time, and now there was a pack of dogs nipping at their heels. The pigeons took to the skies. Goats and dogs raced around the platform and back the way they had come.

Somewhere a boy's voice cried above the uproar, "Haiiii! Haiiii! *Run!*"

Mister Smoke whistled again, and again the birds came down. This time, their claws fastened onto the ropes that bound the captain's arms and legs. A third whistle, and they began to beat their wings so hard that Petrel was driven backwards by the rush of air. For a moment the captain did not move. The wings beat harder. The birds strained. Petrel thought she saw Scroll in the middle of them.

The captain was lifted off the ground.

"Outta the way!" cried Mister Smoke, and as the captain rose into the sky, the rat leaped onto his chest and clung there.

"Where are you taking him?" shouted Petrel.

"To find the Singer," replied Mister Smoke.

"But he's broken!"

Mister Smoke didn't answer. Petrel heard his rough voice one last time. "Full speed ahead, shipmates!"

And the pigeons wheeled as one and disappeared into the darkness.

SHARKEY WAS HOARSE FROM SHOUTING. Every time the goats tried to run out of the quarry, he and Bran sent them back. "Haiiii! Haiiii! *Run!*"

One or two of the masks had fallen off, but most of them stayed where Sharkey had tied them, reflecting the firelight, so that the goats looked not only like hairy demons but like hairy demons with flaming eyes.

All through the quarry, brown-robed men tumbled over one another, trying to escape. Some of them managed to climb a little way up the steep walls, only to slide down again in a flurry of panic. Their frantic cries added to the chaos, and the goats, already unnerved by the fires and the nipping dogs, jibbed and jumped in all directions.

But Sharkey knew it couldn't last. He grabbed Bran and dragged him towards the gibbet. On the way, they met Rain, shaky but singing at the top of her voice.

"Hobgoblins tiptoe through the night
And imp and ghost and evil wight—"

"Quick!" cried Sharkey. And the three of them ran towards the platform.

Petrel was staring up at the sky with a strange look on her face. Fin had his shoulder under Krill's arm, trying to help the big man hobble along. There was no sign of the silver child.

"Where is he?" asked Sharkey, looking around. "Where's your cap'n?"

"He's gone," said Petrel. For a moment she sounded lost, but then her face cleared and she snapped back to practicalities. "And we'd best be gone too. Rain, you coming with us?"

Rain nodded. "Yes, please. And Bran."

"Come on, then." Petrel tucked herself under Krill's other arm and grimaced as she took some of his weight. Sharkey snatched up a discarded cudgel. Bran flapped along in his too-big robes, Rain still sang—though quietly now—and they hustled towards the road.

Sharkey kept expecting someone to stop them. But the demon goats were still cutting a swath from one side of the quarry to another, and the torches were guttering, and the dogs were howling, and not one of those superstitious men could gather his wits long enough to stop the prisoners from escaping. In the middle of the chaos, Brother Thrawn sat in his chair, seething.

The children and Krill reached the road without being challenged, and headed sou'west as fast as they could go, which wasn't nearly fast enough for Sharkey. He looked over his shoulder and said, "Someone'll stop being scared soon and start thinking. And then they'll be after us. Krill can't run, which means we need somewhere to hide."

"What about a horse?" asked Petrel. "If we stick Krill on its back, and maybe Bran too, we *could* run."

Sharkey nodded. "Bran, d'you know where the horses are kept?"

The little boy pointed past the dovecote and the goat pen, and they hurried off the road, dragging Krill over a stile and across a plowed field.

Behind them a dog yelped. Sharkey thought he heard someone shout, "Poosk!"

He hoped the Devouts would be so furious with the man who had fooled them that they wouldn't bother with their escaped prisoners. But he knew it was unlikely. Some of them might go after Poosk. But any moment now, the rest would be on the heels of the escapees.

"Rain," he said, "can you and Bran run ahead and bring back a horse?"

Rain and her little brother set off running into the darkness. The others followed, with Petrel and Fin stumbling across the furrows, and Krill wincing with pain every time he put his bad foot on the ground.

Bran and Rain didn't come back.

"Horse must've taken—one look at Krill and—refused to budge," panted Petrel.

But there was worry in her voice, and worry in Krill's too when he rumbled, "None of your—cheek—bratling. Any horse'd be—honored—to carry me."

"Perhaps they are—lost," said Fin. "Though I—" He broke off abruptly. Ahead of them, looming up against the background of stars, were three enormous round shapes.

"Balloons," whispered Sharkey.

"They must be tethered—behind the stables," said Fin. "Perhaps Rain and Bran—have been caught."

"Then we'll have to—uncatch 'em," said Petrel. "Sharkey, will you swap—for a bit?"

Sharkey gave her the cudgel and took her place under Krill's arm. They set off again.

When they reached the stables, Krill leaned against the

wooden wall, breathing heavily, while Fin slipped inside. He came back with the news that there was no sign of Rain or Bran. "Let us try around the back," he whispered.

"Wait! Listen!" Petrel held up a hand.

Sharkey pinned back his ears, wondering what— Then he heard it too. A shout from the road behind them.

"They're after us," he whispered. "No time for horses. We'll have to take a balloon."

It was a mad suggestion, but the others nodded grimly, knowing what would happen to them if they were caught a second time. Petrel, Sharkey and Fin crept around the back of the stable, with Krill hopping after them, hanging on to the wall for balance.

Sharkey wondered what they'd find. Bran and Rain tied up and helpless? An armed guard blocking the way to the balloons?

The first person he saw was Rain. She wasn't tied up. In fact, she had a knife in her hand and was hacking at the rope that tethered one of the balloons to the ground. Even as Sharkey watched, the balloon jerked, bobbed—and soared up into the night sky with its basket dangling empty beneath it.

Petrel gasped. "What's she *doing*?"

The word *betrayal* tried to slip into Sharkey's mind, but he wouldn't let it. He saw a second figure lying unconscious on the ground. A guard, maybe. And a third, standing next to one of the remaining balloons—

"It's Poosk," he breathed. "He's got Bran."

The little boy was a limp bundle of robes in his uncle's

arms. At his throat was another knife, glinting in the moon-light.

"Hurry up, girl," snarled Poosk. "Loose the other one. I will not have them coming after me."

Rain started sawing at the next rope. Poosk glanced towards the Citadel—and that's when Sharkey saw a stream of torches pouring down the hill towards them.

He nudged Petrel and pointed. There were Devouts behind them—running across the fields—and more Devouts chasing Brother Poosk. They had to get out of here *now*. But the knife at Bran's throat didn't waver, and Sharkey couldn't think of a single way past it, not without causing the little boy's death.

The second balloon disappeared upwards with a rushing sound, like a flock of gulls. The children edged forward, with Sharkey and Fin supporting Krill, and Petrel gripping the cudgel. Rain's eyes gleamed for a fraction of a second, as if she'd seen them.

Poosk hadn't seen them, not yet. He hadn't noticed the men running across the fields either. All his attention was on the river of torches flowing down the hill. And on the sole remaining balloon.

"Get into the basket, girl," he snapped. "Get ready to release the rope. And don't think to take off without me. If you do, your brother will die."

Rain sidled towards the balloon, her head hanging. Sharkey's breath burned in his lungs. *Do something*, he told himself, and he slid out from under Krill's arm.

Behind him, there was a chorus of shouts as the men running across the field saw the torches coming down the hill. "This way!" they shouted. "This way!"

Poosk spun around, startled. At that crucial moment, as the knife in his hand wavered, Rain dashed forward and kicked her uncle in the shins. At the same time, Bran bit his fingers, and Petrel flew across the last few yards and whacked at him with the cudgel.

With a cry of rage, Poosk dropped the little boy and turned on Petrel. His knife slashed the air in front of her. She skipped out of range, shouting, "Bran, get in the basket!"

"No!" growled Poosk, and he tried to seize Bran again, but Sharkey leaped onto his back and clung there, knocking him off balance.

"Bran, go!" cried Sharkey.

Rain grabbed hold of her brother and threw him into the basket. Poosk tried to stab Sharkey in the arm, but Petrel dashed in a second time, swinging the cudgel, and the knife went flying off into the darkness.

Poosk was desperate now, Sharkey could feel it. It was like trying to ride a Massy shark, but he dug in his heels and hung on, determined to keep the man away from the balloon.

A dozen Devouts with burning torches rounded the corner of the stables, shouting, "There he is! And the prisoners too! Stop them!"

Rain clambered up the side of the basket and tumbled in. Krill hauled himself over the edge, and Petrel and Fin followed him. The torches were no more than twenty yards away.

"Sharkey!" screamed Petrel. "Come *on*!"

But now Sharkey was the one who couldn't get free. Poosk held him with one hand and pummeled him with the other, blow after blow, until he was dizzy. In desperation, Sharkey threw his arm over Poosk's eyes. Poosk staggered five blind steps—and fell over the unconscious guard. Sharkey sprang away from him and ran for the basket.

He had his hands on the rim when Brother Poosk, staggering to his feet, grabbed him from behind.

Sharkey saw Fin's blood-streaked face staring at him in horror. He saw the burning torches and the brown robes closing in fast. He saw—

"SHARKEY!" bellowed Krill. And a giant fist shot out of the basket and hit Brother Poosk square on the chin. Poosk's head snapped back, and he fell to the ground.

Sharkey scrambled into the basket more quickly than he had ever moved in his life. "Go!" he gasped.

Rain seized hold of a lever and pulled it down. A rope flew out of its socket. The basket jerked. The leading Devouts threw themselves forward, their faces distorted with effort, their hands grabbing—

And the balloon soared upwards, out of their reach.

CHAPTER 25

THE BALLOON

So the sun rose and they were still alive. Petrel leaned over the edge of the basket and watched the gray sea pass slowly beneath them. Behind her, Rain fed the firepot with scraps of wood, and Bran perched on Krill's knee, talking about goats. His brown robes had been stuffed unceremoniously in a corner of the wicker basket, and he was wrapped in the Head Cook's jacket. Everyone else wore the mittens and scarves that Rain had dug out of that same corner.

"Where are we going?" asked Fin, who was standing beside Petrel.

"I don't know." She looked over her shoulder. "Rain, can you steer this thing?"

Rain shook her head. "It goes where the wind goes, unless it is tethered to a ship."

"In that case," said Petrel, "we're going sou'east."

"Nothing sou'east of here except ocean," said Sharkey. His

lip was swollen, and he'd be covered in bruises tomorrow. But for now he looked happy.

Petrel gazed out over the water. "I hope the cap'n's safe," she said. "I hope Mister Smoke can mend him and that they can find the Singer and—" She broke off, shading her eyes with her hand. "What's that?"

"What?" said Fin.

"Where?" said Sharkey, coming to stand next to them.

Petrel pointed to a dent in the smooth line of the horizon. She wasn't even sure there was anything there. It was just a smudge, slowly growing bigger . . .

"It's the *Oyster*!" she cried.

Krill dropped Bran like a hot fish fillet and hauled himself upright. "Where?"

"There!"

"Looks like a gull to me," scoffed the Head Cook. But his face was wreathed in smiles, and he gripped the side of the basket as if he could make it go faster.

"Our courses won't cross," warned Sharkey. "They'll go west of us unless they turn."

"No," said Petrel. "They'll see us."

"They will think we are the Devouts," said Fin.

Petrel stared at him, horrified. "Then, we'll have to show 'em we're *not*," she said. And she began to wave and shout, though the ship was much too far away for its crew to hear her.

"Dolph!" she screamed. "Missus Slink! It's *us*!" She turned to her companions. "Help me."

They waved until their arms were almost falling out of

their sockets and their voices were hoarse from shouting. But the ship continued on its course. Petrel could hardly bear it. After everything that had happened, to see the *Oyster* sailing straight past, not knowing who they were.

Beside her, Sharkey said tentatively, "Would they pick us up if we were in trouble?"

"What do you mean?" asked Petrel.

"I—" He flushed. "You said I was like the Devouts—"

"Not anymore," said Petrel quickly. "I don't think that now."

Sharkey nodded. "But you said that your people bend to help their friends. Might they also bend to help their enemies, if those enemies were in trouble?"

"What are you thinking, lad?" asked Krill.

Sharkey said, "I thought we might go down. Land in the water."

"But we cannot swim," said Fin. "You are the only one—"

"The basket will float," said Rain. "Even if it turns over, we can cling to it. But if the *Oyster* does not pick us up, we will be lost."

"Aye," said Sharkey. "That's the idea."

Krill's knuckles were white. "If Albie's in charge, he'll go straight past. Probably laugh in our faces."

"He can't be in charge," said Petrel. "If he was, the ship'd be heading south, fast as it could go. It must be Dolph or Hump, or Weddell maybe." She gulped air. "I say we do it. It's either that or keep flying till we run out of firewood."

No one liked *that* idea. Bran stuck his thumb in his mouth, his eyes enormous. Rain picked up the lid of the firepot. "We will have to cut the ropes," she said, "at just the right moment. Otherwise, the balloon will collapse on top of us."

Everyone nodded. She covered the firepot.

Without the heat of the fire to keep it aloft, the balloon began to descend. Sharkey and Fin sawed at the ropes, cutting them just far enough—but not too far—so they could be finished off at the last minute. The basket swayed. Petrel kept her eyes fixed on the *Oyster*, willing it to turn, *begging* it to turn.

"Grab hold!" cried Sharkey.

They hit the water in a long, bumpy skid, sending spray everywhere and throwing Petrel hard against Fin. The two children clung to each other as the balloon began to settle over their heads. Just in time, Rain whipped the lid off the firepot, and Sharkey hacked the final strands of rope apart, and the balloon rose up again, up and up into the sky—

Leaving the basket bobbing in the water.

They were all wet and bruised, but that didn't matter, not now. All that concerned them was the *Oyster*, a couple of miles away and showing no sign of turning.

No one spoke. Petrel's whole being was focused on the ship, on the wind turbines and the cranes and the familiar superstructure of the bridge.

Please turn, she begged silently. *Dolph? Pleeeease turn!*

She closed her eyes and imagined she was a gull and could fly across the waves and beat her wings against the bridge windows. She imagined—

"SHE'S TURNING!" roared Krill, in a voice that almost sank the basket.

Petrel's eyes snapped open. And there was the bow of the *Oyster*, slowly coming around as the ship changed course towards them.

She didn't realize she was crying until she looked at the others. Tears poured down every face—even Sharkey's. They wept, and waved to the ship, and wept some more.

But as the *Oyster* came closer, Petrel wiped her eyes and said, "Soon as we're safe, we'd better pick up the Sunkers. Don't want to leave 'em there for the Devouts to catch again. And then we'll have to see if we can get the *Rampart* afloat."

Sharkey smiled at her. "And retrieve the boxes."

"What boxes?" asked Petrel.

"Just—Sunker stuff."

"Your folk'll be pleased to see *you*, lad," said Krill.

"Nay," said Sharkey, his smile vanishing. "I don't think so. I don't think they'll want me back."

"Don't see why not," said Petrel. "'Specially when you got 'em out of the camp and all. But if they don't want you, you can stay with us, along with Rain and Bran. And then—"

And then we turn south, she thought. *That's what I want, isn't it? We could go back to our old course, as far from the Devouts as possible. And with any luck, one day we'll spot a flock of pigeons, and there'll be the cap'n, as good as new. And Mister Smoke riding on his shoulder.*

The ship was so close now she could see folk standing at

the rail. She waved frantically and heard someone say, "Is that *Petrel*? And *Krill*?"

"Aye, it's us!" screamed Petrel. "And Fin too!"

There was a whoop of joy, and the next minute the rail was crammed with shipfolk, elbowing one another and shouting at the tops of their voices.

"It's Petrel! Look!"

"Where's the cap'n? I can't see him. Can you see him?"

"Here, give way—I was here first."

"Who's the boy with the patch?"

"Where's the *cap'n*?"

"Hey, Krill, cooking's improved since you left. Ha ha ha."

Two voices rose over all the others.

"Da! *Da!*" That was Squid, almost falling over the rail in her excitement.

"Petrel!" And that was Dolph, jumping up and down on the spot, like a bratling.

Krill's grin was so wide that his beard looked as if it were about to split in half. Fin was laughing. Petrel felt like crying again, but she laughed instead.

Sharkey wasn't laughing, and neither were Rain or Bran. They huddled in the back of the basket, glad to be rescued but taking no part in the celebrations.

Petrel thought of Bran when she first saw him, in the quarry. She thought of the whipping posts and the starving Sunkers, and the villagers she had seen, so thin and frightened that it hurt to look at them.

They're Nothing folk, she realized, *just like I used to be. Only there's a whole country full of 'em!*

And then she thought, *We can't just sail away and forget about 'em. That wouldn't be right.*

She took a long, slow breath and said, "We've gotta stop the Devouts."

Everyone in the basket turned and stared at her. "I thought I wanted to go back to the ice," she said, "but I don't. Not yet, anyway. I want to bring back machines, so folk don't have to wear 'emselves out carrying water and suchlike."

"And *feed* 'em," said Krill. "I've never seen so many hungry folk in my life."

Fin was smiling. "And find my mama, so the Devouts cannot harm her. And the captain. And Mister Smoke."

"Aye," said Petrel. "And find the Singer too, like the cap'n wanted. And stop the whippings, and—and—" Her voice trailed off. There was so much to do, and she had no idea where to start.

They were right up against the ship now, so close they could feel the throbbing of the great engines. Four ropes slithered down, each with a strong hook on the end. Petrel and Sharkey jammed the hooks under the rim of the basket, then waved.

Rain started singing, quietly at first, then louder. Petrel joined in, and Bran and Fin and Krill. And last of all, Sharkey, so that as the basket rose slowly up the great vessel's side, they were all singing at the tops of their voices.

"But will we cower, will we hide?
Will we lock ourselves inside?
Or will we hold ourselves with pride
And chase those ghouls away?"

And it seemed to Petrel that just as they reached the rail and fell into all those welcoming arms, a freak wind snatched their voices up and carried the song across the water towards land.

Where it fell upon a thousand starving villages like a promise.

ACKNOWLEDGMENTS

THIS BOOK WAS INSPIRED BY A VISIT TO THE CAPTURED World War II German submarine that sits in the basement of the Museum of Science and Industry in Chicago. As soon as I set foot on that battered old sub, I knew I had to write about life underwater.

The trouble was, I knew nothing about it. The two men who helped me the most were Lieutenant Commander David Jones, RANR, who advised me on steering and navigation, and Commander Ian Dunbabin, RANR, who read the whole manuscript and talked me through various situations on board submarines. Both men gave generously of their time and expertise, and if the world of the Sunkers is a convincing one, it is largely due to them. Any mistakes that remain are mine.

As usual, my publishers in both Australia and the U.S. were brilliant to work with. At Allen & Unwin, the editorial team of Kate Whitfield, Eva Mills, and Susannah Chambers pushed me to make *Sunker's Deep* much better than it would otherwise have been. At Feiwel and Friends, Editor in Chief Liz Szabla has been the best champion of this book that an author could wish for. And Senior Creative Director Rich Deas has worked his magic again with the cover.

Last, but not least, thanks to the excellent Peter Matheson, and to my wonderful agents Jill Grinberg (U.S.) and Margaret Connolly (Australia).